THE MAGIC HORNPIPE

The Magic Hornpipe

"Why has God saved me?
And more than once, at that?"

Gareth Evans

Translated by Jane Burnard

Gwasg Carreg Gwalch

First published in Welsh: 2020
© text: Gareth Evans 2020
© Maps: Greg Caine 2020
© English translation: Jane Burnard 2022

All rights reserved. No part of this publication
may be reproduced, stored in a retrieval system,
or transmitted in any form or by any means, electronic,
electrostatic, magnetic tape, mechanical, photocopying,
recording, or otherwise, without prior permission
of the publishers, Gwasg Carreg Gwalch,
12 Iard yr Orsaf, Llanrwst, Dyffryn Conwy, Cymru LL26 0EH.

ISBN: 978-1-84527-836-6
ebook ISBN: 978-1-84524-472-9

CYNGOR LLYFRAU CYMRU
BOOKS COUNCIL of WALES

Published with the financial support of the Books Council of Wales

Cover design: Eleri Owen
Cover photo: Ann Cakebread
Maps: Greg Caine

Published by Gwasg Carreg Gwalch,
12 Iard yr Orsaf, Llanrwst, Dyffryn Conwy, Cymru LL26 0EH.
Tel: 01492 642031
e-mail: llyfrau@carreg-gwalch.cymru
website: www.carreg-gwalch.cymru

Printed and published in Wales

For Carys and Alaw, two Gwent girls

Preface

The events in the book that you're about to read happened a very long time ago but in a place very close to home – if home is somewhere in Britain or Ireland, that is, because, since you're reading the English translation, home could be anywhere, which is a rather lovely thought.

Back then, English wasn't English but Anglo-Saxon. It wouldn't have got you as far as English today, although you probably could have made yourself understood throughout most of northern Europe, where people spoke similar, Germanic, languages. However, in Ireland and indeed most of Britain it would have got you nowhere, except for into a bit of trouble. No, it was Latin you needed. Although it lives on in many languages like French, Italian, Catalan and Galician, not many people speak Latin today, except for certain politicians who want us to believe they are cleverer than they are.

In this book, you will meet Ina. As you will soon realize, Ina, her family, her friends, and some of her enemies, didn't actually speak English, or even Anglo-Saxon, but rather Brythonic, the language of the Britons. She also spoke Latin, which, as you will see, comes in very handy. Brythonic, or rather a modern version of it – Welsh – is my first language too. And it was in Welsh that I wrote the book. It was translated into English by a fellow author, Jane Burnard. Just as English, together with bits and bobs from other languages (quite a few, actually), developed from Anglo Saxon, Welsh developed from Brythonic – with bits and bobs from other languages too.

As for the world Ina lived in, you will also soon realize that, for better or for worse, some things have changed a lot since then and other things haven't really changed at all.

I

Ina stepped through the rushes by the river – carefully, so as not to dirty her new sandals. She was searching for the perfect stem. Not too thick, and not too thin. From the corner of her eye, she caught a flash of colour and turned to see a kingfisher dart across the river, shimmering in the sun before disappearing from view. She was glad to've seen this shy bird today. There wouldn't be another chance for . . . well, she didn't know how long – and she didn't want to spoil the rest of the afternoon by thinking about it now, either.

Ina forced her attention back to the rushes, with their long, pointed stems. It was hard to choose, so she cut four lengths with her small, sharp knife and, finally, one more, just in case. Then she walked down to the river's edge, to the little nook beneath the canopy of the big silver birch – her favourite place in the whole wide world.

She placed the stems in a row before her, then she chose the longest, folding and weaving it, deftly, just as her older sister, Lluan, had taught her. Ina was the youngest in the family – the chick of the nest. She'd had a brother, too, but he'd died when he was only days old. That's why there were eight years between her and Lluan. Eight years – and then, unexpectedly, Ina had arrived. A gift from God. That's what her mother used to call her, when she was little.

Lluan had been a very patient teacher and had taught Ina a lot, before she'd gone. Ina missed her. Not every day, as she had at first, but often enough for her to feel *hiraeth* – that unbearable mixture of loss and longing – about her still. Ina's world was less colourful without her, somehow, like the old woollen dress she was wearing, that had once been so bright but was now faded and threadbare.

As she worked at the rush stem, she caught a glimpse of herself in the river: a tall girl of twelve years in a plain dress, with dark, curly hair falling across her shoulders. What you couldn't see, in the reflection, was that her dress was too small for her – had been so even before the trees had put out their buds after the miserable, wet winter just gone. Nor that her thick hair, the colour of a raven's wing, was untameable and unruly – as untameable and unruly as her, according to the maidservant, Briallen. If only she'd start behaving sensibly, said Briallen, then she'd grow into a beautiful, graceful young woman, and become a deserving wife to one of the local noblemen.

Ina didn't think she was beautiful. For one thing, her eyes – in her opinion – were too far apart. And then there was her neck, which was too long. The truth was – again, in Ina's opinion – that she looked like the scarecrow in the cornfield opposite the villa where she lived – all thin with sharp, bony angles. One thing was for sure, she would never grow up to be as beautiful as her mother, Heledd, whatever Briallen said. No one was as beautiful as her mother. No one. Apart from Lluan, of course. And, beautiful or not, Ina was glad to know that her guardian and the owner of the villa, Gwrgant ap Ynyr

– Gwrgant son of Ynyr – her mother's uncle, had promised her she never need marry against her will . . .

A sudden sound from the trees above the river cut across her train of thoughts – across one of the many long, serious conversations that she held with herself. There it came again. The sound of someone – or something – approaching through the undergrowth. It wasn't the sound of the wind through leaves, she knew that. Thanks to Gwrgant, Ina was in her element in the woods; she could recite the names of every tree and plant, and recognise and follow animal trails just as well as the most experienced hunter.

Keeping dead still, she turned her attention in the direction of the sound, watching to see what sort of animal it was. A sizeable one, she knew that much. A deer, perhaps? The breeze was blowing away from her, so maybe the creature couldn't smell her. Or was it a wild boar? Woe betide her if it was a boar-sow, with hoglets. Ina swore inwardly – her fighting staff was out of reach. But even a fighting staff was no match, if it was a bear. No one had seen a bear in this area for ages, but it wasn't beyond reason that one had wandered as far as this – after all, the Caerwent forest was thick, and it bordered the vast forest of Gwent Goch . . .

Here she was again, letting her thoughts run away with her, like a yearling foal! Ina forced herself back to the moment, and then she caught sight of something moving in the undergrowth. Frowning in concentration, she saw a pair of green eyes staring back at her and a huge, grey animal slunk into view. Wolf.

The wolf opened its mouth to reveal a row of sharp teeth

before springing at Ina, leaping through the air and crashing against her with its giant paws.

"Bleiddyn! Stop it!" shouted Ina, more sharply than she'd intended. At this telling-off the wolf cowered, instantly, and rolled on to its back, showing its belly and whining. For such a terrifying-looking animal, he was surprisingly tame – at least in Ina's company. Gwrgant had given him to Ina as a present, shortly after she'd moved into the villa, when Bleiddyn had been a little pup of three months old. No one had been sure whether he was a full-blooded wolf or a cross between a dog and a wolf. Ina didn't care. Bleiddyn was Bleiddyn. Her best friend.

"Who's my little baby Bleiddyn, then?" asked Ina playfully, before getting on to her knees and rubbing his belly until he stopped whining. After letting him lick her hand Ina stood, ordering him to lie down and stay out of the water. She needn't have worried. Bleiddyn headed for a shady spot to rest and in no time he was snoring gently.

Ina took up the stem again, weaving quickly, not allowing her thoughts to wander and start another conversation with herself. There was something lovely about this sort of concentration, about losing yourself so completely in the moment. She didn't often manage to quieten the constant voice in her head.

She finished weaving the first stem in no time, and then she chose another. Soon this one was transformed too and now, rather than a piece of rush, she held a little boat, complete with mast, in her hand. She put a kink in the top of the mast to make it different from the other one. Then she carefully placed the two boats on to the surface of the water. Bleiddyn must have realised that something was up, because he opened his eyes and shook himself awake.

"Ready?" asked Ina, smiling, before releasing the two rush boats, grabbing her staff and racing towards the old stone bridge as fast as her new sandals would allow, with Bleiddyn hot on her heels.

Standing in the centre of the bridge where the arch was at its highest, she stared down at the river – careful not to lean too far over, as it had no wall or fence. The two boats had nearly reached the bridge already. Which one would win the race? They disappeared beneath the bridge and Ina spun to see which one would appear first on the other side. The one with the kink in the mast – her boat!

"Ha! I won! Too bad, Lluan!"

In her imagination, the other boat was Lluan's. Lluan always won. But there was no sign of Lluan's boat now. It must have got stuck on a log or something, under the bridge. She saw the victorious boat sailing away from her. On its own. A little, fragile boat, pulled by the current. The smile faded from Ina's face. What was she doing here, playing this stupid game?

Then she heard the approach of easy laughter and saw a gang of children about her own age walking towards the bridge. They came from the fort on the hill. Glancing up through the trees, Ina could see the earth walls of this fort, circling the bare hilltop. She and her sister had played with these children many times. But that was in the past. Before the plague had swept through the land. And nothing had been the same since then – certainly not for Ina.

The laughter stopped as soon as the children saw her and Bleiddyn. They all stood still, staring at her. Their hostility was like a bad smell, rising from the riverbank towards her. Bleiddyn began to growl, low in his throat, lips curling to show his teeth. Ina squeezed the staff tightly in her hand. She knew how to use it – again, thanks to Gwrgant – and she wasn't afraid to, if she had to.

The eldest boy jerked his head at the others – Peblig was his name, if Ina remembered correctly – and then they all turned and headed further down the river to another crossing-place, where the water ran shallow. Some of the younger children looked back at her over their shoulders. It was hard to see who they were more afraid of – Bleiddyn, or her.

The air had turned sharp and chilly, clutching at Ina with its cold fingers, making her shiver in her thin, woollen dress. "Come on," she said to Bleiddyn, before turning to leave the bridge behind and head for the place she called home. The sun hung low in the sky by now. She'd lost track of time, as usual. She'd better hurry, or she'd be late for supper.

The last supper.

II

The villa was visible from afar, its white walls and red roof-tiles shining brightly from the main road that led to the old city of Caerwent and on across the Wysg river to Caerllion in one direction, and over the river Gwy to Caerloyw in the other.

Instead of walking to the crossroad and following the narrow track to the villa, to save time Ina cut across the cornfield that bordered Gwrgant's land, though she wasn't supposed to. This field, like the rest of the land surrounding the villa's estate, belonged to Brochfael ap Cadfarch, their cantankerous neighbour. Part of her was afraid that Brochfael would see her; the other part hoped he would, so she could dare to challenge him. The encounter with the hillfort children had left a bad taste in her mouth, and a fiery quarrel would surely get rid of it.

Long shadows, stretched by the afternoon sun, slunk across the fields and meadows. These were the best lands in all Gwent, according to Gwrgant. And once, the villa's estate had extended to the horizon, in every direction. But, while everything had unravelled in the decades after Britain turned its back on Rome, the villa's land had shrunk, hectare by hectare. Or, perhaps, thought Ina, after Rome turned its back on Britain. She wasn't quite sure who had turned their back on whom.

It was now a century and a half since then. And the villa's land wasn't the only thing to've dwindled. Gwrgant never stopped ranting and raving about the strangers from overseas, who landed on this island's shores and set about snatching land from its native people. From across the sea to the west, the *Gwyddyl*, or the Irish – the peoples of Iwerddon. And from the east, the *Ellmyn*, the Germanic tribes – including the accursed Saxons, who'd killed Ina's father when she was just two years old. She had no memory of him at all, thanks to these barbarians. They were a hundred times worse than the Irish, for there was not one Christian amongst them, according to Gwrgant.

No, there was no order any more – not like in the old days – and the crying shame of it was that some upstart like Brochfael could afford to extend his holdings, while those of Gwrgant (grandson to Pawl Hen, who had been, in his turn, son to the legendary Maximus Claudius Cunomoltus – who had built the villa, for great heaven's sake!) grew ever smaller ... Or, at least, that's how Gwrgant had explained it all to Ina. She loved him without question, but the old man did have a tendency to harp on about the past.

Walking quickly through the rows of wheat with Bleiddyn close at her side, Ina remembered the terrible row that had broken out this time last year, when some of Gwrgant's cows had strayed into this field and wrecked the crop. Brochfael had gone mad, insisting on half of Gwrgant's stock of cattle as compensation for his loss. But although Gwrgant had recompensed him – fairly, in his opinion – he'd refused to give the exact number of cows that Brochfael had claimed. After all, cows were beyond value.

And so it was that not a single word had been shared between the two men since then.

Ina climbed out of the field and over the earthen dyke that Brochfael had built after this unfortunate event – but not before giving the wheat a whopping slice with her staff, smashing several ears of corn to smithereens. She was still angry with the children from the fort – though, after so many years of being shunned by them, she really shouldn't have expected anything more. Slashing at the wheat again, she pretended it was Peblig. *Slash*. If she saw him again, she'd give him a thrashing. *Slash*. So what if he was a boy, and bigger than her? *Slash. Slash. Slash.*

After a bit, Ina came to her senses and realised, with horror, the damage she'd done. Lifting her head, she scanned the empty horizon. There was not a soul about, she was sure – and that was a relief, because she would be in enough trouble already, for being late.

Without lingering any further, Ina headed for the villa's main building. From here, the walls didn't look half as shining white as they did from the main road, and the red roof-tiles not half as smart and tidy, either – in fact, many of them had broken or fallen off completely. In truth, the wretched state of the villa meant that many of its rooms were unusable. And because of that, in the very middle of the villa – where the central courtyard had been – there was now a great wooden hall, as fine as any to be found between the rivers Wysg and Gwy.

At the side of the villa there was a small piece of land

surrounded by a fence, and in this enclosure stood an old, disagreeable-looking horse. As Ina approached, the animal ambled over to greet her. Ina combed the mare's long mane with the fingers of one hand and stroked her neck with the other.

"There you are, old girl – there you are . . ."

The mare was over thirty by now – but her grumpy, unpredictable nature hadn't changed one jot since she'd been a foal. Pennata was her name – which meant 'with wings' in Latin. Her name wasn't very apt. In fact, you never saw a horse less likely to fly like the wind. Pennata had been Ina's mother's horse, but she was Ina's now.

"Ina!" called a familiar voice. "Where in the name of all the saints have you been?!"

It was Briallen the maidservant, full of fuss and flap, her round, short figure bouncing along the path on her little legs, her arms waving in the air.

"To the bathhouse with you – at once!"

Briallen bustled towards the bathhouse at the side of the villa, shooing Ina before her as if she were chasing chickens into a coop. Bleiddyn was wise enough to stay where he was, or Briallen would surely have given him an earful too.

The bathhouse, like the rest of the villa, had seen better days. There was no water supply and the central heating didn't work. Water had to be carried in in pitchers and heated in a pot over a fireplace which had, at one time, held a proper, powerful boiler. Then they had to make do by standing or squatting in a large wooden bucket, instead of lying comfortably in a real bath.

In spite of that, the water in the bucket was scalding hot and in no time Ina was dripping with sweat. Briallen poured perfumed oil from a little vial and rubbed it into Ina's skin. The oil's exotic smell filled the room – the aroma of lavender and wildflowers from the Mediterranean. Then Briallen pulled a little metal scraper across Ina's skin to clean it off, as was the Roman custom, before pouring cold water over her to close her pores and seal the skin.

Now there was only one thing left to do – something that Ina hated more than anything in the world – and that was to wash her hair.

✢ ✢ ✢

Although the dress was new, the wool was so smooth and the weave so fine that it didn't scratch at all. It fitted Ina perfectly, too, unlike the clothes she usually wore. Ina lifted her arm. The green material shone like an emerald as she moved.

"Keep still, in the name of all Dôn's children!" scolded Briallen, invoking an old god as she tried to impose some sort of order on Ina's newly-washed hair.

"I didn't ask you to do my hair."

"Less of your lip, my girl, or you'll feel this brush on even more painful places."

Briallen had never given Ina so much as a clip on the ear, never mind a proper hiding. But this never stopped her threatening to do so, on a regular basis. Ina bit her tongue – not because she was afraid, but because she didn't want this hair-brushing torture to go on for any longer than it had to.

The new dress was supposed to've been a surprise, but Briallen had accidentally let the secret out weeks ago, shortly after everything else had been arranged.

It had been a fine, spring day, a little after Easter, when Gwrgant had told Ina that, now she'd turned twelve, the time had come for her to leave the villa and take up her place as a fosterling, an adopted child at the court of Caradog, king of Caersallog. Ina had known of this plan for a while before then – indeed, Briallen never tired of telling her it was high time she learned to behave like a young lady, after five years of running wild like a boy under Gwrgant's care – but the news had come as a shock, nonetheless. It was usual, she knew, for the noble children of these isles to be sent to other courts for a period of time – sometimes for years – when they were young children but, despite that, it was unusual for someone of her age and status. And even more unusual, because she was a girl. Usually only boys were granted this honour.

It was all thanks to Gwrgant – for his bravery and valour decades ago at the legendary battle of Mynydd Baddon, where the Britons had united against the Saxons and vanquished them, putting paid to their attempts at further western expansion. In this battle, Gwrgant had saved King Caradog's father's life, thus causing the court of Caersallog to be forever in his debt.

"Let me look at you, my girl," said Briallen, who was still fussing about her.

Ina turned to face her. Briallen stared at her, wordlessly, for a moment, and tears formed in her eyes.

"You look like a picture, you do," she said, lifting the

mirror so that Ina could see herself.

Ina stared into the mirror. And, for a fleeting moment, it wasn't her face that stared back – but Lluan's. Ina tore her eyes away swiftly, confused.

"Take a proper look, girl! What's the matter with you?"

But Ina couldn't speak to answer.

"Come here," coaxed Briallen – gently this time, having seen the colour drain from Ina's cheeks.

Ina lifted her head and stared into the mirror once more. Lluan had disappeared. She was looking at her own face now: her own eyes, which were too far apart; her neck, which was too long. And her raven hair, which was a little less wild than usual, thanks to Briallen's efforts.

"I know I'm always saying this, but – as God is my witness – you're every bit as beautiful as your sister. And you'll be as beautiful as your mother too, one day – peace be upon her," said Briallen quietly, making the sign of the cross.

Ina quickly crossed herself too. It'd been five years since she'd lost her mother. And Lluan. Both, at the same time. The *Fad Felen* – the Plague – had stolen them from her, that accursed pestilence that had claimed so many lives. But was it any wonder that the disease hadn't spared those two dear mortals, when it had snatched even the life of King Maelgwn Gwynedd himself, ruler of the most powerful kingdom in Britain?

Five years of not feeling her mother's warm arms wrap themselves around her. Five years of not hearing Lluan's infectious laughter, nor seeing her smile – that smile, that lit up everyone and everything about her. Why had Ina snatched her gaze from the mirror like that, a moment ago? If she'd kept looking, perhaps Lluan's face would have stayed there, smiling sweetly at her.

Thinking of her mother and sister, Ina felt a pang of guilt at her foolish vanity over the dress. But at the same time, she knew that her mother – and Lluan – would have loved seeing her in this beautiful new outfit, just as Briallen did. And one thing was for sure – they definitely wouldn't want her to be sad.

Lifting her head and studying her reflection again, Ina concentrated on the dress this time, rather than her face. It was resplendent, and even she couldn't deny that it suited her down to the ground. In this dress, she thought, she would fit in well at Caradog's court.

But Ina would have exchanged it happily for her old clothes, though they were worn and too small, if it meant she didn't have to leave home at all.

III

Ina stood in the centre of the hall, feeling awkward in her rich, shining green dress. Everyone was looking at her. She stared at the floor, pulling nervously at her sleeves. Candles lit the large room – though the sun had not yet set – and the animal skins that hung from the wooden walls seemed to shimmer and ripple like living things in this dusky hour between darkness and light. Everything was ready. The long table had been set. The best plates were in their places. But where was Gwrgant?

"Gwrgant won't be long," whispered Briallen in her ear, as if she could read her thoughts.

As she continued to wait, Ina became even more aware of everyone's eyes upon her, and of the sound of them whispering amongst themselves. Whispering about her. Then the whispering and the murmuring swelled until they filled her head – like the sound of flies, swarming over a piece of meat.

A hornpipe sounded outside the hall. Although Ina couldn't see who was there, she knew that the person playing the instrument was Gwrgant. He was a master at it. The call of the hornpipe came closer and then Gwrgant strode into the hall, followed by Selyf the slave, who was carrying a bulging sack. Dignified and stately, Gwrgant stepped towards the centre of the room and Ina, a striking figure in his purple cloak and golden collar, surprisingly hale and hearty, and still a strapping man, though he was far past seventy years. Selyf followed his lord in as dignified a way as possible, given the obvious weight of the bundle.

The hornpipe's notes filled the hall, and Ina couldn't help but recognise the tune. It was the lullaby that Gwrgant used to play to her, devotedly, after she'd arrived here five years ago when she was just seven years old. Although at heart a gruff old soldier, who could be really crotchety sometimes – even with her – not an evening had passed during that early, difficult time, without him playing this tune for her on the hornpipe. Because, as he well knew, this was the lullaby that Lluan used to sing to her every night without fail, at Ina's bedside, after she'd been kissed goodnight by her mother.

The magic hornpipe – that's what Gwrgant called it; and Ina believed him when he'd tell her that the instrument had otherworldly powers. The sound of the hornpipe, sharp and penetrating, was completely different to Lluan's sweet voice, but it was the only thing, at that time, that would comfort Ina. In the years that followed, Gwrgant had tried several times to persuade her to take up the instrument, knowing that she used to play it with her mother. But after the plague, and losing her family, Ina had made a vow to herself – a vow never to play a single note again.

Ina's father had owned that particular hornpipe. Only after he'd been killed did her mother start to play it. It wasn't thought seemly for ladies to play such an instrument but, for once, Ina's mother didn't care whether it was seemly or not. This was her way of keeping her husband alive. At least, that's how Briallen had explained it to Ina, later.

Everyone listened, hushed, to the last note of the tune, before Gwrgant put down the hornpipe and signalled to Selyf to put the bundle down. The relief on Selyf's face was obvious.

Then Gwrgant turned to Ina, greeting her formally.

"Ina ferch Nudd. We come together this night in your honour, to wish God's blessings upon you for your journey, and for your time under the care of King Caradog, Lord of Caersallog, at his court."

A lump was growing in Ina's throat, and she found herself unable to look into Gwrgant's eyes. Now he gestured to Selyf, who bowed, pulling something from the sack and handing it to his master.

"Behold a cloak of the finest wool, to keep you warm," announced Gwrgant.

Surprised, Ina took the cloak from him. The patterned material was of the highest quality. And the brooch! This was the same, exquisite brooch that her mother had used to pin her own cloak about her shoulders. Its red enamel and ornate design were dearly familiar to her, the image seared into her mind from early childhood. And then, out of nowhere, a memory: the shining brooch, her mother's cloak wet from rain, and the muggy smell of damp wool. She was struck, suddenly, with a terrible *hiraeth*.

Perhaps Gwrgant realised this, because he gestured quickly to Selyf, urging the slave to give him something else.

"Behold a bag of the finest leather, to keep your belongings safely with you."

Gwrgant handed a large, leather bag to her, before whispering in her ear with a little wink, "You can put the pack across your back, see – or tie it to a horse's saddle."

Ina looked at the travelling bag. This, like the cloak, was of the highest quality. She could tell that there was something inside, but managed to resist opening it – not wanting Gwrgant to think her greedy. Then the older man nodded at Selyf again. They'd obviously been rehearsing this little ceremony.

"And lastly . . ." announced Gwrgant.

There was *more*? Ina couldn't imagine what else Gwrgant could possibly give her. She'd had so much already!

"Behold a sword of the finest iron, a gift to the king, Caradog, and a symbol of the accord between us. May it defend you, that you will return to us, safe and well, when the time comes."

Gwrgant presented a belt, with sheathed sword attached, to her. Stunned, Ina took it from him. And a murmur went through the hall. What a gift! Ina was dying to pull the sword free from its scabbard and admire it. But that wouldn't be a seemly thing for a girl to do – even for a girl who'd grown up with as much licence as her. More than that, she had no right to do so – certainly not once she reached Caersallog – for it was against the strict mores of courtly behaviour for women to carry weapons. So Ina put the scabbard and its belt safely into the leather travelling bag.

Then Gwrgant clapped his hands and everyone sat down at the table.

"Thank you for the gifts," Ina told him, quietly. She was sitting at Gwrgant's right hand.

"Thank *you*," he replied, even more quietly, so that no one else would hear, "for bringing joy into the heart of a grumpy old man like myself."

Next the servants came, bearing food. What a feast! A huge dish heaped with scallops, two whole salmon, meats of all types: venison and wild boar from the forest, and a side of beef – one of their own cows, slaughtered especially for the occasion – a mountain of mashed vegetables, and piles of barley and oat bread loaves. There were even flasks of the best Bwrdios wine from the kingdom of the Franks, as well as local mead. Ina had never seen so much food before, and from the stunned look on the rest of the guests, neither had they. Gwrgant said a short prayer, and then everyone started scoffing and guzzling as if they hadn't had a bite to eat for weeks.

Later on, when everyone had filled their bellies, Gwrgant offered a toast to Ina's health – *Iechyd!* – and everyone drank even more. Ina began to feel more comfortable, but it was too soon to relax completely, because Gwrgant had one more announcement to make. He thumped the table with his fist, and the ring on his middle finger flashed – a ring of thick gold with a piece of green, plasma gemstone set neatly into it. And on the gemstone, two figures were carved, in relief – the twin children of the Greek god Zeus that, according to the old beliefs, protected soldiers and sailors.

"My dear Ina . . ."

Ina sighed, quietly. Not because she was ungrateful, but because she really hated all this attention.

". . . there remains one happy task to fulfil . . ."

For a moment, she was afraid that Gwrgant had asked the local bard to sing a poem of praise to her. What a complete bore! She would have to smile and pretend to enjoy it – in spite of the fact that she never understood half the words he used and that his quivering voice grated on her nerves like a knife. And on top of it all, he smelled.

But, thank goodness, there was no sign of the bard. Instead, Selyf the slave stepped towards her, then went down on his knees. Ina stared at him, open-mouthed.

"I give you this slave, to be at your service in your new home," announced Gwrgant, smiling.

Ina couldn't believe her ears. Selyf? Her slave? At Gwrgant's words, Selyf prostrated himself completely before her, lying on his front on the floor.

"Although there's little in his head, his heart is equal to that of a warrior. He will be a loyal servant to you. When you are older, he will belong to you, and be your property. And then, if it pleases you, you may free him," added Gwrgant, talking about Selyf as if he weren't there.

Ina wasn't sure what to think – after all, he was a slave, with almost no rights; he and his like were right at the bottom of the heap. But she felt a little uncomfortable, in spite of that, because she knew how fond Briallen was of him. Briallen would miss him, Ina was sure. Ina looked across at her and saw that she was staring down at the table. Then she remembered that Selyf was still on his belly on the floor by her feet.

"Get up, Selyf," she said, curtly.

The slave stood and returned to stand at the end of the

table. What's going through his mind? wondered Ina. What does it matter, in the end, she concluded. He has no choice but to obey. Just like her. She wasn't exactly free, either, not by a long shot.

IV

The candles had almost burned themselves out, but there was no sign of Gwrgant doing the same. He was in his element, sailing off on a sea of memories, as often happened when he'd had too much mead – reciting, loudly, the story of the battle of Mynydd Baddon. Although the battle had taken place fifty years ago, it was as alive in Gwrgant's memory as if it'd happened yesterday. His eyes filled with tears as he spoke of how the men of Gwent had fought, sword by sword, shoulder to shoulder, with soldiers from every part of southern Britain.

". . . Briton beside Briton against the Saxon; Christian beside Christian against the pagan. The sky turned black. And do you know what happened next . . .?"

No one said a word. Everyone knew the answer, having heard the story time after time, but they were more than happy to pretend otherwise to please Gwrgant.

"Thunder and lightning struck the earth, right in front of the enemy," came a deep voice from the door of the great hall.

Everyone turned to see who had spoken. Neither Ina – nor anyone else – could believe who was standing there. Brochfael. The quarrelsome neighbour. Perhaps someone had seen her in the cornfield earlier, thought Ina, and Brochfael had come round to cause trouble. She felt the blood flow into her cheeks, blushing scarlet as Brochfael stepped over the threshold into the hall, taking off his sword-belt and giving it to Selyf, before turning to Gwrgant and greeting him formally.

"Hail, Gwrgant ap Ynyr ap Pawl Hen, in the name of God the Highest."

"Greetings, Brochfael ap Cadfarch ap Macsen Hirgoes, in the name of the Almighty," answered Gwrgant. "Come, join our feast," he added, as courteously as he could manage. He didn't want Brochfael anywhere near the place, but extending a welcome to all was a custom that had to be adhered to.

"Forgive me for interrupting. I'm here on account of Ina."

Ina tried to look as nonchalant as she could, but her heart was beating hard.

"To wish her well, that is all; and to present her with a small gift," he added.

Brochfael held out a vial.

"Perfume, all the way from Egypt," he boasted.

Ina was so stunned that Gwrgant had to clear his throat to remind her to reciprocate.

"Thanks," said Ina, taking the present. Brochfael smiled at her. He wasn't usually as pleasant as this. Perhaps she'd been wrong about him. But Gwrgant was watching him suspiciously, before abruptly changing the subject.

"What do you make of these rumours?"

"What rumours?"

"The rumours pertaining to Rhun, king of Gwynedd. That he is looting and plundering his way through the central lands, and that next he means to turn his horses and warriors on Gwent."

"Old wives' tales," dismissed Brochfael. "I know that our lands are rich and productive, but why travel a whole week to steal our cattle and the fruits of our labours, when Môn and her countless cornfields are under his dominion?"

"Because there is no limit to the greed of a king like Rhun, any more than there was a limit to the greed of his father, Maelgwn."

"Be that as it may, there is no cause for concern," insisted Brochfael. He turned to Ina again. "So. Tomorrow, then, you leave for Caersallog?"

"She does," answered Gwrgant on her behalf. "All preparations have been made."

"A good thing too," said Brochfael, taking his belt and sword back from Selyf. "Be mighty, Gwrgant ap Ynyr!"

"Fare well, Brochfael ap Cadfarch!" answered Gwrgant, but Brochfael had already turned his back on him. In the light of the candle above his head, Ina suddenly saw the damage that time had done to Gwrgant's purple cloak – in some places it was worn to threads, and the colour had faded from it. It was also too large for him. It had fitted him perfectly once – as well as this new dress fitted her.

Gwrgant had become smaller.

Brochfael strode out through the door, slamming it shut behind him. The next moment, the candle-flame above Gwrgant's head billowed and snuffed out, shortly followed by another.

✦ ✦ ✦

The wide valley was so beautiful in the light of the moon, and the firmament so full of stars. Snug in her new cloak, Ina stood on the villa's veranda, enjoying the silence. The only sound was that of strong teeth, gnawing at a bone. She'd given Bleiddyn part of a deer's haunch earlier and he was happily chewing on it now, somewhere in the darkness. Everyone else had gone to bed – everyone except Gwrgant. Ina realised that he'd come to join her on the veranda and was gazing wordlessly at her. She turned to face him.

"You fed that cross-breed monster, then," said Gwrgant. He was pulling her leg. Gwrgant was almost as fond of Bleiddyn as he was of Ina.

"Bleiddyn is as much a wolf as the wolves from the Caerwent forest; and as much a dog as the hunting dogs from the king's court," Ina answered in a flash.

Ina had mentioned the king on purpose, to goad Gwrgant. She knew he hated making the yearly payment of meat, grain and honey to the local king, who, in Gwrgant's eyes, was a no-good, worthless layabout. To Gwrgant, everything had been in much better order years ago, when there'd been no kings at all.

But instead of taking offence, Gwrgant laughed. Hardly anyone dared to answer him back, usually. Ina was one of the privileged few.

"*Cum mentior et mentiri me dico, mentior an verum dico?*" he asked her in Latin: If I tell lies and say that I'm telling lies, am I telling the truth?

"*Dear teacher,*" answered Ina, also in Latin. "*It is impossible to answer that puzzle.*"

Gwrgant smiled fondly at her. Ina was a good pupil and had mastered Latin as well, if not better, than he'd dared to hope. He'd insisted on her education, even though she was a girl. Latin had become a sort of private language between them, something playful, to enjoy – their secret language, unless an educated person happened to call by, like the two learned monks, Pasgen and Uinseann. They too had been teachers of a sort to Ina, though neither of them had been able to maintain any discipline over her.

According to Gwrgant, every person worth their salt knew Latin. Apparently, there were even some, over the river Hafren, who spoke it daily. It was the language of learning. And the language to use if you met someone from a different country or lineage from your own – if they were civilised people, that is. Gwrgant doubted that many Saxons or their kind could speak Latin. Small wonder, when, belonging to different tribes, they babbled in a confused mish-mash of Germanic tongues and were unable to write, either – at least not using a sensible alphabet.

Gwrgant and Ina stood side by side for a long spell, in silence. Sometimes, there's no need for words, thought Ina. Sometimes it's good to share silence with a dear friend.

"Time for bed, my girl," said Gwrgant at last. "You've a long journey ahead of you."

He turned to go back inside, and Ina was about to follow when something made her lift her head and stare up at the firmament again. Would the stars be this clear and bright in Caersallog?

V

Ina woke suddenly, to the sound of voices outside her room. Voices full of fear. Bleiddyn was awake already, ears up, sniffing nervously at the air.

Someone was at the door. A moment later Briallen rushed in.

"Get up! Rhun ap Maelgwn and his soldiers are laying waste to our lands!"

She tore the blanket off Ina. "On your feet! Get dressed!"

Ina rubbed at her face, trying to come to her senses.

"Now, Ina! There's not a moment to lose!"

Ina fell out of bed and started, clumsily, to dress herself, while Bleiddyn turned circles and whined in distress.

"Get your things – and take the horse to the woods. Selyf will meet you at the cave – you know which one."

"What about Gwrgant?"

"Someone has to watch the property, and the cattle. Don't worry – plenty of serfs are ready to stand with him."

Briallen disappeared through the door and Bleiddyn approached Ina, licking her hand to ask for reassurance. Hurriedly, Ina stroked his head before pinning her cloak about her. Like Briallen said, there was no time to lose.

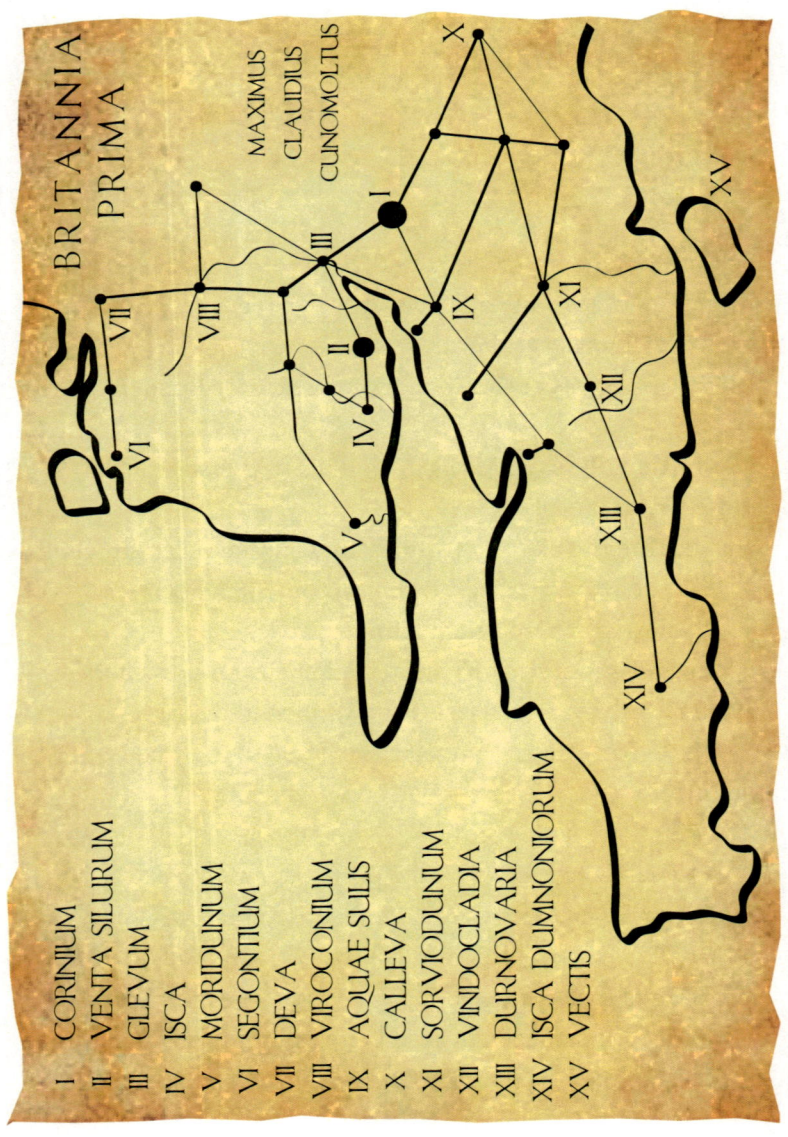

MAXIMUS CLAUDIUS CUNOMOLTUS
LIST OF PLACE NAMES

NUMBER	LATIN	WELSH	ENGLISH
I	CORINIUM	Caergeri	*Cirencester*
II	VENTA SILURUM	Caer-went	*Caerwent*
III	GLEVUM	Caerloyw	*Gloucester*
IV	ISCA	Caerllion	*Caerleon*
V	MORIDUNUM	Caerfyrddin	*Carmarthen*
VI	SEGONTIUM	Caernarfon	*xx*
VII	DEVA	Caer	*Chester*
VIII	VIROCONIUM	Caerwrygion	*Wroxeter*
IX	AQUAE SULIS	Caerfaddon	*Bath*
X	CALLEVA	Caergelemion	*Silchester*
XI	SORVIODUNUM	Caersallog	*Salisbury*
XII	VINDOCLADIA	xx	*xx*
XIII	DURNOVARIA	Caerdorin	*Dorchester*
XIV	ISCA DUMNONIORUM	Caerwysg	*Exeter*
XV	VECTIS	Ynys Wyth	*Isle of Wight*

Ina had been in the cave for ages, but there'd been no sign of Selyf. He'll surely be here soon, she thought, and Gwrgant too. She just couldn't believe that this king, Rhun, would be stupid enough to attack the villa and challenge one of the heroes of the battle of Mynydd Baddon, when there were so many other estates nearby, undefended and there for the taking. On the way to the cave, Ina had passed many fleeing people, all of them desperately searching for temporary hideouts in the woods. Then they would crouch and pray that their animals and property would still be safe – after the men from the north had collected their spoil and set off back to Gwynedd.

With nothing better to do, Ina opened the travelling bag she'd had as a present from Gwrgant, which she'd attached to Pennata's saddle. As well as the sword, there were more clothes and useful things like pieces of flint to make fire, and hunting tackle. At the bottom of the bag was a travelling set of the game *Ludus latrunculorum* – or latrones, as everyone called it – the game that she and Gwrgant had played incessantly at one time.

But the most valuable thing was the parchment map, which Ina had pored over endlessly with Gwrgant – the map of Britannia Prima, the Roman province of western Britain. Not the original map, of course – that was far too precious – but a copy of it, a very fine copy indeed, which was just as good. The original was one of Gwrgant's most prized possessions, belonging originally to his great grandfather – Cynfawl Hael, the legendary Maximus Claudius Cunomoltus. Gwrgant always referred to him by his Latin name. And the full Latin name, at that. 'Cunomoltus', on its own, would not do.

Although Britannia Prima didn't exist any more – except for on maps – Gwrgant was fiercely patriotic about this part of Britain. As opposed to Gwynedd. Nothing good ever came out of Gwynedd, in his opinion. For hadn't King Maelgwn been served his just deserts when he'd died of the plague, after vowing to become a priest and devote himself to the Lord and then breaking his word? Ina didn't understand how Maelgwn's death could be God's punishment, while Lluan and her mother, Heledd, had died because God had loved them so much that he wanted them to join him in heaven. But when she asked Gwrgant about it, he'd changed the subject.

Ina let her finger wander over the parchment. She knew the names of all the towns and cities – in Latin, of course – because she'd learned to read with the help of this map. They were seared into her memory: Segontium, in Gwynedd; Moridunum, in Dyfed; Isca Silurum and Venta Silurum in Gwent; Glevum, up the river Hafren; Aquae Sulis and its famous baths across the mouth of that river . . .

"And here we are now, arriving in Corinium," said Ina out loud, pulling her finger from the map as Bleiddyn stuck his nose in, wanting to know what was holding her attention. Corinium – or Caergeri, in Ina's language, Brythonic – was once the capital city of the whole province.

She was about to trace the journey that she and Gwrgant would begin today when she noticed that Pennata, who was standing in the damp mouth of the cave, was becoming jittery. Cautiously sticking her head out to see whether Selyf was on his way, she saw a figure striding on short legs through the trees towards her. Briallen.

For someone so round, she could move surprisingly fast. She had a sack on her back and an expression of the utmost seriousness on her face. Ina stepped out of the cave with Bleiddyn at her heels, leading Pennata into the light of day and tying her reins securely to a nearby branch.

"Where's Selyf?"

Briallen paused before answering. Ina noticed, with a stab of panic, that her eyes were filled with tears.

"Briallen . . .?"

"Poor Selyf . . . He is in heaven, with the angels."

"Selyf's been *killed*?" asked Ina, stunned.

Briallen nodded her head. Ina knew how much she'd cared for the slave. She reached out a hand to comfort her.

"I'm so sorry . . ."

Briallen brushed her hand away and when Ina saw how deathly pale her cheeks were she was seized, suddenly, by the most terrible fear. The maidservant took a deep breath. Then,

"Gwrgant has been killed, too."

"No. You've made a mistake," Ina insisted, in a voice she hardly recognised.

"Listen, Ina my love . . ."

"No. You listen! Gwrgant will be here any minute now. We need to be ready . . ."

Ina made to seize the horse's bridle, but Briallen grabbed her arm to stop her.

"Ina, my darling. I saw his body with my own eyes. He's

left us – he's in the kingdom of the Lord now."

Ina stared at her, stupefied. She saw Briallen's tears, falling freely now, and realised that she was telling the truth. Her legs sagged beneath her and she would have collapsed in a heap to the ground, if Briallen hadn't caught her.

Her head spun. Dear Gwrgant. The person who had been the centre of her world, who had done so much for her, had died, and she hadn't even been given the chance to say farewell to him.

But as much as she wanted to cry, she couldn't. Something beyond her control was strangling her grief, choking her with a fist as hard as an iron glove. Exactly the same thing had happened when Lluan and her mother had died. And she had not shed a single tear since then.

"What will I do without him?" whispered Ina hoarsely, as much to herself as to Briallen.

"Leave for Caersallog. Quickly."

"On my own? I can't!"

Bleiddyn, realising that something was wrong, nuzzled at her side. But instead of comforting her, Briallen grabbed her shoulders and shook her, hard.

"It's what Gwrgant wanted you to do! Are you going to insult him by going against his wishes, and his body not yet cold?"

"Of course I'm not. But perhaps it'd be better to ask Brochfael for protection, instead of starting out on such a dangerous journey. He might be an unpleasant, angry man but . . ."

"No, Ina!" Briallen cut across her. "Forget Brochfael!"

"He's not all bad. He gave me a present, after all."

"Have you got the vial?"

"Yes. Why?"

"Give it to me."

Ina pulled the vial from the bag and Briallen snatched it from her hand, hurling it against the nearest tree and shattering its glass into fragments.

"Briallen!"

"It wasn't King Rhun's men that killed Gwrgant. It was Brochfael," said the maidservant, quietly. "I bet you all the gold in Gwynedd that the vial contained not perfume – but poison."

Terror swept through Ina. "Why would Brochfael want to kill me?"

"In case you take revenge on him one day."

Gwrgant, Briallen explained, knew that Brochfael planned to attack him, and that was why he'd been so keen to send Ina away. Rumours had been flying for ages that, come what may, Brochfael would lay claim to Gwrgant's estate because, in his eyes, Gwrgant hadn't fully compensated him for the damage to his cornfield. For sure, said Briallen, Brochfael had schemed with King Rhun, promising him half Gwrgant's cattle to secure his support.

Ina was only half listening. As soon as Briallen had said the word 'revenge', she'd felt something terrible swelling inside her.

Ina delved into the travelling bag for the sword belt. She pulled the blade from its scabbard and drew it threateningly through the air.

"If he wants to kill me, let him try!"

"Calm down! And put that sword away, at once!" commanded Briallen. "No good can come of a girl raising a sword. It's against God's will."

Ina ignored her, turning to jump into the horse's saddle, but Briallen was quicker, blocking her way.

"Move!" spat Ina.

"I won't."

Bleiddyn was agitated too by now, barking fearfully.

Then Ina stepped towards her maidservant, sword in hand. Briallen cowered, letting out a scream. In that moment, Ina realised what she was doing. She stared dumbly at the blade and the rage retreated, as quickly as it had come. She let the sword fall to the ground. She'd scared herself as much as she had Briallen.

"I wouldn't have . . . I didn't mean to . . ." stumbled Ina.

"I know that full well, my darling," said Briallen, her own voice shaking. She bent to pick up the sword. "I'll put this away, safely."

Briallen lifted the sword carefully by its hilt, slotted it back in its scabbard and put the belt into the saddle bag. Ina stood, motionless, watching her.

"But what about our own king?" asked Ina, when she'd found her voice again. "Can't he do something?"

"Our puny kinglet will do nothing to challenge the will of the ruler of Gwynedd. Of course, if Brochfael had killed you, he'd have been made to pay compensation – no one's above the law. But if the price of a soldier's life is but three cows, how much cheaper is an orphaned girl's?"

Ina's heart sank. Briallen was right, she knew that. As a girl, she didn't have the same rights as a nobleman like Brochfael. And as an orphaned girl, even less.

"Don't lose heart," said Briallen.

How on earth was she not to lose heart? For, apart from what she carried in the travelling bag, she had nothing left in the world.

"Perhaps you'll return some day, years from now, and claim justice," encouraged Briallen. "Who knows? With all the misrule and disorder that's upon us, perhaps Rhun ap Maelgwn and Brochfael will both be in the grave by then. And I'll be praying daily that I live to see the day you tread Gwent's soil safely once more."

Ina was trembling all through her body. Although Gwrgant had trained her well, nothing could've prepared her for the terror that now seized her, fast in its fist.

"In the meantime, do your best in Caersallog. Do your best to win the favour of King Caradog."

"Who there will believe my story? I have no proof."

Briallen delved into her sack, pulled something out and gave it to Ina.

"Here's your proof."

Ina stared at the ring in her hand. Gwrgant's ring. She didn't ask how Briallen had managed to get it off his finger – she was afraid to know. This ring had been in Gwrgant's family for generations and, though a staunch Christian, Gwrgant had always insisted that it'd saved his life during the great battle of Mynydd Baddon. But the ring didn't save him today, Ina thought, bitterly.

Then Briallen gave her a little pouch, heavy with silver.

"A while ago, Gwrgant showed me where he hid this bag. He told me I was to give it you in an emergency."

Gwrgant had thought of everything. It was so typical of him, as was the fact that he hadn't breathed a word to Ina about his concerns, so as not to worry her. A wave of *hiraeth* swept over her, almost knocking her off her feet.

Briallen was delving once more in the sack. "Here's the only other thing I managed to save."

She passed something to Ina. It was the hornpipe.

"I know you don't play it now; but I also know that Gwrgant would've wanted you to have it."

"Thank you," said Ina, stunned, taking the instrument.

"Dearest Ina . . ." said Briallen, tears pooling in her eyes again. "If you could defeat the plague, you can survive this – believe me."

Then the maidservant pulled Ina to her, embracing her tightly.

"Now. Head for the ferry boat. God be with you, my treasure, and all Dôn's children too."

Ina turned, nodded at Bleiddyn to follow and undid the horse's reins before climbing on to her back. Digging her heels into Pennata's sides, the horse began to walk, before breaking into a trot. Ina looked straight ahead. She dared not look back and see Briallen, sobbing fit to break her heart. She dared not.

VI

"Can you pay me?" snapped the boatman, eyeing Ina doubtfully.

"I can," she answered, offering him a piece of silver. These days, coins were only worth their weight in metal. The time when everything had a price in money and every coin was worth the sum stamped upon it was long gone, as Gwrgant had explained to Ina more than once.

The boatman took the coin and spun it through his fingers, before putting it between his teeth and biting into it. Then he grunted and pocketed it. But instead of letting Ina into the boat, he held out his hand again, palm up.

"One more, for that there monster, and two for the old horse."

Ina sighed. But she could tell from the expression on the boatman's ugly face, tanned and wrinkled by the weather into old leather, that there was no point arguing with him. She gave him three more pieces of silver and witnessed the same performance as he spun, bit and put away each one. Then he set about undoing the boat's rope.

"Get in. No time for loitering – tide's on the turn."

Ina seized Pennata's bridle and led her to the landing place called the Craig Ddu – the Black Rock – which was a huge, flat stone that stretched out, low, into the water like a hand with just one finger – its thumb. The boat, which was about ten metres long with a mast at the front and a large steering oar at the back, was tied up in the narrow channel between the 'thumb' and the rest of the rock.

Still gripping the mare's bridle and with Bleiddyn following obediently, Ina stepped off the Craig Ddu and into the boat. That was easy enough, because the sides of the boat were low and its hull was flat and comparatively wide. This was the first time Ina had ever been in a boat, and it was an unsettling experience to be within something that was solid, yet moving. A small wave hit the boat, rocking it from side to side, and Ina's stomach began to turn.

"Is this boat safe?"

"Safe as any other boat."

That didn't really answer her fears, especially as Ina couldn't swim.

"Is it strong enough to carry a horse?"

"Enough with your nonsense, stupid girl! She can carry five tons, easy, so I'm sure she'll manage your bony old mare."

Anxious not to annoy him further, Ina turned to Pennata and tried to coax her into the boat, doing her best to hide her own nervousness.

"Come on – good girl."

But Pennata stood her ground. She didn't move an inch. Then Bleiddyn pushed past and jumped without hesitation into the boat, as if he were showing her how to do it. At long last, Pennata doubtfully placed one front hoof into the boat, and then the other. She neighed, uncertainly.

"The back legs now. Come on," Ina whispered in her ear.

Pennata neighed again, before giving a little leap and then, at last, she was fully in the boat, from her nose to her tail. But her hooves had barely touched the hull before she was champing at her iron bit, throwing her head up and squealing, loudly and anxiously.

"Silence that there creature!" barked the boatman.

Though Ina did her best, nothing worked. If anything, she seemed to be making things worse, and the mare was panicking so much by now that the boat was rocking wildly and threatening to capsize. Ina lost her grip and fell to the hull. Pennata kicked out with her back legs then jumped over the side of the boat into the water – *splash!* – soaking the boatman, who roared like a bear, grabbed the huge oar and waved it threateningly at Ina.

"Out with you! Before I throw you into the water myself!"

He lurched towards her and perhaps if Bleiddyn hadn't snarled at him, baring his teeth, he would have kept his word and thrown her overboard. In the meantime, Ina struggled to her feet and jumped back on to the landing place, with Bleiddyn at her heels. Then she turned to the boatman and stuck out her hand.

"The silver."

"What about it?"

"I want it back."

"No chance. That's the payment for wasting my precious time."

With that, the boatman shoved off from the stone with his oar and started out for the far side of the estuary while the tide was in his favour.

"May all the angels curse you!" shouted Ina, once the boat was far enough away. Turning round, she saw Pennata grazing contentedly on a clump of seaweed in the grey mud of the estuary.

"Tasty, is it, that seaweed?" snapped Ina.

The horse took no notice of her. Then Ina's legs suddenly became heavy. She needed to sit down for a bit, and regroup. Looking about for a dry spot, she stumbled over a long, straight piece of wood. Taking it up, weighing it in her hands, she thought that this would do for now as a makeshift fighting staff. In her haste, she'd left the proper one back at the villa. She might need it, to defend herself. Of course, she already carried the sword in her travelling bag, but that had better stay in its scabbard. Too dangerous. Whatever, used properly, a fighting staff was almost as good as a sword and, after many years of training, Ina had a whole repertoire of self-defence moves.

Still gripping the staff, she sat down on the large stone with Bleiddyn at her side. Gazing across the water, she could see the hills of the kingdom of Caerfaddon. They seemed close enough to touch, but yet they were so very far away. And down the estuary, towards the fort of Dinas Powys, the hills of Dumnonia on the opposite side looked amazingly clear and defined too – so much so, it was almost as if they were mocking her.

Dumnonia was a powerful realm, one of the few countries on this island strong enough to take the place of Gwynedd as the principal kingdom of the Britons, now that Maelgwn had died.

Ina pulled the map from the leather bag and studied it, and her heart sank even further. Hearing her sigh, Bleiddyn lifted his head and placed his chin on her knee, staring up at her with his big eyes.

"Dear Bleiddyn. I'm afraid we've got a long journey ahead of us."

Thanks to the horse and her tantrum on the boat, they would now have to travel all the way up the river Hafren to Caerloyw before being able to start the real journey down the far side of the estuary to Caersallog. The three-day journey had just doubled into almost a week.

But first she needed, somehow, to avoid Brochfael's men, who were surely out looking for her – not to mention Rhun ap Maelgwn's soldiers, who were busy plundering the whole region . . .

VII

The path along the coast from the Craig Ddu was pretty bleak and uneven, but Ina didn't dare use the main road again, because Brochfael's lands bordered on it. What's more, they stretched eastwards all the way up to the ford across the Nant-oer stream and inland to Pwll Meurig and the banks of the river Gwy. Once she reached the Gwy, she'd need to cross this wide river somehow, before following the Roman road up the Hafren estuary on the other side.

"That is, if I arrive at the river Gwy at all," said Ina to herself.

Pulling on Pennata's reins, she drew the horse to a halt. The path before her was turning inland, because a small river-mouth lay straight ahead. This must be the Nant-oer, she realised – but it was no longer a stream. On its arrival at the Hafren estuary, it had turned into a river, wide and fast-flowing. Its banks were filled with rushes. Ina imagined Brochfael's men lurking within them, or in the bushes of the copse beyond it.

Staring into the distance, Ina followed the path with her eyes, past the turn in the mouth of the stream to what had to be the crossing place, some hundred metres away – a shallower, stony section. But she saw nothing suspicious, only the flashes of red on the beaks of oyster-catchers, who were searching for food on the grey shores. Bleiddyn obviously hadn't sniffed any danger either, because he continued to walk at a leisurely pace ahead of her along the path. So, though the feeling of unease hadn't left her, Ina decided to keep going, taking the lead once more.

But as they crossed the stream, Bleiddyn stopped, suddenly, staring ahead and whining, low in his throat. Following his gaze, Ina saw two figures lurking in the bushes further up the path. So her instinct had been correct! Ina swallowed. Her throat was dry.

The next moment, Bleiddyn was tearing towards the bushes. Gwrgant had given her enough lectures about never attacking if there were any other choice, but she couldn't leave Bleiddyn on his own. Digging her heels into Pennata's sides, she drove the horse after him, at the same time pulling the makeshift staff from the saddle. Gwrgant had also warned her how difficult it was to actually attack someone – especially for the first time. As she galloped towards the men, Ina felt a cramp in her stomach. Playing imaginary war games was one thing. Doing it for real was something else.

Ina saw the wolf-dog jump into the bushes. She heard a shout, followed by loud barking. But the barking was more like a greeting than the attacking sound Ina had expected. And when she arrived at the bushes, she realised why. Who should be hiding there but Gwrgant's great friends, the monks, Pasgen and Uinseann! Ina sighed with relief, pulled on Pennata's reins to draw her to a halt and put her staff away.

"By the grace of God! You're safe!" shouted Pasgen,

happily. "I've never been so happy to see that bad-tempered old mare in my life!"

"Me happy see Wolf too," said Uinseann in his shaky Brythonic, though he didn't actually look very happy to have Bleiddyn jumping all over him, relentlessly licking his face. "Good Wolf!" he said, nervously, to the wolf-dog, before reciting the same thing in Latin: *"Lupus bonum! Lupus bonum!"*

"Bleiddyn! Let poor Uinseann be," commanded Ina. Uinseann was a *Gwyddel*, an Irishman from across the sea. And although he was a great, broad-shouldered man, he had a fear of dogs.

"Thank you, my dear child," said Uinseann in Latin, wiping his brow.

At once, Pasgen grabbed his wooden cross, which he'd hidden in the bushes, and kneeled before it. Uinseann and Ina got to their knees with him. Then Pasgen recited a prayer, asking God to welcome Gwrgant into the kingdom of heaven. After the prayer, the three continued to kneel for a little while, their eyes down, quietly invoking memories of Gwrgant. Bleiddyn sat motionlessly with them, as silent as they, as if he were remembering Gwrgant too.

Pasgen was the first to get to his feet, rising hesitantly as his joints were not as supple as they used to be.

"We hoped you'd come this way," he said, also in Latin. This was the language they used most often with each other, for Uinseann's sake.

"Not hoped, Pasgen. Prayed. We prayed you'd come this way. And the Virgin, in her wisdom, was merciful enough to listen to our plea."

"Be that as it may . . ." said Pasgen abruptly, pulling himself up to his full height – which was about the same as Ina's – *"you are alive and well, Ina, in spite of Brochfael and his devilish plan."*

The two of them always corrected each other, and Gwrgant used to joke that they were like an old married couple, delighting in pulling their legs. Pasgen didn't have much of a sense of humour, being a little pious – although he had a great heart. Uinseann had an impish sense of fun, however, and Gwrgant had loved to tease him by telling him that the Irish were second-hand Christians – those of them who'd had seen the light, of course, as many of them were still pagans – because the legendary saint who'd taken Christ's message to their land – Padrig Sant, or Saint Patrick – was a Briton, from these isles. Uinseann had laughed every time, without taking any offence. Ina smiled to remember this, then sobered, instantly, as she realised that she would never again hear the two of them laughing together.

"We a have plan too!" said the Irishman, animatedly.

"We do indeed. By great good fortune, we are on our way . . ." Pasgen began, before Uinseann cut across him.

"To Caergeri. At the request of King Cynddylan. At last! We are Christ's pilgrims!"

Ina had heard many times of Uinseann's dearest wish, which was to leave the abbey near Caerwent and spread God's word – *peregrinari pro Christo*, as the Irishman called it, in Latin.

"As you know, Caergeri is halfway between here and Caersallog . . ." Pasgen continued.

"But first, of course, we must get you past Brochfael's men, who are patrolling the crossing place on the river Gwy . . ." interrupted Uinseann again.

"I'd thank you to allow me to finish what I wish to say!"

"If you'd be so good as to express that politely, I'll be more than willing to do so!"

The bickering was starting to get on Ina's nerves, especially with the situation being so serious.

"Perhaps you could stop disagreeing for long enough to tell me what the plan is, exactly?" Ina suggested.

The two monks looked at each other in embarrassment. And then, before Uinseann could interrupt him yet again, Pasgen explained what they had in mind and Ina listened, agog.

✦ ✦ ✦

After walking for over three hours – it wasn't possible for the three of them to ride on Pennata's back – the Roman bridge across the river Gwy came within sight in the distance. Pasgen, who was leading the way, held up his hand.

"We should stay here, in case Brochfael's men notice us," he said. *"This is a good place for us to prepare ourselves to cross the bridge,"* he added in Latin.

The plan was a daring one: to fool Brochfael's men by dressing Ina as a monk.

"I agree," said Uinseann. *"Pasgen – give Ina the habit."*

"Which habit?"

"The spare habit, of course."

"I don't have a spare habit."

"Neither do I!"

It was true that the plan was a daring one – but perhaps it wasn't terribly practical.

"What about crossing further up the river instead?" suggested Ina.

"The nearest ford is six miles away," answered Pasgen. *"And I've heard that King Rhun's soldiers are on hand there, demanding payment from all who try to use it."*

"Too dangerous," said Uinseann, emphatically.

"We'll have to cross the bridge, then," said Pasgen. *"Uinseann, give your habit to Ina. You'll have to swim across the river and meet us on the other side."*

Uinseann stared at him, open-mouthed.

"My own habit? But I'm much taller than Ina. Yours would fit her better."

"True," ventured Ina. *"After all, we don't want to attract even more attention to ourselves."*

After further discussion, Pasgen gave in and agreed to take Bleiddyn with him too, in case the wolf-dog raised suspicion. The relief on Uinseann's face was obvious.

So it was that Pasgen pulled his habit off and handed it to Ina. He looked very awkward in his holey underclothes, which came down to his knees. Then he gave the cross to Uinseann.

"God be with you," he said quickly, before hurrying away, Bleiddyn following faithfully behind.

"Dominus tecum!" called Uinseann after him. God be with you.

Ina put the monk's habit on over her own clothes. It was a little big, but it covered her completely, and when she pulled up the cowl – the bit that covered the head – her face was well hidden.

"*Splendid! Brochfael's soldiers will never recognise you now,*" said Uinseann, with an encouraging smile.

But Ina could see from the unguarded fear in his eyes that he wasn't as confident as he was trying to make out.

✦ ✦ ✦

"Halt!" shouted the soldier, raising his spear as Ina and Uinseann approached the bridge. Ina was sitting on Pennata's back – ready to gallop through the battalion of men if need be – and Uinseann was leading her.

"Good day to you, in the name of God the Highest," said Uinseann, in his Irish accent.

The soldier stared suspiciously at Uinseann.

"You're no Briton."

"Irish, I am – but a Christian, like you. Uinseann, one of Cadog the Wise's *discipuli*," answered Uinseann, forgetting the Brythonic word for 'disciples'.

This holy man, Cadog – along with his abbey in Llancarfan – was well known to all, even one of Brochfael's henchmen.

"And who is the brother on the horse?"

Ina stared down, careful not to show her face. They'd agreed earlier that Uinseann would do the talking.

"I . . ." began Uinseann.

For a moment Ina was afraid that the Irishman would ruin everything by giving her real name, but she needn't have worried. Although he was a little naïve sometimes, Uinseann wasn't stupid.

"Ibar mac Lugna. Irishman. Also a *discipulus* of Cadog."

"*Dominus tecum!*" said Ina in a deep voice, raising her hand to bless the soldier.

Instinctively, the soldier returned her words by making the sign of the cross then stepping aside to let them pass.

"*Dominus tecum,*" repeated Uinseann, the relief clear in his voice, before leading Ina over the bridge.

Ina's heart was beating like a hammer. To make matters even worse, as soon as Pennata saw the water either side of her, she began to get the jitters again. Ina managed to subdue her by leaning forwards to talk soothingly in her ear but then a sudden, violent gust of wind caught her cowl, so that she wobbled on Pennata's back, letting go of the reins as she tried to pull it back in place. Her head released, Pennata shied and reared up, threatening to throw Ina off.

Uinseann's reaction was instant. He lifted the wooden cross in his hand, and the wind subsided immediately. Ina grabbed the reins again and Pennata quietened down. Then Ina turned to stare at Uinseann, stunned. He returned her look with a cheeky little grin, as if to say that he and God were on very good terms.

"*Dominus tecum,*" said Ina, quietly. She meant it from the bottom of her heart.

A few moments later, they were across the river and safe on the other side.

VIII

"Are we nearly there?" asked Ina, as nonchalantly as she could. She wasn't one for complaining, but her feet were crying out in pain and the leather of her new sandals was biting hard.

"Do you see those hillocks in the distance, to the left?" said Pasgen. "Caergeri is just beyond them – less than a mile away, if my memory has not altogether deserted me."

The relief was obvious on Ina's face, though she tried to hide it. But Uinseann, who was riding Pennata, noticed it. Since crossing the river Gwy, they'd been taking it in turns to ride the horse.

"Have a turn on Pennata, if you like."

Ina shook her head. Uinseann was surely tired too, and she didn't want to take advantage of his generosity. After all, without the monks' help who knows what would have become of her?

Ina smiled to herself quietly, as she pictured Pasgen's wretched appearance when he'd rejoined them after she and Uinseann had fooled Brochfael's soldiers and crossed the bridge. The monk had been shivering from head to toe after swimming across the river, his thin underwear soaking wet and his knees turning blue with cold. Bleiddyn, on the other hand, had obviously relished the challenge of crossing the

Gwy, and was as pleased to see her as she was him. Ina knew that Uinseann was just as glad to see Pasgen too, though he would never admit that, of course.

The first part of the journey through the vast forest of Gwent Goch towards the city of Caerloyw had been cheerful enough, once Pasgen had thawed out and come to himself. But the paths were steep and the woods were thick, and very soon the merriment and the chatter quietened down. Then Pasgen and Uinseann started bickering again. But, to Ina's relief, after a while even the two squabbling monks were too tired to quarrel.

Although the evenings were long at this time of year, it soon became obvious that there was no hope of reaching Caerloyw before nightfall. So they took refuge at a nearby farm, lodging in the cowshed with the animals after a simple supper of porridge in the farmhouse. As the plague had shot its bolt by now, most people had returned to the kindly tradition of giving shelter to strangers and sharing food with them – all you need do was knock on the door and ask.

As she lay on a pile of straw, her new cloak wrapped tightly about her, Ina heard a wolf howling from far within the belly of the great forest, and she gave thanks that they hadn't had to sleep out under the stars. Bleiddyn, agitated by the wolf's cry, bristled beside her and began to growl. She stroked his head to soothe him, so he didn't wake Pasgen and Uinseann. His body was lovely and warm, as warm as the smile of the farmer who'd opened the door to them. He'd been a deliberate, gracious man, so different to his wife, who was full of fuss and flap, just like Briallen.

Though she had no way of proving this, Ina knew that Briallen was still alive because, although it was so difficult to accept that Gwrgant, and Selyf, for that matter, had died – and both alive and well, only this morning! – Ina felt, somehow, that they weren't here any more. But Ina could still sense the presence of Briallen. And she prayed to God to keep Briallen safe from harm, as he had kept her – up till now, anyway.

The strange certainty that Briallen was still alive, had not been killed, was enough comfort to allow her to fall asleep in the bleak cowshed, in spite of the cry of the wolf that continued to howl, somewhere, deep in the forest . . .

✢ ✢ ✢

Ina stumbled, almost falling. Her thoughts had wandered again, and she hadn't been watching where she was going. She stared at her sandals. The strap around her ankle was filthy. Briallen would surely have scolded her, if she were here. Although she got on her nerves sometimes, Briallen was a small, round ball of kindness. Ina would never forget the smile Briallen had bestowed upon her when she'd arrived to live with Gwrgant, and the fact that she'd allowed little Ina to comb her hair for hours without complaining once, in the same way that Ina had used to comb her mother's hair. Without realising, she let out a sigh.

"What's worrying you, my child?" asked Uinseann kindly, pulling on Pennata's reins.

"Nothing," answered Ina. *"My sandals,"* she added, when

she saw that the Irishman didn't believe her.

"Ina! Look!" said Pasgen, interrupting.

Ina turned to follow his pointing finger. Then she stood still for a moment, savouring the view before them. A fair way ahead of them yet, but clearly visible, loomed the proud and imposing walls of Corinium Dobunnorum, former capital city of Britannia Prima and home of the king Cynddylan, ruler of Caergeri and all its lands.

✦ ✦ ✦

Ina stepped towards the city's gate house at the end of the road, awed by its size. It was as tall as a castle's tower, and it made even the high walls on either side of it look puny. As she entered its wide mouth she obeyed an urge to unleash a loud yell, which echoed endlessly around the ceiling and walls of the stone passage – that was as damp as the cave near her home in Gwent, and almost as dark.

"Settle down, old girl," said Uinseann to Pennata, who was threatening to bolt at the noise.

"Forgive me," said Ina, quickly.

There was no need to worry that he'd taken offence. The familiar, ready smile was on Uinseann's face, as ever.

"Not to worry. I've forgiven much worse."

But the Irishman slipped quickly from Pennata's back, just in case she grew even more skittish.

Ina knew that it was her turn to take the mare from Uinseann, but she couldn't wait to see inside the city. Rushing through the gateway she stood, stock-still in wonder, on the other side. Bleiddyn bounded over to stand at her side. But for once she took no notice of him.

The city was enormous. Although the walls of Caerwent were high and thick, that old Roman stronghold wasn't quarter the size of Caergeri, which stretched far before her.

To her right, throwing its shadow across the street, was a huge building in the shape of a half circle – the biggest building she'd ever seen. Bigger than the gatehouse tower, even. But it wasn't the magnificence of these buildings that most surprised Ina, it was the fact that most of them were in ruins and that the streets were totally empty.

"Here we are then, in Caergeri. I can see you're not disappointed," said Pasgen, who'd come to join her.

"Where is everyone?" asked Ina, stupidly.

"Long gone, my child. Hardly anyone lives within the walls of the old city these days."

"But where's King Cynddylan's court?"

"Nearby. You'll see, in a bit."

Ina didn't understand. The way that Gwrgant had sung the praises of Caergeri – or Corinium, as he insisted on calling it – Ina had taken it for granted that the city was still an important one.

"The striking building over there that caught your attention is the theatre. Or, rather, was the theatre," explained Pasgen. "Who knows what it's used for nowadays, if it's used at all. Would you like to see the forum?"

"I would," said Ina, finding her voice. The forum was the centrepiece of every Roman town or city; a large square where a market was held, as well as other important public events.

With Pasgen leading the way, Ina walked down the street, astonishment still written all over her face. Bleiddyn trotted after her, keeping close at her heels. They left Uinseann behind, staring up at the enormous cliff-face of the theatre.

Ina looked about her. The buildings on either side were in ruinous condition; thorns and brambles scrambling through the ground-floor windows of one, a tree growing from the roof of another, and the house on the corner of the street had collapsed entirely. These buildings should have been brimming and the streets bustling busily with people. But instead of that, there was deadly silence. A shiver ran through her. Bleiddyn must have felt uneasy too, because he began to whine for attention. Ina remembered Gwrgant telling her that the Saxons believed these old towns to be full of ghosts, and so avoided them. She understood why, now.

"Careful!" called Pasgen.

But it was too late. Ina had stepped into a pool of stinking water in the middle of the street. She staggered out of the hole with her sandals dripping wet, the leather soles covered in some sort of foul slime. If Briallen had been here, Ina would certainly have had a telling-off now, if she hadn't had one before. And Ina would have put up with the scolding happily, just to hear her voice again.

She strode ahead, half-listening to Pasgen as he lectured her on how these ditches had once kept the city hygienic and flood-free by channelling away waste water, and how most of them were blocked up now, like bogs – but she was unable to concentrate properly. Especially when Uinseann, who'd just joined them, kept questioning and correcting him. Even when they reached the forum, which really was something to behold, she couldn't for the life of her give it the attention it deserved. Because Ina felt terribly uncomfortable. Every sinew in her body wanted to leave the city, and that immediately.

Then Bleiddyn began to bark and, before Ina could stop him, he was racing towards the giant column at the far end of the square. Ina saw someone peeking out from behind it. A slim figure, with a face as pale as a spectre, which let out a terrified yell when it saw Bleiddyn rushing towards it.

"Bleiddyn!" shouted Ina, her voice sharp with shock. "Come here! At once!"

Bleiddyn stopped in his tracks before creeping back to her in a comically shame-faced way, his tail between his legs. There was no sign of the phantom, which seemed to have disappeared into thin air. Ina turned to Pasgen.

"Was it a spirit, behind the column?"

"If it was, it was the spitting image of Sulien."

Uinseann laughed heartily and Ina began to feel a little silly.

"So who's this Sulien, then?" she asked.

"King Cynddylan's son."

The son of a king? A real prince? Ina had never seen one of these before – and she found it very hard to believe she had just now, either.

IX

Ina gripped the piece of meat and tried to eat it in the most civilised way possible. She was starving and she'd have loved to lay into it, noisily – tearing and scoffing to her heart's content – but she was well aware that she ought to behave like a young lady. The trouble was, she didn't have much idea how to. The main guests, Ina included, were sitting on a *lleithig* – a kind of sofa spread with down cushions and arranged in a horseshoe shape, in the Roman way.

From the corner of her eye, she watched Eurgain, Cynddylan's wife, and tried to copy her. Everything about her was so graceful. The lady noticed her staring and gave her a friendly smile. Ina smiled back. Eurgain had made a point of praising her dress earlier, and Ina knew she'd done this to make her feel at home. Because, although Ina's dress would do fine in this company, it was nothing but rags in comparison to the costly robes of the king's wife.

Then, to Ina's huge embarrassment, Bleiddyn put his big, muddy paws on her knee, sniffing at the piece of meat.

"Get down!" she hissed.

Bleiddyn sat down again. Ina glanced about her to see if anyone had noticed, but the only person watching her was Sulien, the king's son, with a stupid look on his face. When she caught his eye he looked away, quickly.

Cynddylan's son was a strange creature, in her opinion. This afternoon, when she and the monks had been officially welcomed to the court – which was located within the walls of Corinium's old amphitheatre, outside the city – this youth had taken it upon himself to pretend he hadn't seen them in the forum earlier, denying that he'd been there at all. He must've felt ashamed, thought Ina, for hiding like a coward.

"How much for the wolf-dog?" Ina heard Cynddylan's voice. And then she realised, with a jolt, that he was addressing her. Cynddylan was handsome man with a commanding gaze, younger than Ina had expected. She had no idea how to answer him. She looked to Pasgen, who was sitting at her side, for direction, but the monk was too busy licking his fingers to notice.

"Don't tease the poor girl," said Eurgain. "It is plain for all to see that Ina wouldn't sell that hound for all of old Maelgwn's gold."

Ina smiled thankfully at her, but Cynddylan hadn't finished.

"Then perhaps we should take Ina on as a paid soldier. I'll wager she's as good a warrior as her wolf-dog. After all, it's not every day that a girl has to take her sword off before coming into this hall."

"My dear king, you know full well that the sword is a gift for Caradog," said Eurgain. It was obvious that the king liked to pull a leg or two.

Ina squirmed, embarrassed. There'd been an awful confrontation after they'd arrived, when one of the king's war-hounds had dared to challenge Bleiddyn – and had been put, unceremoniously and swiftly, in its place, courtesy of Bleiddyn's strong, sharp teeth.

"I'm sorry about what happened," said Ina, awkwardly. She wanted to be polite; but she wanted to tell the truth too, "but Bleiddyn doesn't usually attack without reason."

"So the king's hounds are to blame?" retorted Cynddylan, in a flash.

Not sure whether he was still joking or not, Ina decided that the wisest response was silence.

"Better she play the hornpipe that's about her neck than pretend to be a warrior, in my opinion," said Sulien, not troubling to look in her direction this time. This wasn't the first time he'd spoken, but it was the first time he'd referred to Ina. His squeaky voice pierced her eardrums like the sound of a knife-blade scraping against stone.

Ina frowned at him. It was difficult to believe that this was Eurgain and Cynddylan's son – they were so good-looking. Nothing about Sulien was appealing – in Ina's opinion – and the fact that he was no longer a boy, nor yet a man, made him look like something left half-done, like a lump of dough that'd been taken out of the oven before it'd properly baked. Perhaps he wasn't their son after all, Ina thought, but an adopted child. Some ugly, disagreeable nobleman had sent him to them as a baby and forgotten to organise his return – or chosen not to bother . . .

"What is more, my dear king, I wonder who could possibly have thought it a good idea to arm this young lady with a sword, even if it is a gift to Caradog, as she claims. It is surely more likely to be a toy."

For some reason, Sulien insisted on speaking like someone of Gwrgant's generation, instead of a normal, young person. Ina's blood was beginning to boil. She turned to face him.

"Toy?! Let me tell you, Gofannon himself couldn't have made a finer sword."

Sulien guffawed with laughter at this. "And how, pray, would *you* know that?"

Ina paused before answering. She knew that she'd create a scandal then and there if she breathed a word about pulling the sword from its scabbard yesterday.

"Gwrgant told me."

Sulien laughed again, scornfully. "I hardly think that Gofannon, the Great Smith, would have broken sweat making a girl's sword."

"What about Buddug then, queen of the Iceni? She was a woman. Unless you're going to tell me she was a man in a dress."

The smile on Sulien's face disappeared. He obviously wasn't used to being spoken back to. Perhaps she was imagining it, but Ina was sure she could hear Cynddylan chuckling under his breath.

"I'm sure that wasn't what the young prince meant," said Pasgen, frowning slightly at Ina, warning her to calm down.

"*Aquila non capit muscas,*" recited the youth in Latin, obviously hoping to throw Ina. 'Eagles do not hunt insects' – meaning he wasn't going to bother replying to her.

"*Lupus non timet canem latrantem,*" shot back Ina; 'The wolf fears not the barking dog' – to show him that he didn't scare her.

Sulien's jaw dropped to hear Ina's flawless Latin, but Cynddylan was laughing loudly now, no longer able to contain himself.

"*Watch out,*" he said to his son, also in Latin. "*Her tongue is as sharp as her sword. You'd better keep quiet, or she'll deal you a mortal wound.*"

Sulien was blushing from ear to ear, glaring at Ina. Was she imagining it, or was Eurgain staring strangely at her too? However, despite the fact that his son looked as happy as a rabbit caught in a trap, Cynddylan seemed to be enjoying himself enormously.

"*I agree that your sword is bold and valiant,*" he said cheerfully to Ina, continuing to speak Latin, "*but I agree with my son also. It would indeed be a pleasure to hear you play your instrument after the feast.*"

"*I wouldn't want to offend the bard of this court, by stealing all the attention,*" answered Ina, also in Latin, trying to think of a way to refuse the king's request without looking disrespectful. She wasn't going to break her vow, not even for Cynddylan.

"I'm sure he wouldn't mind at all," said the king, turning back to Brythonic.

"Not the slightest bit, my dear king, shining sovereign of all Caergeri," said the bard, bowing low. If he did mind, he was shrewd enough not to show it.

"I'd rather not," said Ina. "I haven't played since . . . years ago."

"Would you disappoint the king?" asked Cynddylan. Ina was quite sure he was pulling her leg again, but she felt uncomfortable nonetheless.

Uinseann cleared his throat. He was seated on the other side of Ina and had managed to follow the first part of the conversation.

"Perhaps you might remember us mentioning the unfortunate event that forced Ina to join us on our journey," he said, diplomatically.

"Of course," said Cynddylan. For the first time, his voice was serious. "I heard tell, many times, of Gwrgant ap Ynyr. One of the heroes of the battle of Mynydd Baddon, as was my own father. Peace be upon him."

"Peace be upon him," repeated everyone, making the sign of the cross.

"He was from Cynfawl Hael's line, if I remember rightly. One of the most illustrious noblemen in all Gwent."

"Maximus Claudius Cunomoltus was one of the most illustrious men in the whole of Britannia Prima," said Ina in Latin, to underline the point.

"Gwrgant was a good teacher, I can say that much. Your Latin is excellent. What other subjects did he school you in?"

"How to fight," answered Ina, staring in Sulien's direction, hoping he'd taken note of this.

"Against whom?"

"The Saxons, of course."

"I'd better warn our neighbours in the Cymer, then," said Cynddylan, turning back to Brythonic again.

Ina stared at him, uncomprehending.

"The Cymer – a village a few miles down the river Tafwys, where two riverlets flow into the great river. I forget what the Saxons call it. Something no one else can pronounce, I'm sure."

"*Saxons* live there?" asked Ina, astonished. "As close as that?"

"It's possible to travel up the river as far as the Cymer from faraway Londinium. And so they can sail the whole way here from Germania – over the sea and up the mouth of the Tafwys – without letting their feet touch land."

Ina was horrified. "And you allow that?"

Cynddylan laughed, a little too loudly. "They've lived there since my grandfather was a child, if not before. What would you have me do – exterminate them like mice?"

"But isn't that the duty of every good Christian?" asked Ina, repeating the words she'd heard time and again from Gwrgant.

The hall went quiet – and Ina knew she'd gone too far. Her and her big mouth.

"I like your brooch," she said to Eurgain, saying the first thing that came into her head, desperate to change the subject. The brooch was round and had been overlaid in gold, its edge raised like a saucer, and its skilful, intricate pattern demanded admiration.

"Thank you, my daughter," said Eurgain, smiling, but without the warmth that had been there earlier.

"You like it, do you?" asked Cynddylan, nonchalantly.

"I do. It's really beautiful."

"Even though it was made by a Saxon?"

Not for the first time during this feast, Ina wasn't sure how to respond.

"Not every decision is easy, Ina. You must weigh and measure before deciding whether it is time to fight, or whether it is time to co-exist. You will understand better when you're older, I'm sure of that. Indeed, I wouldn't be at all surprised if there were the makings of a leader in you, like your famous forefathers. But I must tell you now, the situation in Caersallog is not a simple one, either."

Caersallog? This wasn't good news. Cynddylan saw the concern spreading across her face.

"Caersallog is secure – no need for you to worry," he reassured her. "As stands the old Britannia Prima, so stands Caersallog."

Ina let out the breath she'd been holding.

"But I'm less confident about your journey. I've heard tell – from the Saxons of the Cymer – that some of the more warlike amongst their leaders are stirring, yearning to break the peace. This isn't the time for a young girl to be travelling on her own, even if she is from the line of Maximus Claudius Cunomoltus. You'll need a travelling companion."

There was a pause. Then,

"I am willing to take up the mantle." A familiar, strident voice spoke out. Ina turned to stare at Sulien, astonished. And she wasn't the only one to do so.

The king paused before answering. Eurgain gripped her husband's arm, as much as to tell him out loud to give her son the chance. Then Cynddylan gave in.

"Very well . . ."

Ina's heart sank and Sulien smirked proudly, sitting up very straight.

"I shall not disappoint you," he said to his father, the king, before turning to Ina. "Do not be afraid. I shall keep you safe."

Ina knew that everyone was staring at her, especially

Eurgain. So she smiled back at Sulien so hard that her cheeks hurt. It would be better to suffer all the torment and flames of hell, she thought, than have to spend two days in the company of this youth. But even she knew better than to argue with a king.

Cynddylan clapped his hands and turned to the court's bard, who picked up his harp and cleared his throat self-importantly, ready to sing the praises of the man who kept a roof over his head. From the look of things, there'd be no stopping him once he'd got started.

Ina's heart sank even further.

X

Ina did all she could to delay leaving Cynddylan's court. After giving Pennata a bag of oats, she brushed the mare's coat until it shone and then cleaned her hooves, even though the stable-hand had done all this the night before. Bleiddyn stood guard at the stable door, in case anyone should come too close to Ina. Not that there was much danger of that, after he'd put the king's favourite hound firmly in its place yesterday.

At last, Ina climbed on to the horse's back and rode towards the court's main gate, where everyone was waiting for her – including Cynddylan, who was busy giving instructions to Sulien.

". . . once you've crossed the ford at Rhyd-y-grug, you'd better leave the road and follow the shepherds' path up the Esgair Las ridge towards Dinas Berian, then follow the path over the hills to the long stones at Meini Hirion, in the direction of the Clawdd Mawr – that is, the great dyke . . ."

Ina saw Sulien turn to watch her approach. He was frowning peevishly, because she was late.

"Sulien," said Cyddylan, and there was a hard ring in his voice. "This is important."

"Forgive me, my king," he replied, limply.

The king beckoned Ina closer. Quickly dismounting the

horse – in case he was annoyed with her, too – she listened carefully to what he had to say.

"Go past Meini Hirion and cross the Cynedd river. You'll see the great cairn of Carnedd Beli before you and, beyond that, the earthworks that are called the Clawdd Mawr. By the ford, there's an old, crooked oak. Follow the path that starts at the trunk of this tree, keeping the Clawdd Mawr on your right-hand side. In no time, you'll arrive at the estate of Tegid ap Gwyddien, my cherished friend and a Briton to his very core. You'll receive a warm welcome there. But beware – they say that one or two Saxons have lately settled in the area, and we've no guarantee that they'll be as peaceful as their cousins in the Cymer."

Sulien swaggered. "If any Saxon dare to trouble us, he shall have a taste of my sword!"

Empty words, if ever she'd heard them, thought Ina. It was obvious that Cynddylan didn't think much of his son's comment either, because he acted as if he hadn't heard, turning to Pasgen and nodding his head. At this, Pasgen stepped forward, his wooden cross in his hand, and blessed the two young travellers before whispering in Ina's ear.

"Remember, there will always be a place for you in the Lord's house, if for any reason you need help . . ."

"Thank you," Ina whispered back, before looking over at Uinseann, who was trying his best to smile at her, though tears shone in his eyes. He too stepped forward, putting his great arms around her.

"*Dominus tecum*, dear Ina. God be with you."

Ina couldn't say a word. The lump in her throat was too big.

Then the queen, Eurgain, embraced her son hastily and gave him a little kiss on the cheek. Sulien went bright red.

"Take good care," Eurgain warned him. Turning to Ina, she said, "I know you will be a dependable and responsible companion." Then, bending her head closer still, she whispered: "Hopefully you will be patient, too."

Ina smiled feebly at her.

"I'll do my best."

It was obvious that Sulien had heard every word, for his cheeks were now crimson, as if the fever were upon him.

Cynddylan raised his hand and made a fist. "May God protect you both. Farewell, dear son. Farewell, Ina ferch Nudd."

Bowing to his father, then to his mother, Sulien mounted his horse and set off down the slope in the direction of the city's walls and the Roman road towards the south east, without saying a word to Ina. After bowing her head at the king she climbed on to Pennata's back and urged her into a trot to catch Sulien up, with Bleiddyn tight on the mare's hooves.

"It would be more seemly if you stayed behind me," said the youth once she'd drawn level with him, urging his own horse to trot to prove his point.

Ina felt herself begin to seethe and she had to remind herself of Eurgain's words before retorting angrily. She may have promised his mother not to lose her temper with him, but if Sulien carried on talking to her like this she would have to teach him a lesson – son of the king or not.

✦ ✦ ✦

The shepherd's path wasn't half as good as the highway but it was easy enough to follow. Having said that, the climb to the old hillfort of Dinas Berian was so steep that Ina dismounted and walked, leading Pennata by her reins. Bleiddyn was already on the summit, stepping lightly around the earthworks of the stronghold. Sulien insisted on riding to the top, though his own horse was grumbling and beginning to hobble. Ina couldn't help but notice that Sulien was careful to leave a wide berth between himself and Bleiddyn.

"We should take a break," Ina suggested, after they'd reached the peak. "And you need to tend to your horse. I wouldn't be surprised if there's a stone stuck in one of his hooves."

"I had noticed," was Sulien's prickly answer, then he set to, clumsily lifting each of his horse's legs in turn. He's got no idea at all, thought Ina. She could see at once which hoof was troubling the animal.

"Let me," said Ina, nudging him out of the way and kneeling at the horse's side.

She quickly got rid of the stone. Without a word of thanks, Sulien pulled a piece of oat bread from his saddle bag and bit into it. Ina did the same, then took a swig of water from her goat-skin flask. She was sweating, and the water was very welcome – cold and refreshing.

Bleiddyn came over to see what he could scavenge, so Ina went back to her bag and pulled out a piece of meat, wrapped in a cabbage leaf to keep it fresh. She'd been given it by one of

Cynddylan's cooks. As soon as he saw it, Bleiddyn jumped up at her, placing his front paws on her shoulders.

"Wait!" scolded Ina, without a trace of reproach. From the corner of her eye, she saw Sulien staring suspiciously at Bleiddyn. Then she threw the meat in the air and Bleiddyn leapt up to snatch it, gulping it down in one. Sulien had seen enough, it seemed, because he climbed impatiently back on to his horse.

"Onwards," he said abruptly, not bothering to see if Ina was ready or not. She wasn't going to hurry on his account, so she took her time finishing the piece of bread. She didn't care about having to ride behind Sulien any more. At least then she didn't have to look at his annoying face.

The wind was keen up on the ridge, but the view from the path along the Esgair Las was stunning, and Ina began to relax. Though she would never have admitted this to Sulien, she'd worried they might meet some of the local Saxons after the crossing at Rhyd-y-grug, but they'd come across no one on the shepherd's path – neither Saxon nor Briton.

After a good hour, the path gradually brought them down into the wide valley where stood an enormous circle of standing stones – the Meini Hirion – surrounded by a high, earthen dyke. From up on the path, they could see over this dyke and, from a distance, the large stones looked like people, standing motionless as if they were waiting for something, or someone. Sulien went ahead to get a better look. Bleiddyn ran off, sniffing for rabbits. There was something about the stones that made Ina feel uneasy, though she had no idea why. However, after pausing for a moment, she urged

Pennata into a trot and followed them both.

When she reached the stone circle, Sulien had already gone in through a gap in the dyke. Ina dismounted, leading Pennata through it. Riding into the middle of the stones didn't feel right, somehow. The circle was even bigger close up than it looked from a distance, the huge stones looming over her head. Ina tried counting them, but soon gave up. She saw Sulien on the other side of the henge, trying, uselessly, to climb one of the stones. He really doesn't have a clue, she thought.

Then a memory, from somewhere. And suddenly, it wasn't Sulien who was struggling up one of the standing stones, but her. The stone was so big, and she was so small. Two arms held her tight around her middle, lifting her up. She knew at once the arms belonged to Lluan, her sister. Other children were there too, laughing and messing about. The children from the hillfort. Lluan and Ina had called on them and they'd all climbed the mountain of Mynydd Llwyd to play. Ina was hugging the top of the wide stone now. But the supportive arms about her waist suddenly vanished. Her little hands were too small to grip it properly and she fell to the ground.

"Lluan!" called Ina, her voice for once small and afraid.

She looked about for her sister. But this wasn't Mynydd Llwyd. Realising this, she felt the same, crushing disappointment as when the rush boat got stuck under the bridge, three days ago. The same void. Lluan wasn't there. And she would never come back. Ina stood still, as motionless as the standing stones, before running back towards the gap in the dyke.

"Do not be afraid! For they be but stones!" Sulien called after her.

Ina didn't have the patience to explain that she didn't feel fear, but something much worse – that grief and longing called *hiraeth*. Sulien wouldn't understand anyway, Ina was sure of that.

✢ ✢ ✢

The ford across the river Cynedd was easy enough to find. And you couldn't miss the crooked oak, either. It stood alone, as solitary and as bent as an old witch. Further down the river, there was an enormous, stony mound. That had to be the cairn called Carnedd Beli. And, running along the sides of the hills in the distance, Ina saw an outline. This was the Clawdd Mawr – the great dyke – without a doubt. Ina pulled at Pennata's reins to steer her in the direction of the dyke, but Sulien was going the other way.

"Sulien! You're going the wrong way!"

Either he didn't hear, or he was ignoring her.

"Sulien!"

At last, Sulien pulled at his horse's reins.

"I know very well what my father, the king, said. We are to keep the Clawdd Mawr to our right, and the river on the sinistral," he said, drily.

Did he have to speak like a dictionary? "Sini-*what?*"

"On the left," answered Sulien impatiently. "Keep the river on the left."

"No. Your father said otherwise."

Sulien turned and continued ahead. Ina knew she was right, so she went in the other direction. There was no need to tell Bleiddyn to follow her. The path was clear, starting at the tree trunk, exactly as Cynddylan had said. If Sulien wanted to put himself in danger by riding towards the no-man's-land between the Britons and the Saxons, good luck to him.

When she'd calmed down a bit, Ina began to worry. She wasn't at all fond of Sulien, but what if he was ambushed, or killed? After a bit, she heard a horse, neighing in recognition and blowing hard behind her. Ina let out a little sigh of relief, but as soon as Sulien opened his mouth, her blood began to boil again. She'd never met anyone who got on her nerves so much!

"Intractable girl! I have a duty to protect you!"

Although he was trying to sound authoritative, he was so agitated that his voice started to break again. He was screeching like an old woman by the end of the sentence. Then he cleared his throat, full of embarrassment. If he hadn't been a fool of the first order, Ina would've felt a little sorry for him.

"Pray you look, respected prince," said Ina, copying him, "here lies the path. And behold – the estate of Tegid ap Gwyddien, but a little distance from yonder hillock, I shouldn't wonder."

Sulien didn't breathe another word until they reached the estate, which suited Ina just fine.

XI

Their welcome at the home of Tegid ap Gwyddien was as warm as Cynddylan had foreseen. But for some reason, he was very anxious to hear which way they'd come.

"Over the Esgair Las and past Meini Hirion – just as my father, the king, instructed," answered Sulien.

Ina had to bite her tongue to avoid blurting out that they'd have gone the wrong way and not arrived at all, if Sulien had had his way.

"Excellent," said Tegid, without explaining further. "You two must be starving. We will prepare food for you at once."

He called out and two servants arrived to take their horses to the stables. These servants were so different from each other – like Pasgen and Uinseann, thought Ina, missing the monks.

The servant who led Sulien's horse away was pretty sullen. But the other man was much friendlier, and he smiled amiably at Ina. She half expected the mare to have a tantrum, but she accompanied him quietly.

Tegid explained that one of the men was a slave, a Saxon who'd come to him for refuge after being exiled from his village, following a brawl. He'd been willing to sacrifice his freedom for a safe roof over his head.

"Why?" asked Ina in astonishment.

"Because he had nowhere else to go. He would have starved otherwise, or been killed."

Ina wrinkled her nose. She would rather die than be a slave. "He'd been injured, you see, in the brawl," added Tegid. "His leg had the worst of it."

Ina stared in the direction of the men, and saw which one limped. And she realised, in surprise, that it wasn't the sullen man with the bad leg, but the other one. This was the Saxon, then. The man that had smiled at her. The first Saxon she'd ever seen. If she'd known he was a Saxon she'd have looked at him more closely, but from the back he looked just like any other man.

How strange! Ina had always imagined that meeting a Saxon in the flesh would be more of an event. A Saxon, who shared the same nature, the same soul, as the person who'd murdered her father. Her mother had never been the same, after losing him. That's what Briallen said, anyway – Ina had been too young to remember how she'd been before then, of course. But Ina, even though she'd been very young at the time, had seen that some overwhelming sadness hung over her mother. She'd never seemed completely happy, even when she smiled – wrapping her grief about her like a heavy shawl which she never took off. Lluan had been more of a mother to Ina, in truth. Not that Ina had minded that at the time – she'd idolised her older sister and treasured every moment in her company.

Tegid took them into the main building, giving them the chance to wash and rest before they ate. Bleiddyn stuck tightly to her side the whole time, and Tegid's hounds kept a good distance. Perhaps they were wiser than Cynddylan's dogs. When Ina had washed her face properly – and her feet, that were all over in dust – she heard Tegid calling for her to come and eat.

Sulien was there before her and had finished his first bowl of soup already. He was offered another straight away, and another after that. And then a fourth. He tore into a whole loaf of bread too, and an enormous piece of cheese. Ina had never seen anyone eat so much and she wondered where all this food went, for there was hardly any meat on his bones at all. He was even skinnier than her.

Ina managed to eat quite a bit too, but she felt stuffed full after her second bowl of soup. And although Tegid encouraged her to take another piece of bread, she couldn't manage another crumb.

After making completely sure that the two had had enough to eat, Tegid cleared his throat. He had an announcement for them.

"Sulien, did your father the king say why you should take the path to Caersallog, instead of the main road?"

"He said there'd been some talk of Saxons breaking the peace."

"Then I'm sorry to have to tell you that the situation is much more serious than that."

Ina looked at him in concern. Tegid continued,

"There are rumours – credible enough, worse luck – that something major is afoot. We hear that the Saxons beyond the Clawdd Mawr have been given orders to send a man from each house, and to raise arms."

"Why?" asked Ina, her voice suddenly hoarse.

"To form an army."

Ina felt the soup turn in her stomach. She looked over at Sulien. His face had turned a deathly white.

"If the rumours are true, then the Saxons intend to attack. Perhaps they mean to seize those parts of the lands of Caer Gelemion, way to the east, which are still in our hands, or . . ." Tegid paused, ". . . or even Caergeri."

Sulien jumped to his feet.

"We cannot be sure of their intent – I hasten to emphasise that," said Tegid swiftly, clearly trying to put Sulien's mind to rest, but the fear was clear to be seen in his own eyes.

"I have to return – at once," Sulien blurted, heading for the door.

Tegid moved quickly to block his way. "Calm yourself! You have a task to fulfil for your father, the king – that is, to carry this girl safely to Caersallog. The best thing would be for you to continue on your journey, and that tonight, without staying here."

"Is it safe for us to travel?" asked Ina, her voice shaking.

"Safer than staying here, my child," answered Tegid.

His answer wasn't of much comfort to either of them.

✦ ✦ ✦

It must be after midnight by now, thought Ina, staring at the sky. But the clouds hadn't begun to clear yet and, without seeing the stars, it was hard to know how much time had passed. Worse than that, she couldn't tell whether or not they were heading in the right direction.

"Can we stop for a bit?" she called to Sulien, who was leading the way.

"We shall stop presently, when we reach the top of the next hill."

"I'm not sure if we're still on the right path," said Ina.

Sulien didn't answer.

"Did you hear me?" persisted Ina.

Sulien pulled on his horse's reins, stopping.

"We shall wait here," he said authoritatively, avoiding Ina's question.

Ina pulled on Pennata's reins. The old mare would surely be glad to have a break. Bleiddyn, on the other hand, was full of energy. He loved roving about at night with Ina.

Sulien dismounted his horse, opened his saddle bag and took out a piece of bread, stuffing it whole into his mouth. How on earth can he eat, Ina wondered, when they might be riding straight into the middle of a Saxon army?

She got down from Pennata and took a gulp of water. Thinking about food made her feel sick. She was on tenterhooks. Then, a hideous scream rang out. Ina nearly jumped out of her skin, and Bleiddyn shivered, all through his body. In the silence of the night, it was impossible to tell how near or far was the sound.

"Reynard," explained Sulien, pretending he hadn't been scared.

"Who?"

"Not who. What. A fox, to you."

"I knew it was a fox," answered Ina shortly, annoyed with

herself for letting him get the better of her. Why couldn't he just have said so, instead of using some stupid word that no one used, except for poets and boys who thought they were much cleverer than they actually were? She gulped down another mouthful of water and looked up. The clouds were still thick. Why couldn't it have been a clear night – tonight, of all nights?

The two of them stood still for a bit, not saying anything. This was nothing like the contented silence that Ina had felt on the veranda with Gwrgant. *Hiraeth* pricked her, like the blade of a sharp knife. She looked over at Sulien. He seemed miles away.

"Worrying about your family?"

"I should be in Caergeri – not here, on some fool's errand," said Sulien, more bitterly than he'd intended and forgetting for once to use grand words.

"Go home, then. I'll be fine on my own."

"My father the king's wish was for me to protect you, and I must do my duty. If you are afraid of a reynard, how then will you react to real danger?"

There was that word again! What was wrong with saying 'fox'? Every time she began to warm towards him, Sulien uttered something to make her seethe with anger. He seemed to want an argument, so she bit her tongue. She wasn't about to give him the pleasure.

But perhaps Sulien really should go home to Caergeri, in case Cynddylan's court needed defending. Then there'd be no need for her to put up with him any more, either. And then she remembered Pasgen and Uinseann. If the Saxons really intended to attack Caergeri, they'd be in danger – and she'd be heartbroken if anything happened to them.

"*Dominus vobiscum*," said Ina out loud, without thinking. God be with you.

"What did you say?" asked Sulien, stuffing another piece of bread into his mouth.

"Nothing."

"You did. I heard you."

"*Dominus vobiscum*," said Ina, louder this time. "Just a word of blessing for Pasgen and Uinseann. It's thanks to them I'm still alive. Without Uinseann, I wouldn't even have been able to cross the river Gwy."

"Why? What did he do? Carry you on his shoulder, like Saint Christopher?"

"Better than that. He performed a miracle and calmed the wind, in order to save my life."

Sulien laughed scornfully, and Ina's blood began to boil once more.

"If Uinseann were here, he'd say a prayer and the clouds would part!" she blurted.

"Ask him, then. If he be as much a saint as all that, he'll surely hear you."

Ina frowned at him before shutting her eyes tight and, making sure not to speak aloud this time, begging Uinseann to help them – and to prove this mouthy milksop wrong.

One. Two. Three . . . Ina opened her eyes. She looked up at the sky. The clouds were as thick and impenetrable as ever.

"Perchance he's deaf," said Sulien, a spiteful smirk on his lips.

Ina turned her back on him. He was lucky she didn't use her staff on him. If he wasn't careful, she might yet . . .

Then something caught her attention, silencing the words in her head. She saw the moon peek shyly from behind a cloud and, to the left of the moon, a star. Then another. And another. The clouds were breaking up and thinning out, and the firmament was coming into view.

"Look!" shouted Ina.

Sulien stared upwards, open-mouthed.

"He heard me! Thank you, Uinseann! Thank you!" shouted Ina, overjoyed, jumping on to Pennata's back.

Then she looked up again, searching for one particular star. First, she located a cluster of stars in the shape of a crown: Caer Arianrhod – Arianrhod's Fort. From here she drew a line with her finger until she reached the milky streak that made up Caer Gwydion and within this the M- or W-shaped constellation of Llys Dôn – Dôn's Court –and then . . . there it was: the North Star. So. If that was north, she now knew where south was.

Without waiting to see if Sulien would follow, Ina urged her mare to trot southwards.

XII

Ina woke as the first of the dawn's rays tickled her nose. She'd not had much sleep because they'd spent most of the night travelling, but she felt refreshed nonetheless. What's more, despite Tegid ap Gwyddien's concerns, they'd not seen a single soul for the rest of the night, let alone a band of marauding Saxons.

She closed her eyes again and turned her face to the sun, enjoying the warm, welcoming smile of the dawn on her cheeks. There was not one cloud to be seen, and the sky was a soft blue. Bleiddyn was at her side, still asleep, his legs twitching every now and then, as he surely dreamed of chasing rabbits.

She turned to see Pennata grazing contentedly. And behind her, Sulien's horse, who was tied to a tree. Under the tree was a pile of clothes – which she realised was Sulien, sleeping soundly, his hair falling across his forehead and his face as pale as marble in the wan light of the early morning. He looks quite sweet when he's asleep, Ina thought, surprising herself by thinking such a thing – it had to be because he couldn't speak and because his face was still, in sleep.

Then she had an idea, giving Bleiddyn a little shake.

"Wake up, lazybones!" she said gently, careful not to speak too loudly.

The dog opened his mouth in a wide yawn before fondly licking Ina's face.

"Stop it!" she laughed quietly. "You stink!"

Bleiddyn didn't seem to mind this insult, turning on his back so she could tickle his belly.

"Later. Go and wake Sulien first."

Ina pointed in the youth's direction and Bleiddyn slunk towards him to lick his face. Sulien let out a high scream and jumped to his feet as if someone had placed a red-hot iron across his cheek, and Ina laughed out loud this time, so hard her sides hurt.

"Do not be afraid!" she called, throwing his own words back at him. "I shall keep you safe."

Sulien scowled at her, before stomping to the nearby stream to wash. Ina decided to gather last night's left-over food together to make breakfast. But when she opened her travelling bag all the bread had gone, and so had the cheese. The only thing left was a little bag of nuts.

Marching to the tree, Ina searched through Sulien's saddle bag. There was nothing in that, either. The greedy pig! Bleiddyn had followed her and was now lying on his back, expecting her to tickle his tummy.

"Later, I said!"

She was too furious with Sulien to think about stroking the dog. Lifting her head, she saw him striding back towards her from the stream, a self-important look on his face.

"You have no right to interfere with my belongings."

"You finished all the food while I was asleep!"

"I was starving."

"So what are we going to have for breakfast, you idiot?"

"Providing food is a woman's responsibility," answered Sulien, airily. "You have some nuts, do you not? And these bushes are full of blackberries and bilberries."

Ina glared at him, speechless, too furious to say a word. Sulien avoided her blazing gaze by turning to head for the nook where Ina had slept and rummaging through her things. Bleiddyn started barking, but Sulien took no notice.

Ina strode behind him, picking up her fighting staff. Without pausing to think, she lifted it, ready to strike. Sulien turned, the bag of nuts in his hand, and saw her. He froze. Ina swiped the staff at him, threateningly.

"Put that bag back. Now!"

"You dare to threaten the son of King Cynddylan, commander in chief and leader of all the people of Caergeri?" challenged Sulien, his voice starting to break again.

"If you dare take one little nut I will break your hand, like the low thief you are."

They eyed each other wildly, like two stags squaring up in the autumn, ready to gore each other with their antlers.

Then, with a sly little smile, Sulien put his hand in the nut-bag. Before she knew what she was doing, Ina brought the wood down, swift and hard, to within a hair's breadth of his hand.

In his fear, Sulien dropped the bag. Ina stared, stupefied, at the staff, which was hovering like a kestrel above his arm, then she pulled it away hurriedly. What on earth had come over her?

"Sulien . . . I wouldn't have . . . not really . . ." said Ina, unable to finish the sentence. She had complete control over the staff but she could so easily have injured Sulien, smashing the bones of his wrist to pieces. Just as she could have injured Briallen, with the sword.

"There's something wrong with you! You're mad!"

Ina saw that there were tears of indignation in Sulien's eyes. She had made him cry, and she felt even more ashamed.

"Help yourself to the nuts," said Ina, limply. "I'll go and collect blackberries for us."

"Stuff your nuts!" Sulien sat down and rubbed his eyes.

Despite everything, it was a relief to hear him speaking like a normal boy. Ina turned to Bleiddyn. "You coming?"

But, for once, instead of obeying the dog stayed where he was. She had frightened him too. That's a lesson for me, thought Ina, before turning and walking towards the brambles and picking blackberries, though she wasn't hungry any more.

Perhaps Sulien was right. Perhaps there was something wrong with her. After all, she was different to everyone else – that's what most people thought. Perhaps they were all right.

The remains of the old fort rested on the ridge of the hill, like the body of some enormous animal. It was obvious that no one had been near the place for years, apart from to use it as a livestock enclosure, thought Ina, staring down at sheep droppings.

Before nightfall, Ina had taken care to note the point on

the horizon that marked the south. And as the weather was fair today, she'd been able to navigate using the sun's position, too. So a few miles after leaving the stream they'd arrived at the old fort, exactly as they'd hoped. She'd managed to follow Tegid ap Gwyddien's instructions to the letter.

"The river Gwili can't be far. Why not have a little break here?" suggested Ina.

"Very well," said Sulien, drily. These were the first words he'd thrown in her direction since 'the incident' – although Ina, unusually for her, had tried more than once to draw a conversation out of him.

After a brief rest they set off again, arriving before long at the river Gwili. The remainder of the journey was easy, according to Tegid. Follow the river for an hour or two before arriving at the high road. And no more than an hour after that, they'd reach Caersallog. At last.

Suddenly, Ina felt hungry. She'd eaten almost nothing at breakfast and neither had Sulien, for obvious reasons. Ina dismounted Pennata and led her to the river so she could drink, and Sulien did the same thing.

Then Ina offered a handful of blackberries to him, which she'd stored in her bag. While he stuffed them unceremoniously into his mouth, Ina ate a handful too – one by one, to enjoy their rich, sweet taste. Sulien had already swallowed his and dark red juice was smeared all around his mouth. Ina laughed.

"You've got a moustache!"

Without thinking, she stretched out her hand to wipe the juice away. Sulien jerked his head back.

"Don't," he said, desperately embarrassed.

Ina blushed, straightaway regretting her impulse. What had she been thinking of? Without saying another word, she passed him a fistful of nuts then walked hurriedly away towards the river, where she filled her leather flask with pure, sweet water and made sure that Pennata and Bleiddyn had drunk their fill too. But mostly, she made sure not to look in Sulien's direction.

When she got back, Sulien was on his horse already. His lips were wiped clean by now, though he'd missed a bit. Ina decided it'd be better not to say anything. Without waiting for her, Sulien urged his horse into a trot and Ina followed, like a good little girl, without so much as a word of complaint.

She was going to do her very best to behave like a young lady, as was expected of her, and not to make a fool of herself in Caradog's court. Caersallog would be a chance to start afresh. She should take this opportunity and fulfil the wish of her dear Gwrgant, peace be upon him.

Ina tried to imagine just what sort of a place Caradog's court would be. She'd been doing this for a while – ever since Gwrgant had told her of the plan. But she had a better idea now, after being in Caergeri and meeting a real king. Caersallog was a huge fort, bigger than Caergeri, she knew that much. And so Caradog's court was sure to be more luxurious than Cynddylan's. Hopefully she wouldn't look awkward and out of place in her emerald, woollen dress. Perhaps she'd be expected to dress in satin clothes? Her mother had had a satin dress, of a shining, deep red. Ina had only ever seen her wear it once. She'd looked so beautiful.

Swiftly, Ina pushed the image from her mind. This wasn't the time to reminisce. It was the time to look towards the future . . .

Then Ina realised that something was wrong, in the same way you sense that a storm is about to break. Bleiddyn began to bark – two low, nervous yaps. Looking down at him, Ina saw that his ears were pricked up and his tail was low. She felt Pennata's gait change, her muscles tightening and her nostrils flaring wide before she snorted, fearfully. Ina gripped the staff, which she'd attached to the saddle.

"Sulien! Wait!"

But Sulien had already pulled up. He'd sensed something too.

Ina stared into the distance. The sun had long risen by now and the heat haze made it difficult to see far. She shaded her eyes with her hand. Was that smoke on the horizon or was it the heat, creating shapes?

"Can you see anything?" she asked Sulien.

"Smoke, perhaps? I'm not sure."

"That's what I thought, too."

Then Ina heard a sound behind her. She turned to see something coming towards them along the path – an ox-drawn cart.

"Sulien! Someone's coming!"

"Stay where you are," said Sulien, pulling his horse about and digging his heels into its sides, setting off at a canter towards the cart.

There'd been a different note in his voice – something that Ina hadn't heard till now – a firmness, which made her do as he said. She could see that there was a small family on the cart – husband, wife and two children. The smallest wasn't much more than a baby and it was crying, its mother gripping it tightly to her. The cart stopped as Sulien approached. The man had a whip in his hand. He raised it, as a warning. Perhaps he feared that the plague was upon them – Ina knew that isolated cases of the disease still flared up, here and there. At her side, Bleiddyn growled, showing his teeth at the strange man. Instinctively, Ina gripped her staff even tighter.

"State yur name, and yur purpose hare," the man shouted at Sulien.

The way he spoke sounded strange to Ina's ears, and his voice was hoarse with fear. She saw Sulien sit up proudly on his horse, though she could tell that he was afraid too.

"Sulien, son of the king Cynddylan. And this is Ina daughter of Nudd. She has a place in the court of King Caradog."

The man brought his whip down. Ina let her staff go, and Bleiddyn quietened.

"Furgive me, Sulien son of Cynddylan, but you must return to Caergeri. At once!" said the man earnestly, in his strong accent.

"For why?"

With a sinking of her heart, Ina knew the answer before the man spoke another word.

"See that smook? The fields are aflame, the crops destroyed. The Saxons came at dawn this murning. Caradog's dead, murdered. And all the best of his sons – dead, murdered. Theer's no one left to defend Caersallog. Everyone who can has fled."

So. The Saxons hadn't been intent on taking Caergeri. All along, they'd had their eyes on the bigger prize – Caersallog.

The man lifted his whip and snapped it in the air. The ox began to pull the cart again. The older girl, who was sitting next to her mother, raised her hand at Ina and smiled, tentatively. Ina didn't move.

"Better take the highway! It isn't fer. God be with yuh!" shouted the man over his shoulder.

Ina hardly heard him, gripping Pennata's reins tightly. She felt unsteady, as if she might fall from the back of the mare.

"Ina," called Sulien. "We had better follow his advice."

She looked at him, stupefied. In her anguish, she'd forgotten he was there at all. He was afraid, of course, as was she, but something else was evident on his face. Relief. Ina felt something inside of her explode.

"You're glad, aren't you?"

"Of course I'm not glad. This is a tragedy!"

"You're glad that it's not Caergeri that fell, I mean." Sulien squirmed.

"Go away," said Ina, her voice rising. "There's no reason for you to be here any more."

"But . . . what will you do?"

"It's none of your business what I do!"

"But I can't leave you like this!"

"Why? You afraid of what your father, the king, will say?"

Sulien shifted in his saddle, his cheeks flushing red.

"He thinks you're a fool. You know that, don't you?" added Ina. It was a very cruel thing to say, but by now Ina had lost it completely.

"Get lost! Get out of my sight! Go running back to Caergeri, back to Mummy – you big baby!"

Sulien opened his mouth to say something. Then he shut it without a sound and, swiftly turning his horse, he galloped away.

"And a fair wind follow you – you milksop!"

Ina regretted the heartless words immediately. She wanted to gallop after him and say sorry, beg him not to leave her on her own. But she was far too proud to do so, even at so fateful a moment as this.

She gripped the mare's reins even more tightly. If only she'd been able to cry, she would've been sobbing her heart out.

Her former home was in Brochfael's hands; her new home in the hands of the Saxons. What in the world would become of her now?

XIII

Suddenly, Ina heard a groaning rumble that seemed to be rising from the belly of the earth, as if the very ground were in pain. She felt the tension return to Pennata's muscles and heard Bleiddyn bark again, sharply. Then she realised that the sound was coming from the direction of the high road. Cautiously, not knowing where else to go, she continued down the path towards the sound. Could it be the people of Caersallog – or . . . the Saxons?

The fort came into view – set firmly, like a crown, on the head of the hill. The proud city of Caersallog – now lost to the enemy. The Roman road was now within a stone's throw, and it was overflowing with people. Ina edged closer, staring, stupefied, at this procession. People of all sizes, colours and shapes. Some rich. Some poor. Some on horses. Some in carts. Some dragging their belongings behind them on improvised sledges, but most walking, sagging under the weight of their baggage. Ina realised, numbly, that these were the people of Caersallog – those who had chosen to flee rather than take their chances under Saxon rule.

There was something unreal about the whole thing, as if a huge gap had opened up between her and these refugees, although by now she was almost near enough to touch them. She stared at face after face as they passed. The wide, empty eyes of people who had lost everything.

Pennata began to squeal and kick up her hooves. Ina held tightly to her reins to try to subdue her, and threw a word of comfort to Bleiddyn. Although so very wretched, at least these people were still alive, unlike the men who'd fought against the Saxons – those men would never tread any road again, apart from the golden one that led to heaven.

"The stallion!" someone shouted in her face. "How much do you want fur him?"

Ina jumped in fright. Glancing down, she saw a beautiful woman looking up at her. But although her face was very pretty, there was something chilling about her striking eyes, made even more piercing by their outlines of black makeup. The lady was dressed in satin from head to foot, with costly beads about her neck and finely-worked bracelets on each wrist. Unlike the rest, she carried nothing but the jewellery she wore. Behind her, two slaves crouched and staggered under the heavy load of her possessions, like a pair of pack-mules.

The woman thrust a leather pouch into Ina's hand.

"Feel its weight. There's mur than enough siller in theer to compensate you fur him," she said. Her accent was strong, not unlike the man with the cart's. The woman was trying to smile, but there was something false about her expression, something that made Ina bristle with distaste.

"Her," said Ina, pointedly. "Not him. And she's not for sale," she added, pushing the pouch back into the woman's hands. Without hesitating, the woman pulled off one of her bracelets and offered it to Ina.

"What about this? It belonged to my gran-mum. A lady at the court of no less a king than Caradog himself."

"The answer's still no," said Ina. "And just so you know – this mare belonged to no less a person than my mother, niece of Gwrgant ap Ynyr ap Pawl Hen, the highest of the noblemen in all Gwent."

Once she realised that Ina wasn't going to give in, the woman's smile vanished.

"Then I sharl claim her fur myself!"

The woman turned to her slaves, shouting orders. Before Ina could react, one of the men had grabbed Pennata's bridle and the other had hold of Ina's leg, pulling her off the horse. Bleiddyn sprang at him, but in panic Pennata lifted her hooves and kicked him, unintentionally. Ina could feel herself slipping from the saddle. She tried to reach for her fighting staff, but the slave holding Pennata's bridle grabbed her arm and twisted it. Pain shot up to her shoulder. If only Sulien were still here, he could have helped her, or at least attempted to. But, of course, Ina had sent him away.

Suddenly, a murmur ran through the crowd, as if a swarm of bees had sensed danger.

"The Saxons!"

"Theer after us!"

"Run! Run for yur lives!"

At that, everything went crazy. People started running, pushing. Something struck the slave holding Pennata's bridle and he fell, face-first, to the ground. Her head freed, the mare reared her front legs and clawed her hooves through the air before her, throwing the other slave to the ground. Ina gripped the horse's mane hard and leant forwards, managing, just, to stay on her back.

With a scream, the woman leapt at Ina, trying to drag her off the mare. But Ina was back in the saddle, her hands tight around the reins. She galloped away, leaving the rich lady rolling in the dirt.

✦ ✦ ✦

After riding far enough from the road to feel sure that no one was following them, Ina pulled at Pennata's reins and slowed down. The mare was breathing heavily. So was Bleiddyn. But he was none the worse after the horse's kick, thank goodness.

Ina's heart was beating hard. She tried to control her breathing, to exhale the fear from her body and clear her mind, as Gwrgant had taught her. She had to have a plan, and that straight away.

She couldn't return to Caergeri, not after the unspeakable way she'd treated Sulien. She found it hard to understand how she could've been so nasty to him. She wondered whether Sulien would find his way back to the road. She really hoped he wouldn't get lost, and wander on to land snatched by the Saxons . . .

"Concentrate, Ina!" she said to herself, annoyed, forcing her fears for Sulien aside and trying to think. Pasgen had offered his help if she were in trouble, by finding her a place in one of the Christian communities in Gwent. Under the circumstances, that had to be the best thing. Even Brochfael wouldn't dare do anything to her if she was under the wing of the church.

Then she remembered the map, delving in the bag to find it. Her hands were shaking. She found Caersallog – or Sorviodunum, as it appeared on the map – and saw that many roads crossed it. The road to the west, in the direction of Caerfaddon and the legendary hillfort of Caercado, was the one filled with refugees. If the Saxons really were out for blood, it'd be better to avoid that road altogether. She didn't want to meet the mad woman again either, in case she tried to steal Pennata a second time.

Studying the map, Ina saw that there was another road, heading south-west towards a stronghold of the Britons – Caerdorin. From there, she could reach Caerfaddon from the other direction, then return to Gwent when the situation had settled down. The trouble was, even riding hard, Caerdorin was too far to reach in a day. And she couldn't risk spending the night out here, with the countryside crawling with Saxons . . .

Forcing her attention back to the map, Ina saw that a little over halfway to Caerdorin stood an old Roman town called Vindocladia. For some reason, the name rang a bell – but Ina couldn't for the life of her remember why. Even if no one lived there any more, perhaps this town would offer her safe refuge.

✦ ✦ ✦

The main road to Caerdorin was in good condition, allowing Ina to travel many miles before lunch time. But the road was steep, especially to start with. Now Pennata had begun to slow down and was blowing hard again, and even Bleiddyn wasn't as lively as usual, trotting wearily at her side. So Ina decided to rest under the shelter of a tree by the lane – the three of them badly needed a break.

After a simple snack of nuts (there were no blackberries left), Ina filled her leather flask at a nearby stream, giving the animals a chance to drink their fill too, before resuming their journey.

The sun blazed scorching hot through a cloudless sky for the rest of the day. It was unusually hot. And unusually good for the crops, which had failed many times in the previous years. But this was scant comfort for Ina. The beating sun made her feel heavy and tired. She was tempted more than once to beg Uinseann for help again – to make the clouds appear this time instead of making them disperse. But she was afraid to do so in case she offended God. This was a black day for the whole country – the day the pagans had taken Caradog's city. The Lord had more important things on his mind, that was for sure.

By the time the sun began to set, Ina's mouth was as dry as a bone and the leather flask was empty. As was the horizon – there was no sign of the old Roman town. How on earth was she to reach Vindocladia before nightfall? Had she made a mistake, perhaps? She was about to reach for the map again when she saw something before her – a cart, and on it a woman, three children and a pile of belongings. A farmer walked before the ox, leading it. Ina lifted her hand in greeting.

"Good day, in the name of the Lord!"

"Not a gud day hare," said the farmer, shortly.

"Where are you going?"

"To the greet furt, we are."

Ina knew, by now, that he meant 'great fort' by this. Here was another of the people with the strange accent.

"Fleeing the Saxon. They say theer on the merch, after the fall of Caersallog."

"Is there a fort nearby, then?" asked Ina, hopefully. Better than hiding in an old Roman town, all by herself.

"Wheer you frum, gal? The mun?"

"No. Not from the moon. From Gwent."

"Gwent?!"

The farmer stared at her in astonishment. He'd couldn't have been more shocked than if she'd said she *had* come from the moon.

"The fort's nearby, is it?" persisted Ina.

"Yes, gal. The furt of Caer Faddan."

"Caerfaddon?" It was Ina's turn to look surprised.

"Not the furt of Caerfaddon. The furt of Caer Faddan. No one lives theer any mur, but it's a safe place. You know – wheer the glorious baddle took place."

"The battle of Mynydd Baddon?"

"Theer you are – Menedd Baddan."

And then Ina remembered why the name Vindocladia had rung a bell. The town was very close to the site of this famous battle.

"My guardian, Gwrgant ap Ynyr, was at that battle, fighting side by side with King Caradog's father."

"Was he really? God bless you then, my gal. To the furt! And quickly too!" said the farmer, his face lighting up at the thought of this victory and he gestured, with eyes that sparkled with tears, for Ina to move ahead of the cart.

She passed a long line of people on the way, every one of them greeting her courteously. They moved purposefully and without panic, as if it were fairly normal for them to make for the great fort in times of trouble – just as the people of Gwent found temporary refuge in their land's forests and caves.

Night fell slowly. Ina began to fear that they'd never arrive when the stronghold of Caer Faddan emerged through the twilight before her: a great fort on top of a hill, defended by three high earth dykes. Staring about her, she felt a shiver zigzag down her back. To think that it was here, on the wide field before the hillfort, that that fateful battle she'd heard so much about had taken place. If only Gwrgant were at her side to share the moment! She sighed, feeling the first prickles of *hiraeth* and forcing herself not to let them develop into full-blown grief – Gwrgant wouldn't want that.

She bent to comb Pennata's mane with her fingers, whispering in her ear, "There you are, old girl. We've arrived at last." Then she turned to Bleiddyn, who was staring up at her. "Don't worry – I haven't forgotten you."

She smiled at the dog's shaggy, dusty appearance. Then he stiffened, beginning to bark. Ina heard raised voices and lifted her head to see that the people nearest the fort were starting to run – and then she saw why.

Galloping towards them, their swords and battle-axes held aloft, was a band of Saxons.

XIV

Something darted past Ina. An arrow, and then another – closer this time. She heard it hiss through the air and land heavily on the ground behind her. The men defending the fort were attacking the Saxons. Perhaps they thought she was an enemy too, because she was on horseback. But it was hard to tell what was going on, through the dusk and the fleeing people.

"Out of here!" Ina shouted at Pennata, kicking her harshly. She galloped away down the slope, Bleiddyn bounding at her side.

After a few minutes, Ina pulled on the mare's reins, judging they were far enough away to avoid the arrows. But before she had time to come to herself and decide what to do next, there was a commotion behind her. Turning, she saw three terrifying-looking figures, galloping towards her. The Saxons had noticed her too.

Ina froze. She knew she must flee, but she was paralysed.

"Dearest Ina, they're real! And their weapons too! Away with you – at once!"

Ina turned in the direction of Gwrgant's voice, but there was no one there. She knew the voice had been in her head; and she knew that these warriors would drag her off her horse and hack her to death, but still she could not move. All she could do was stare, stupefied, as they raced towards her.

Then she realised that Bleiddyn was barking at her. She saw him bare his teeth and nip Pennata's flank, who reared then galloped away, squealing wildly. Ina, clinging to her back, was almost thrown for the second time today, but the shock was enough to bring her to her senses. She leant down low, gripping the reins tightly.

Bleiddyn raced at their side, his ears flying backwards, his long legs moving smoothly. In no time he was ahead, his furry tail waving as he passed them, but he looked back continually, as if making sure Ina was still safe.

Ina twisted her head to see that the Saxons were within a stone's throw of her by now. She was beginning to lose hope when something appeared to her right – an outline of stone walls, lurking in the dusk. The silhouette of a Roman temple. So the old town of Vindocladia had to be close by. Then she remembered. Of course! The Saxons were afraid of deserted Roman towns! If she could reach it before they caught her up, perhaps she'd be safe.

Digging in her heels, Ina urged Pennata to gallop even harder. In no time, the rectangular walls of Vindocladia were straight ahead of them. There was a large hole in the wall before her. Turning again, she saw that the Saxons had almost reached her.

There was not a moment to lose. Ina yanked the reins to aim the mare's muzzle straight at the gap in the wall then closed her eyes tightly. Somehow, Pennata managed to clear the rubble and land safely on the other side. A moment later, Bleiddyn hurled himself through the gap to join them.

Then Pennata slowed, without Ina having to pull her up. The horse was dripping with sweat and blowing heavily from wide nostrils. Ina jumped from her back, running her hand across the mare's long neck.

"Good girl!" whispered Ina into her ear, before hurrying to stroke and praise Bleiddyn too. But there was no time to waste. She gripped the horse's reins and ran with her into the enclosing ruins of some large building, with Bleiddyn hot on her heels.

Once she'd pulled the saddle off Pennata's back, Ina heard shouting from beyond the town walls. The harsh voices of the Saxons tore through the silence, as they berated each other like quarrelling dogs in their fierce, foreign tongue. To Ina's ears, it sounded like the language of the devil himself.

Taking a quick peek through one of the building's remaining windows, she saw that they were standing outside the hole in the wall. The moon had risen by now, and Ina could make out enough of the men to feel even more terrified of them. They were tall and thickset, their faces sinister and each one's hair was pulled back in a greasy knot. There wasn't a trace of kindness about them, unlike the Saxon slave on Tegid's estate. The tallest one lifted his arm and something caught the light of the moon and flashed. A short sword. The weapon that Ina had heard so much about – the seax. The fearsome blade that had given them their name – Saxon.

But although the Saxons continued to snarl at each other, it didn't look as if they wanted to venture through the wall. They seemed to be afraid, exactly as Ina had hoped.

Her relief lasted only seconds, however. The next moment,

Ina saw a spark of fire. They were busy lighting torches, that soon flared brightly in the darkness. The tallest of them stepped across the rubble, flaming torch in one hand and sword in the other. Bleiddyn began to bristle, lifting his lips to bare his teeth.

"Shh," warned Ina, quietly.

The Saxon raised his torch high, and in its light Ina saw a deep scar on the man's face. A shiver went through her. He beckoned to the others to follow him, but they didn't move a muscle. Exasperated, he shouted at them, the strange words blazing and jarring through the darkness like the sparks of his torch. Then, one after the other, the two warriors stepped reluctantly through the hole behind him. Now the first man was walking down the street towards the building where Ina hid. Her fighting staff would be useless against him. She put her hand on the hilt of the sword, ready to pull it. Perhaps she would have a right to under the circumstances? Without realising she was doing so, she held her breath.

All of a sudden, Bleiddyn crouched, stretched out his neck and howled. One long howl after the other tore from his throat, each more terrifying than the last, sending shivers down Ina's spine until the last, dreadful cry that would have caused even the dead to tremble with fear. At once the two Saxons at the back scurried for the wall, hurling themselves out through the gap. In his fear, the big scarred man dropped his torch and scrambled out too.

By this time, Pennata was shivering from her ears to her hooves and her wide-open eyes bulged from her head.

"Don't be afraid. It's only Bleiddyn," Ina whispered,

running her hands across the mare's back to try to soothe her. And perhaps she would have succeeded, if only Bleiddyn hadn't chosen that moment to let loose a last cry from the heart and howl for all his lungs were worth, as if he were making completely sure that the Saxons wouldn't dare come near the place again. Pennata was panicking now. And this time, there was no calming her. Although Ina tried to rein her in, the mare was much too strong, knocking Ina to the ground and galloping away from her.

"Pennata!"

Ina scrambled to her feel and sprinted after her, but it was no use. Pennata leapt through the hole in the wall and disappeared into the darkness beyond. Ina couldn't follow, in case the Saxons were still outside. She could only hope that Pennata wasn't galloping in their direction. There was nothing for it but to stay here, and hope for the best.

So she turned and walked back down the street to the building. In the corner, Bleiddyn was waiting for her with a guilty look on his face.

"Did you have to?" asked Ina, sharply. Bleiddyn looked up at her with his big eyes and Ina felt herself softening as relief began to flow through her veins. She couldn't manage to stay angry with him for long – after all, he had saved her life.

"Come here, you silly beast."

Bleiddyn came to her and licked her hand before lying down at her feet. Ina crouched to stroke him, realising that her hands were shaking. She lay down at his side, and the big wolf-dog shoved his nose towards her before settling, his deep breathing slowing gradually as he fell asleep.

Ina tried to drift off too, but she was too worried to sleep. Worried about Pennata. And – this was a surprise to her – worried about Sulien. She turned on her side and put her arm around the dog. Who knew what the morning would bring?

XV

Ina woke to the sound of something scratching by her ear. She turned and found herself eyeball to eyeball with the beady black gaze of a staring rat. She screamed, leaping to her feet, and the rat scrambled away. Bleiddyn opened a lazy eye to see what all the fuss was about.

"You just missed breakfast."

The wolf-dog stretched and shook himself upright, sniffing at the rat's scent-trail. Then he crept, furtively, after it.

"Don't go too far," warned Ina, as he disappeared from view. Then she remembered that Pennata had fled last night. Perhaps she was back already! Ina followed Bleiddyn out into the street, but there was no sign of the mare. Maybe she was grazing outside the walls?

Ina walked cautiously to the hole in the wall. The Saxon's torch was still lying in the rubble, now burned to ashes. Peeping through the hole, she saw a landscape covered in thick, morning mist, which the rising sun hadn't yet burned off. There was no sign of the Saxons, which was a good thing; but no sign of Pennata either, which was a bad thing.

"Pennata . . . Pennata . . ." she called, careful not to raise her voice too high. Again and again she called. In vain. The mare had disappeared from the face of the earth.

Ina tried to comfort herself. Perhaps the Britons in the hillfort have found her, she thought, hopefully. The first step would be to go to the hillfort and ask. Of course, there was another possibility: the Saxons . . . But Ina didn't even want to consider that.

She went back to collect her things. She didn't want breakfast – didn't even feel thirsty, though she hadn't drunk anything since yesterday afternoon. She was too worried about Pennata to think about food and drink – unlike Bleiddyn, who had just returned, happy as a lark, licking his bloodied lips. Obviously, he'd caught the rat and made a fine breakfast of it.

✣ ✣ ✣

The mist was starting to clear as Ina walked up the slope towards the hillfort, the travelling bag across her shoulders weighing heavy already. Her fighting staff was in her hand and the sword safe in the bag on her back – ready to pull out, if she had to. Bleiddyn stuck close to her. At times like this, Ina was truly grateful for the dog's company.

On the ground before her, she could see several piles of clothes. People must have thrown them aside as they fled the Saxons last night, she reasoned. But as she stepped closer she realised that they were not piles of clothes – they were bodies.

Ina stood stock-still and so did Bleiddyn, who began a low whining. Nausea rose, suddenly, in her throat, and she retched. Then the mist withdrew a little further, revealing more bodies to her left. She caught a glimpse and averted her eyes in horror – but not before the image of a whole family, lying motionless and bloody, was seared into her mind.

Her blood seemed to freeze. And she saw herself, at seven years old, waking from fever, from the clutches of the plague. Beside her lay her mother and her sister and, for the life of her, she couldn't understand why they were lying so still, why they wouldn't answer her . . .

A horn sounded through the fog, dragging her back to the present. Perhaps the horn was a sign that the Britons in the hillfort were coming to collect their dead, to bury them. The horn sounded again. A strident blast, threatening. And again. This time its call seemed savage, vicious, and Ina knew, instinctively, that this was not a horn of peace, but a war horn.

The fog lifted further still. In the distance, she saw a large group of men, gathering purposefully together, about some business. Men with horses. Soldiers. She understood, in horror, that this was the Saxons' camp. They were still here. And worse, they stood between her and the hillfort.

She had only one choice now. To flee.

"Dear Pennata . . ." she whispered. The thought of leaving without the mare was enough to break her heart. Pennata was her mother's horse. And leaving without her was almost as hard as saying farewell to her mother again. In her imagination, she saw once more the still bodies of her mother and sister. She forced herself to push the picture from her mind. If she wanted to live, she had to concentrate.

Ducking behind a shrub, she beckoned Bleiddyn to follow. Then she pulled out the map and studied it with shaking hands. And saw, with relief, that she should be able to reach Caerdorin before nightfall – even on foot.

The map showed that the main road to Caerdorin crossed a river. Good – she'd be able to fill her flask there. Then she thought it would be safer to find another, less obvious, crossing place and rejoin the road somewhere beyond the river, having put enough distance between herself and the Saxons' camp.

The war horn sounded again, making Ina jump. Its shrill call penetrated her flesh like a jagged blade. Quickly, she looked about once more in the hope that, through some miracle, she'd see Pennata. But there was still no sign of the horse. Heavy-hearted, she crept quickly down the slope, crouching to make herself as small as possible with Bleiddyn trotting silently at her side. She prayed with all her heart that the mist didn't clear completely until she was well clear of the Saxons.

✦ ✦ ✦

After crossing the river, Ina easily made her way back to the main road – though this section was much poorer, its cobbles missing or jumbled underfoot. However, she reasoned, no matter the state of the road as long as it led them safely to Caerdorin. But as the road continued to deteriorate, becoming overgrown with grass and brambles, she began to wonder whether she was on one of the minor roads that weren't on the map at all. Going back wasn't possible now, so she had no choice but to head on across the uneven stones.

After walking for ages, the scorching sun beating down on her, Ina saw a strip of blue in the distance. The sea. Her heart sank. Caerdorin wasn't by the sea. She'd taken the wrong road. Reaching for the map, she realised, in panic, that it wasn't in the travelling bag. Her heart sank further. She must have dropped it when the war horn had pierced through her. Without the map there was no way of working out where she was. Hope began to drain from her and she slumped to the ground, before shaking herself.

"Come on, Ina! Think!"

The sea was straight in front of her, so Caerdorin, which lay to the west, must be somewhere to her right. As long as she headed west after reaching the sea, she'd be fine. There would surely be another road leading in the right direction, further along the coast. She smiled with relief, thinking that Gwrgant would be proud of her logic.

Then she took a sip from the flask before pouring water into her hand and letting Bleiddyn lap it up.

"I'm sorry, Bleiddyn. This is turning into a much longer journey than I'd hoped."

But Bleiddyn didn't seem to mind much. He'd just slaked his thirst and, for a dog in the heat of the sun, there was nothing better.

Ina lifted the flask to her lips once more, but it was empty already. Dragging herself to her feet, she began to walk cautiously towards the end of the road, and a natural harbour came into view. She was pretty sure by now that they were on the right side of the border between the Britons and the Saxons, but she also knew it was dangerous to relax too early.

The road petered out and before her she took in a bay in the shape of a circle, broken by a narrow throat which led out to sea. In the middle of the bay lay a little island. The tide had to be out, because the sea had retreated to reveal the harbour's mud. On this mud, she saw a tatty-looking boat, resting on its side. To the left of this was an old stone building, some sort of store house or warehouse. From the tumbledown look of it, it hadn't been used for many years. Beyond the building there was a collection of poor, wooden huts – but there was not a living soul to be seen.

Ina stepped warily towards the huts, signalling to Bleiddyn to follow her quietly and keeping a tight grip on her staff. She saw a wooden cross by a small, earthen mound, facing the sea. These were Christians, then. Britons. People like her.

"God be with you!" called Ina, in the direction of the buildings. She waited for an answer. Nothing but silence. She tried once more.

"Good day to you in the name of the Lord Jesus, he who died to save us."

Not a peep of a sound in return. There was something overpowering about the silence. Something unnatural. Ina felt relieved to give up and walk away from the huts towards the sea.

By the time she'd reached the mouth of the bay, her head was splitting and her chapped lips were painfully dry in the blazing sun. Bleiddyn wasn't much better either – his tail was low and his tongue hung limply from his mouth. Then Ina saw a little strip of silver, shining in the sunshine. A stream was spilling its way from the sand dunes to the sea. Walking quickly towards it, she soon broke into a run with Bleiddyn racing ahead. Falling to her knees, she plunged her head into the cold, clear water, too thirsty to bother using her hands to cup it into her mouth. She drank deeply, draught after draught, until she choked. Then she surfaced, taking a moment to come to herself before drinking again.

When she'd finally slaked her thirst, she filled the leather flask with water and looked about her. Opposite was a long beach, the sand as white as snow in the bright sunshine. To the right of her was a stony shore, laced with seaweed. Ina's stomach began to rumble, and she realised how hungry she was. Fortunately, there were a few nuts left in the little leather bag but after she'd swallowed them she felt even more hungry.

So she pulled the hunting tackle from her travelling bag and walked over to the dunes, hoping to find a bird's nest or a rabbit hole.

She came across a promising-looking hole more or less straight away and placed a trap over it. Bleiddyn had been watching carefully, obviously longing to follow the rabbit's trail, so Ina had to drag him away.

Keeping a tight grip on the scruff of his neck, Ina walked back to the shore, weaving her way through mounds of seaweed to the water's edge. Lifting a stone, she threw it into the sea. Without hesitation, Bleiddyn chased after it, leaping into the waves. On impulse, she hurriedly placed her cloak and bag on a nearby rock. Then, pulling off her sandals and lifting her dress, she stepped into the cold water. She could almost hear her feet shouting in joy as the first wave washed over them, splashing up her ankles.

She took a step forwards, letting the water reach her knees. But no more. That was deep enough for her – unlike Bleiddyn, who was far out of his depth and swimming as confidently as a seal – a very furry seal. Ina closed her eyes, enjoying the cool sea breeze on her forehead. She felt her headache gradually clear.

And she began to feel terribly tired. It wouldn't do any harm to have a little nap, she thought. Perhaps by the time she woke there'd be a rabbit caught in the trap. At this thought, her stomach began to rumble again and she did her very best to ignore it.

Finding a clear, dry spot further up the beach, she lay down, using her bag as a pillow. She was so tired her bones hurt. She didn't even know it was possible to be so tired. Pulling her cloak over her head, she listened to the sea's murmur, lulling her to sleep.

XVI

Ina woke to see the rich woman from Caersallog looming over her, threateningly.

"Wheer's the mare?"

"I don't know," answered Ina sleepily, trying to get up. But the woman placed her foot on Ina's chest and pushed her back down.

"You sharl carry me, then!"

The woman lifted her foot. Ina tried to move, but something was wrong. Very wrong. She didn't have hands at the end of her arms, but hooves. Like a horse's. The rich woman laughed to see her astonished expression. And as she laughed, a mass of bees came swarming from her mouth, landing thickly on Ina's body and covering her with sharp stings.

Ina woke – properly, this time – waving her arms about to fend off bees that weren't really there. The skin of her face felt prickly, because she'd fallen asleep while the sun was high in the sky. She stared upwards, lifting her hand to avoid looking directly at the sun, and saw that it hadn't moved much, so she couldn't have been asleep for very long.

The dream had shaken her, reminding her that Pennata was no longer with her. Thank goodness Bleiddyn was still by her side. She had no idea what she'd do without him.

Pulling the flask from her bag, she took a swig of water to try to soothe the hunger pains in her stomach. But what she needed was food, not drink, and that as soon as possible. So she decided to make a fire. Then, if the trap had done its job, she could roast the rabbit straight away, without having to wait.

She collected a handful of brittle seaweed, bone-dry as charcoal, and a heap of sticks. Making a circle of stones, she tore the seaweed into small pieces before stacking it within. Then she took a piece of flint from the bag and scraped her knife down the stone in the direction of the seaweed, until sparks flew from it. The sparks caught the seaweed and in no time smoke was spiralling upwards. Then she arranged the sticks over the seaweed like a tent, and small flames jumped from the seaweed to the sticks. She had a fire.

Next, Ina walked swiftly back to the dunes, holding Bleiddyn tightly by his scruff to stop him rushing ahead. Something seemed to've excited him. Perhaps he could smell something. Perhaps the trap had really worked. Presently he began to bark, yanking her towards the rabbit hole with such strength that she was forced into a run. There, its neck stuck in the trap, was a rabbit.

"Bleiddyn! Sit!"

Obediently, the dog sat at once, although he couldn't resist a little whine of frustration. Ina turned her attention to the rabbit – a big, fat one. Its eyes were open and it seemed to be staring, accusingly, at her. But, from the awkward way it lay and its crooked neck, Ina knew it was dead. She picked it up. Its body was still warm and its fur felt as smooth as silk.

As soft as the little ermine shawl her mother used to wear across her shoulders. At this sudden memory, Ina swayed, nearly dropping the rabbit.

She hurried back to the beach. The fire was still alight, thank goodness. She set to at once, skinning the rabbit and cutting it open, throwing everything but the meat to the ground so Bleiddyn could eat it. Amongst the hunting tackle was a skewer. Ina held the thin piece of metal and pushed it through the remains of the rabbit's body, before placing it across the fire, resting the skewer's ends on two sticks.

Bleiddyn stared at her the whole time with his big eyes, licking his lips. Ina felt for him. He was starving too. The leftovers she'd given him hadn't been enough to fill him.

Motioning with her hand, she said, "Off you go. Go on."

Barking thankfully, Ina watched as Bleiddyn raced straight back to the dunes before disappearing from view.

Then she turned back to the fire, twisting the meat to make sure it didn't burn. The rabbit's flesh was starting to change colour already and beginning to smell good, but there was some time to go before it'd be ready to eat. Ina put more sticks on the fire, just in case.

To kill time, she stared at the sea. The thought of its great depth filled her with horror. But, despite that, there was something about its vastness that held her spellbound. This was the first time she'd seen so much of it – and it was unimaginably huge. There were no hills nearby to lessen its impact, like the hills of Caerfaddon and Dumnonia, that you could see from Gwent when you looked over the river Hafren. There was nothing at all to be seen beyond the watery flatness, apart from the horizon – and that was the most frightening thing of all.

The breeze picked up and a meaty gust filled Ina's nostrils.

Her stomach rumbled, even louder and more painfully than last time. She had to eat, this moment. She couldn't wait a second more.

Grabbing the skewer, she burned her fingers and almost dropped it.

"Be careful, Ina!" she snapped, reprimanded herself, before picking up a piece of seaweed – one that was still damp, this time –and wrapping it around the thin piece of metal to stop it burning her again.

She sunk her teeth into the meat and tore at it, like a wolf. Then she chewed contentedly, not minding one bit that the flesh was rather tough and bloody, from not being well-enough cooked. She devoured the whole thing. Every last morsel. When she'd finished, she sucked on the bones. And if her teeth had been as sharp and tough as Bleiddyn's, she would have eaten them too. Then she remembered that it'd been a while since the dog went to the dunes.

"Blei-ddyn!" she called, expecting to see him leaping towards her, but there was no sign of him. Perhaps he'd wandered out of earshot. She'd better go and look for him. Ina wrapped her cloak about her and set about packing the travelling bag. As she lifted the sword belt, the hilt shone brightly in the sunlight, dazzling her for a moment.

The temptation was too much. She tied the belt around her waist and gripped the hilt, which fitted her hand perfectly. She hadn't noticed this, the other evening. Perhaps because she'd been so scared. Pulling the sword from its scabbard, she realised that it was comparatively short and light, but a dangerous weapon nonetheless.

The blade flashed as Ina turned and admired the sword. It filled her with wonder – it was obvious that it had been wrought, sharpened and polished by a craftsman of the highest order, with its bright, even sheen and the patterns created in light and dark grey that ran like fine fishbones along its length.

Ina lifted the sword and whipped it through the air. She felt a thrill – the excitement of doing something she had no right to do and the shiver of realising the power of the sword. It was surprisingly easy for her to wield, just as if Gwrgant had ordered it especially for her, and not as a gift for Caradog.

Ina turned to face the endless sea, lifting the sword high and shouting across the waves:

"I am Ina ferch Nudd! Ina daughter of Nudd! Ina! Ina! Ina!" over and over, until her voice was hoarse.

Then she put the sword back in its scabbard and turned towards the dunes. And that's when she saw the two men walking towards her.

✜ ✜ ✜

"Don't be afraid," said one of the men. He spoke in Ina's language, but with a strong unfamiliar accent, and he was smiling. The other didn't say a word, just stared at her through his shaggy red hair: he was huge and made the leader of the three Saxons look like a weakling. Meanwhile, the first man was looking about him.

"Here on your own, are you?" he asked.

"No," answered Ina, finding her voice. "I'm with my travelling companion – Bleiddyn ap Gwrgant. Strange that you didn't see him in the dunes."

Under her cloak she kept a tight grip on the sword. She could tell from their clothes and their hair that they weren't Saxons, but they weren't her people either. The man turned to the other and said something in a tongue that was foreign to her, yet somehow familiar. Then Ina remembered where she'd heard it before. From Uinseann's mouth.

"Are you Irishmen?" she asked.

"We are," answered the man, surprised. "You've a good ear."

"*Cid dot ucai?*" Ina asked him, in the Irish tongue. What you up to here?

The man looked even more surprised, then he laughed, and Ina began to relax.

"Who taught you that?"

"Brother Uinseann. Sorry, it wasn't a very polite thing to ask. But that's what Uinseann always asked me, as a joke. Do you know him?"

"Uinseann? From Dyfed?"

"No. From Iwerddon – Ireland. That part you call 'The Land of the Spears'."

"Then he'll be a Leinster man, sure. We're from Britain, like you. Dyfed, to be exact. Ardál Mac Domnhaill, at your service," he said, bowing. Under her cloak, Ina loosened her grip on the sword. "And this feller's name is Garbhán Rua," he added, jerking his head to indicate the surly giant behind him. "The Rough One With the Red Hair, if you need a translation."

"Good day to you," said Ina politely, to no response from the red-haired man.

"Garbhán doesn't speak your tongue."

"But I thought you were from Dyfed?"

"Aha. Not everyone can speak Brythonic, see? Even in our village – Neugwl – which isn't far from the church of one of your holy men, David – or Dewi, as you people call him."

The big man – whom Ina now christened Rough Redhead – said something impatiently to Ardál, as much as to suggest that he was wasting time. Ardál replied sharply, before turning to Ina.

"Forgive him. He's no manners on him at all, nor patience."

"Have you ever been to David's church?" asked Ina, curious. Everyone had heard of David. Some said that one day he'd be even more famous than Cadog the Wise.

Ardál laughed. "No, I haven't. I'm not sure how much of a welcome I'd get."

"There's a welcome for all in God's house. Apart from Saxons."

The Irishman laughed again.

"Who told you that? Brother Uinseann?"

"No. My dear guardian, Gwrgant ap Ynyr, one of the heroes of the battle of Mynydd Baddon."

With that, Bleiddyn came into view, barking.

"And here's his son, Bleiddyn, I shouldn't wonder," said

Ardál, his smile fast disappearing. "That brindled hound is your 'travelling companion', so."

He stepped towards her, his eyes fixed on hers.

"There's no point trying to escape."

Ina took a step backwards, glancing quickly over her shoulder. The giant, Rough Redhead, was now behind her, ready to catch her if she tried to run away. There was nothing for it but to hold her ground. She turned to face Ardál, opened her cloak and raised her sword.

The Irishman froze, the shock evident on his face. Then Ina stepped forward, and he stepped back.

"Put your sword away, girl, before someone gets hurt. You don't want to cross Garbhán, believe me. He's as rough as his name."

But instead of yielding, Ina took a further step towards him, forcing him and the giant to back off. From the corner of her eye, she saw Bleiddyn racing towards them. The giant saw him too, shouting a warning to Ardál just as Bleiddyn threw himself through the air at him.

Ardál turned, but too late – Bleiddyn was already sinking his teeth into his arm. The Irishman screamed in pain and fell to the ground. The other one shouted again. Ina turned to face him, but Bleiddyn was there before her, snarling ferociously. But instead of defending himself, the giant stood his ground, challenging the dog. Ina saw Bleiddyn's whole body tense, ready to attack. And saw, too, that the large Irishman was holding a long knife at his side.

"Bleiddyn! No!"

But the dog was too wild with rage to hear her. He leapt at

the man. Ina saw the knife flash, and the blood. And the next moment, Bleiddyn lay on the beach, trembling and whining.

Without a thought for herself, Ina rushed to embrace him. Bleiddyn tried to lick her face but he was already too weak to lift his head. The trembling worsened, before stopping altogether. Although Bleiddyn's big eyes were still staring insistently into Ina's, she knew that he could no longer see her.

"Bleiddyn!"

She knew that he couldn't hear her any more either. He had gone. For ever. Her best friend. The sound of howling filled her ears – her own cries, baying at the unrisen moon.

Then she jumped to her feet and turned on her heel, slashing wildly with the sword at the red-haired giant. Instinctively, he stepped back, roaring as the blade swiped at his leg. If he hadn't moved in time, it would've split his hip to the bone. But instead of retreating, the man seized Ina's staff, which was lying on the beach, and raised it. He was fearless. He laughed, showing his front teeth, which were as sharp as a wolf's.

Now Gwrgant's voice sounded in Ina's head, warning her to be careful. But she was too maddened to take any notice, just as Bleiddyn had been, moments earlier. There was only one thing on her mind – and that was to make this bearded beast pay. She flung herself – fearlessly, recklessly – at the giant. She didn't stand a chance, in truth, not against him.

Effortlessly, he struck the sword from her hand with the staff, with such force that Ina fell on to her back.

Then the man grabbed her legs and pulled her towards

him. He bent over her, his body heavy, his breath hot and sour, spitting incomprehensible words through his thick, red beard. Ina saw the flash of the knife again and closed her eyes tight shut. Whatever was about to happen, she didn't have a hope of stopping it. All she could do was try not to look.

Then Ina heard the other man shout something and the two began to argue loudly with each other. The next moment the redhaired giant gave in, getting to his feet – and kicking her viciously in the side, for good measure.

Ina opened her eyes. Ardál was standing over her now, the marks of Bleiddyn's teeth dripping blood from his arm. He reached out a hand and she allowed him to help her up. She had no strength to carry on fighting.

"You're much too valuable to let that great hairy bear ruin you."

"Valuable?"

"I'll have an excellent price for such a spirited creature as you, sure. You're easily worth a cumal."

He saw that Ina hadn't understood.

"A cumal's worth three cows in Ireland."

The same as a soldier in Britain, thought Ina. She was worth the same as a soldier, after all. Not that that was any comfort to her.

Ardál nodded at the big, bearded man, who grabbed Ina's arms, unceremoniously snapping shut a pair of heavy iron manacles about her wrists.

And that's when Ina fully realised the raw horror of her fate: she was to be sold as a slave.

XVII

Ina didn't know which was worse. The heat, or the crying and groaning of the girl at the far end of the boat. She just wouldn't shut up.

Ina knew that she should also be very afraid. But she felt almost nothing at all, not even the cuffs on her wrists, even though the skin around them had been rubbed red-raw already. The shock of losing Bleiddyn was still with her. She knew that the pain of his death would hit her again soon, and that it would be unbearable. Part of her was jealous of the girl at the front of the boat, and her endless tears. Ina's tears for Bleiddyn had frozen within her before she'd had the chance to shed them, frozen into a bright, glittering stone of ice that she feared would lie heavy in her heart, weighing her down forever. Just like the tears for her family, and for Gwrgant, rock-hard inside her.

From the corner of her eye, Ina studied the girl at her side, who was chained fast to her. She was a pitiful creature in shabby clothes not much better than sack-cloth, her hair shorn so short you could see her scalp in places. She hadn't looked in Ina's direction yet, never mind spoken to her – she just stared, dumbly, at the hull of the boat.

At least she doesn't cry non-stop, thought Ina, looking towards the round-faced, red-cheeked girl who was still wailing at the front of the boat. None of the others were crying. Perhaps their tears had long dried. Or maybe they couldn't, for whatever reason, shed tears at all, like Ina. They were all young people, most of them girls – apart from a woman who looked about thirty years old, who was staring at the horizon as if she were expecting someone, or something, to save her.

It was difficult to count them but there had to be twenty, if not more, captives all told, every one of them crammed either between the wooden oar benches or around the mast in the centre of the boat. And then there was the Irish crew, who were the sailors of the boat, of course. Two of them stood at each end, watching over their prisoners. The rest were sleeping on the boat's hull, on top of sacks and animal skins – including the two men who'd captured Ina.

The one who could speak Brythonic, Ardál, had explained to her – while he transported her from the beach to the boat in a small coracle – that they'd set sail after nightfall. Ina had been surprised to see that the boat – which had been hidden behind the small island in the middle of the bay – was round and made of animal hide stretched over a wooden frame, like the coracle. It wasn't much bigger than the ferry across the Hafren either – but its sides were higher, because this boat was shaped more like a bowl or dish, whereas the ferry had been more or less flat.

Suddenly, the vessel began to shake from side to side as Rough Redhead, the bearded giant, abruptly got to his feet and strode, kicking captives out of his way, towards the girl at the front of the boat, who was still crying. She turned in time to see his approach, but not in time to dodge the terrifying blow he dealt to the side of her head with his fist. Ina had never seen such a blow. The girl's body fell down limp, and that was an end to the crying.

The man growled something in his own tongue and made his way back to lie down again, giving a few additional kicks – even more vicious this time – to anyone unlucky enough to come between him and his resting place.

Ina forced herself to look somewhere else. Anywhere but the front of the boat and the still body of the girl. She stared, wordlessly, at the floor, exactly like the girl at her side, and waited for night to fall.

✦ ✦ ✦

The boat slipped swiftly through the waves. Although there was hardly enough breeze to ruffle the sail, never mind fill it, the Irishmen's oars were all that was needed on such a mild evening. The sun had set, extinguishing the blazing light on the far horizon, but pink and purple hues still coloured the darkening sky. Turning her head, Ina could see the outline of the Dumnonian coast receding in the twilight, a long, crested black strip to the south of her. She'd never seen the sunset from the sea before. It was a magical sight, and at any other time she would have been entranced by it. But not tonight – not here – with her hands in manacles.

The other captives were either sleeping, or trying to. Everyone apart from the girl next to Ina, who continued to stare silently at the hull. Ina looked over at the girl in the front of the boat. She was still as limp as a rag, and the young woman who was chained to her had turned her back on her as best she could, the horror obvious on her face, even in the gloom.

Ina pulled her cloak tightly about her. Ardál had allowed her to keep it, for now. He would take it from her when the boat reached Ireland, for that was where they were sailing. The emerald dress – that was all she'd have left. Her sandals were still on the beach, and everything else had been taken by the Irishmen as spoil, including Gwrgant's ring. Without the ring, she wouldn't be able to prove who she was. Not that that would make any difference, now. She was a slave. Worth three cows. If she was lucky she'd be allowed to keep her name, but she'd better not hope for more than that.

Hugging her cloak still tighter about her, from the corner of her eye she saw that the ragged girl had lifted her head to stare shyly at her. Her face was so very pale. Like marble. Like Sulien's face . . .

Ina turned to face her, but the girl looked down again at once. There was something about her, her jerky little movements, that reminded Ina of a small, wounded bird, and she felt a sudden urge to protect her. Lifting her arm, Ina drew the cloak across the girl as well. As her arm touched her, she jumped as if Ina had burned her.

"I'm sorry I frightened you," whispered Ina. The girl didn't say a word. Did she choose not to, or was she unable to speak? Perhaps she'd been struck dumb by the dreadful experience of being captured. From her wretched appearance, Ina wondered if she'd suffered and seen things that no one – especially not a child – should.

She tried to wrap the cloak around her again. This time, the girl sat quietly. And, after a little difficulty, Ina managed to spread the cloak over the two of them like a blanket.

"Sleep well," Ina whispered.

At that, the girl lifted her head and stared at Ina as if understanding her for the first time. Ina held her breath. Although her face was so pale, the girl's eyes were dazzling, all the more so because of her crudely-shaven head. But the reason Ina held her breath wasn't because her bright eyes were so penetrating and observant but because they were green. Just like Bleiddyn's.

The girl bent her head to lean it against Ina's shoulder and Ina pulled the cloak tighter about her. The girl was trembling all over. Every part of Ina's body shook too, from the most overpowering exhaustion. Only moments later Ina fell into a sleep that was heavier than anything she could possibly have imagined.

XVIII

Ina opened her eyes suddenly, before shutting them again at once. She wasn't ready to wake yet. She could feel the warm body of Bleiddyn at her side. He must still be asleep. Ina tried to put her arm across the dog, to stroke him. But for some reason, she couldn't move it.

Opening her eyes, properly this time, she saw that it wasn't Bleiddyn at her side at all, but a fearful, frail-looking boy. No, not a boy. A girl, with hair shorn painfully short. But those eyes! She recognised them from somewhere . . .

Ina stared at her, uncomprehending, and tried to stand up, but she was stuck fast to this girl and her wrists were in manacles. Then Ina remembered where she was, and that Bleiddyn had been killed. A sound came from her mouth, a sound like the agonised whining of a dog. Then she said the one word, over and over:

"No . . . No . . . No . . . No . . .!"

Ina felt something on her cheek. The palm of one of the girl's hands – which were also in cuffs – trying to comfort her. Ina turned her face away and closed her eyes tightly.

The rocking motion of the boat made her stomach turn, so she opened her eyes once more. She could still clearly see the outline of a coast, but she had no idea whether the kingdom of Dumnonia was beyond the black strip or whether they were now sailing past some other land. Dyfed, perhaps. She doubted that they'd reached Ireland yet. Fat, bulging clouds rolled in the sky above, flame-red in the dawn light.

Ina looked up at the sail. It was filled with wind now, carrying the boat, flying, across the waves. She realised that the red-cheeked girl was no longer at the front of the boat. She stared about, unable to see her anywhere. Then Ina realised what had happened. She had not woken after the redheaded giant's hideous blow and then they'd thrown her body into the sea while everyone slept. Hopefully her soul would reach heaven, despite everything. Lluan and her mother had not been laid to rest in a grave, either. Their house, and all it contained, had been put to the torch – burned to ashes to destroy the plague.

Her mother had insisted on welcoming the young man who came to the door, though he had a terrible look about him. Some of the household had tried to warn her not to, for the plague was widespread. But according to her mother, Heledd, it was Christ's will to help the poor and wretched. It soon became clear what was troubling the sick young man – to everyone except Ina. She'd felt that something was wrong, of course. She hadn't understood how, suddenly, no one could go out. And why everyone kept away. Or why Lluan kept bursting into tears. Then the fever came over her and, when she woke, days later, she was the only one still alive.

How would things have been, she wondered, if her father hadn't died? Would he've allowed the young man to cross the threshold? If the Saxons hadn't killed him, perhaps the whole family would still be alive. Living happily together . . .

The boat rose in the water, then fell suddenly. Ina felt the girl shifting at her side. And felt ashamed that she'd ignored her earlier. She turned and smiled at her, and received a small, shy response. Not much more than the shadow of a smile really, but it was better than nothing. Ina realised, looking more carefully at the girl's eyes, that they glowed blue-green in the light of day. Perhaps they only turned pure green by the light of the moon.

"Good morning," said Ina, but the girl looked away and stared at the floor again, silently. Perhaps she really couldn't speak at all, and all Ina's efforts at conversation were futile.

The Irishmen had stopped rowing, letting the sail do the work for them. Only one oar was needed now – the large one at the back of the boat, behind Ina – to steer the vessel. A short, hairy man was at the helm, smiling from ear to ear, obviously in his element as he wielded this rudder. Then he broke into song, his voice surprisingly pleasing. Another man joined the singing, then another. Before long, all the Irishmen were at it, even the sullen Rough Redhead. Ina didn't recognise the song, but the tune and the rhythm were familiar. It sounded a bit like one of the melodies Briallen would sing when she did the laundry, or the serfs, as they worked in the fields. Or maybe it was one of the tunes her mother used to play on her hornpipe. But these memories were too painful, so Ina tried to think about something else.

The wind lifted again, billowing the sail. The men sang louder still, shouting the words defiantly into the teeth of the wind, laughing to see that some of the captives were afraid as the waves lifted and fell roughly all around the boat. Ina stared into the sky and saw that the clouds were changing colour from red to black.

After several hearty shanties, the singing stopped. Ardál said something to the others, then everyone looked in Ina's direction. Ina tried to ignore them but she couldn't help feeling their eyes staring strangely at her. The girl next to her had noticed too. She was trembling again. Ina swallowed hard as Ardál stood and made his way towards her, with Gwrgant's hornpipe in his hand. He passed it to her.

"Play us a song."

Ina shook her head.

"Play us a song," said the Irishman again, this time without the hint of smile.

"No," said Ina, emphatically.

"If I were you, I wouldn't be disappointing Garbhán, now."

"I haven't played for many years."

"High time you did, then."

Ina shook her head again. The girl at her side fidgeted anxiously. Ardál leaned down and whispered in Ina's ear.

"If you don't play that hornpipe, Garbhán will snap your neck – and I won't be stopping him this time."

"I have vowed an oath never to touch the hornpipe again."

Ardál put his hand to the back of her neck and squeezed.

"It'd sure be a sin to break such a graceful, valuable neck."

"It'd be a sin to break an oath," answered Ina, quietly.

Then Ina felt a nudge in her side, and turned to see the girl staring pleadingly at her with her big blue-green eyes.

"Your travelling companion wants you to play too – see?" said Ardál. "You realise, I hope, that Garbhán won't be sparing her, either. She won't be much of a loss to us, but you're too valuable to waste. And we've lost one of our cargo already, of course . . . So, for the love of Lugh, the all powerful . . ."

"How can I," asked Ina, "when my hands are manacled?" Ina half hoped that would be the end of the matter. But to her surprise, Ardál unlocked her manacles – or at least, one of them. Ina felt the blood flow back into her freed hand and she tried to flex her fingers. She found she could hardly move them.

"That's enough practice," said the Irishman, forcing the hornpipe into her hand.

It was difficult to hold it, never mind play it. But Ina knew she had to. Her mouth was dry. She tried as best she could to wet her lips and lifted the instrument to her mouth. It felt so strange and, at the same time, so familiar. Five years had passed since she'd held a similar instrument – almost half her life. But at the same time it felt like yesterday.

When her lips touched the reed, her heart began to beat hard. She breathed in deeply and blew into it. A harsh tone blasted from the horn, like a pig being jabbed by a sharp knife, and Ardál made a show of pressing his hands to his ears.

"What tune is that? The song of the Gobsmacked Goose?" Turning to the rest of them, he translated what he'd just said. The Irishmen laughed. Their stupid chortling infuriated Ina. She'd show them how to play the hornpipe. She closed her eyes, concentrating, and she heard her mother's voice, patiently encouraging her, just as she'd done every time Ina made a mistake. Then she lifted the hornpipe to her lips once more and began to play a lullaby – the lullaby her mother had taught her, the song that Lluan had sung to her every night and the tune Gwrgant had played in her honour at her farewell feast, five days and forever ago.

Although the notes stumbled a little – not having been played for so long – something wonderful began to happen as the tune spread across the boat. The girl next to Ina seemed to light up all through, beginning to murmur the words quietly to herself, obviously knowing the song. A smile danced on her face and the pain disappeared from her eyes. The Irishmen's laughter quietened. Everyone was listening intently, everyone remembering a dear voice singing them a song like this one – the voice of their mother, their grandmother, their aunt.

Ina knew she wouldn't be able to reach the end of the song. She had no more breath left in her lungs and her cheeks hurt dreadfully from the effort. But she battled on, regardless. Then, from the corner of her eye, Ina saw her mother. She was within touching distance. Ina almost dropped the hornpipe in shock. Her mouth dried and the string of notes ended abruptly. She turned her head, quickly, but her mother wasn't there any more.

Then the rain came. One moment it was dry, the next it was pouring down. And then a flash of lightning and a deafening clap of thunder. A storm. From out of nowhere. A fearsome one. Another flash. And another clap. The wind was gusting hard and within seconds it was roaring. At this point the sea really began to surge.

Some of the captives screamed. The Irishmen had no time to quieten them. Some were trying their best to row, while others scrambled in vain to lower the sail. They could hardly stand, so wild was the wind.

Ina remembered that her right hand was still free. She put the hornpipe's strap around her neck, and held tight to the bench in front of her. The mute girl huddled against her. Although her expression was fearful, she smiled at Ina before pressing even more closely to her side. At least she wasn't afraid of Ina any more. Not after she'd played the lullaby. Ina smiled back as best she could.

The sea was churning furiously. Ina hadn't known that waves could be so huge. When the boat dropped, the waves around them were higher than the villa, and some were even higher than Ina's favourite old birch tree, down by the river. And when the boat lifted, it felt as if they were on the brow of a hill, while the water around them boiled and splatted like lava.

By now pure panic had spread like wildfire across the boat – both sailors and captives were screaming and shouting, praying and pleading. Many were being sick or had wet themselves in fear, but no one took any notice. Everyone was too busy trying not to be thrown overboard into the sea. Everyone apart from Garbhán – Rough Redhead – who was staring straight at Ina.

The next moment he was striding towards her, stamping over those in his way. Before Ina could react, he'd grabbed her arm and lifted her to her feet, shouting enraged words in her face. It was as if he were blaming her for the storm. Perhaps he was right. Perhaps the hornpipe had made it happen . . . Because God was angry with her for breaking her oath, thought Ina, fearfully. And also, for daring to wield the sword.

When the man saw that her right hand was free, he became even more enraged and yanked her arm so hard that Ina was afraid he'd rip it from her shoulder. If Bleiddyn had been here, he'd have tried to help. But there was no one here to save her. No one, except the feeble girl at her side. The man lifted Ina until she was off the floor. He was so strong, and so tall, that the mute girl hung in the air at her side – like a pair of chickens hanging from a butcher's hook.

The boat fell suddenly again, and the man dropped them. But only for a second. Grabbing Ina's arm a second time, he began tugging her to the side of the boat. Ina understood in that moment what he intended to do. Throw her into the sea. And the mute girl with her. That would be her punishment for breaking her oath. This was what she deserved.

The moment Ina gave up trying to resist Garbhán's strength, another flash lit up the boat, accompanied by a deafening thunder clap. Then the mast broke free, whipping across the deck and hitting the bearded giant, sweeping him over the side of the boat and into the sea in a single neat, smooth action. As long as she lived, Ina would never forget the look on his face. Not fear, but surprise.

Then Ina heard the mast splitting. Heard screams and felt the boat lift under her feet. And the next moment, she too was flung, headlong, into the waves, the mute girl after her.

She hit the water hard, and began to sink into the black depths.

XIX

The cold sea stole Ina's breath. If she'd tried to breathe under the surface her lungs would've filled with salt water and she'd likely have drowned on the spot – and perhaps what happened next wouldn't have made any difference.

Ina felt something lift her back to the surface. She was above the waves again, gratefully gulping down air. She saw what had saved her – it was the ship's mast, which had somehow become entangled in the chain attaching her to the girl. The next moment, the girl came into view, dragging herself on to the mast, sitting on it as if it were a horse's back. Grabbing hold of Ina's cloak, she pulled her up and on to it too. Ina had no idea where she found the strength.

Then the girl disappeared underwater again and Ina was afraid she'd lost her, but she soon surfaced on the other side of the spar – the piece of wood attached to the mast that held the sail. And Ina realised what she was trying to do. She was wrapping the chain around the spar, so that the two of them could lie on the sail without the waves throwing them off. She can swim amazingly well to do all this with her hands in manacles, thought Ina, helping her back up.

The sky was so black and the waves so high that they couldn't see the boat. They couldn't see anything. On the boat, Ina had accepted that her life had ended. But, after being thrown overboard, she realised that she wasn't ready to die after all. She'd prayed for forgiveness and for God to bring her – and the girl – to safety. And it looked as if – please God, let it be so – he may have heard her prayer.

Ina gripped the spar tightly. The sail lifted and plunged wildly, at the mercy of the waves. But it was beginning to dawn on Ina that the mast wasn't going to sink; that the sail was easily strong enough to hold the two girls' weight. And as she thought this, she realised that the hornpipe was still around her neck. Perhaps playing it hadn't offended God after all, but pleased him. And perhaps he'd raised this storm not to punish her but to save her. Perhaps Uinseann had had a quiet word in his ear, on her behalf.

At that moment, without being able to explain how, Ina knew without a shadow of a doubt that they were going to survive. She felt so filled with gratitude that she could've screamed with happiness. She began to chant, praising the Supreme Being in the words that Gwrgant had taught her:

"He is the guardian of the forest, the master of the mighty stag, who reigns sovereign over all other creatures of the woodland. He is the breeze, that murmurs to the bees and the birds. He is the river, home to the salmon. He is the earth, that sustains our crops. He is the fire, that warms our hearths. He is the Lord of all creation – let praises be sung to him by all creatures, great and small, on earth and in the heavens."

Ina stared up towards the sky. The black clouds had begun to disperse and the wind was dropping.

"We're going to be all right, you hear me?" Ina shouted joyfully to the girl.

The girl stared back at her as if she'd gone completely out of her mind.

+ + +

Ina had no idea how much time had passed, but the faith that had come from somewhere was beginning to wither and die. She'd never been so cold in her life and she could feel the strength flowing slowly from her body. The girl at her side lay like a rag in the sail, drowsy and lifeless.

Then Ina saw the cliffs. Towering walls of solid stone, rising out of the sea. She felt her dwindling spirits light up from within.

"Look!"

The girl turned her head and she, too, seemed to light up when she saw the cliffs, which were rapidly approaching. The tide had taken hold of the mast and was pulling it towards the shore.

Ina's next concern was the rocks beneath the cliffs. But it looked as if the current was dragging them towards a beach to the left of these sharp, stony teeth. When they were almost within reach of shore, the girl dived under the spar to free the chain, in case they got stuck in the mast and dragged underwater as they beached. Then she jumped into the water again, obviously expecting Ina to follow her. Ina hesitated.

"I can't swim."

Without a word, the girl grabbed her, dragging her into the waves. Ina shouted, throwing her arms in the air, ducking under the surface before rising again. The girl had hold of her and was supporting her, swimming on her back and holding Ina's head above water.

Surprisingly quickly, the sea disgorged the two girls on to the sand. In shock, Ina lay there, immobile, but the girl gripped her hand, pulled her to her feet and dragged her up the beach. The next moment, the mast came charging up the shore behind them, flung by a wave. If the girl hadn't insisted that they move, this heavy piece of wood would've smashed into them.

"Thank you – again," Ina told her, before falling to her knees.

The last thing she saw before exhaustion wiped her out was the hornpipe, still hanging around her neck.

✦ ✦ ✦

When Ina came to, the sky was blue and the wind had dropped completely. The girl was sleeping at her side, looking even more ragged and fragile than she had on the boat. Yet, thanks to her, the two of them were still alive.

The last time she'd been on a beach, Bleiddyn had been at her side. The best friend she'd ever had. Her only friend. Apart from Lluan – if a sister counted as a friend. They were two different things, perhaps: a friend with a blood tie; and a friend of choice . . .

Gwrgant's voice cut across her mind, warning her that this wasn't the time to start another conversation with herself, however interesting the question. They needed to leave the beach as quickly as possible, in case any of the Irishmen had also survived the storm.

"You're right," said Ina out loud, without thinking, and she gave the girl a little shake to wake her. Her eyes opened, full of fear.

"It's only me," said Ina, gently. "We'd better go. But first, we have to break this chain."

Ina helped the girl to her feet. Shackled together by the chain, they walked to the top of the beach where Ina found a sharp stone. Then they laid the chain across a rock and Ina used the stone to strike at it with all her strength, like a blacksmith. Tonk. Tonk. Tonk. And the chain broke. Ina pulled it free from her manacles, then the girl did the same. Ina turned to her.

"Let's go."

The girl stared back, without making the least effort to move.

"We have to go," said Ina, urgently.

Still the girl stood there, motionless. What was the matter with her? Ina pointed towards the steep slope that led down to the beach.

"That way. Quickly!"

Finally, the girl nodded her head and began to walk towards the slope, without looking back. Perhaps she's a little bit deaf, thought Ina – that's why she doesn't understand me. She obviously had some sort of hearing, because she'd heard the hornpipe. But the hornpipe was so loud that even the dead would hear it. She'd need to remember to make signs when she talked to her from now on . . .

Then Ina realised that the girl had reached the slope and was beginning to climb up it, so she hurried after her, running to catch her up.

"Hey!"

The girl turned. She looked surprised to see Ina behind her.

"You didn't think I told you to go away, did you?"

The girl stared at her with her big eyes. Had she heard enough to understand? How could Ina make her realise that she wanted to look after her? She lifted her arms and placed them around the girl's shoulders, hugging her as best she could with one hand in a cuff. It felt a little awkward, especially as the girl was looking at her in astonishment. And she hadn't given anyone a hug for . . . for years. Bleiddyn, yes – but not a person. Then the loveliest smile spread across the girl's pale face. Resting her head on Ina's shoulder, she began to cry.

"Hey, don't . . ." said Ina, tenderly, putting her arms back around the girl. "I'm not going to leave you. Understand?"

To Ina's huge relief, the smile had returned to the pale face. The girl dried her tears clumsily with her arm, before determinedly turning to lead the way up the slope. Thank goodness that's sorted, thought Ina, following in her steadfast footsteps.

After reaching the top of the cliff, the two of them paused for a moment to catch their breaths. As their breathing quietened, Ina became aware of a faint sound carrying towards them, murmuring on the wind. It was so soft that she almost couldn't hear it at all. She listened intently. It was the sound of animals, bleating in the distance.

"You hear that sound?"

The girl stared at her, mutely. Ina regretted asking such a stupid question. Then she bleated, loudly, in the girl's ear, making her jump back in fear. Ina had no idea how to tell her that there were animals in the distance, so she simply grabbed her arm and pulled her hurriedly in the direction of the noise.

In no time, they came across a flock of sheep and, in the middle of them, a shepherd. He hadn't noticed them yet. Ina hesitated before stepping towards him, dragging the girl – who was watching him suspiciously – with her.

"Good day!"

"Gud day to you," answered the shepherd, obviously surprised to see the two of them, his eyes widening even further when he noticed their manacles. Ina gave a sigh of relief. Two sighs of relief, to be exact. The first because he spoke the same language as her. And the second because he looked like a harmless, sweet old man. Not someone who would try and capture them.

"Where is this?"

"Wheer? The meen land."

The accent was pretty familiar to Ina by now; so, they were safe, in Dumnonia!

"What main land?" asked Ina, just to be completely sure.

"The meen isle, of curs."

Isle? Ina's heart sank. Not somewhere on the coast of the kingdom of Dumnonia, then.

"The meen isle of Syllan," added the shepherd, earnestly.

The Isle of Syllan? The name rang a bell. Then Ina remembered Gwrgant speaking of it, in Latin. Scillonia Insula. It was an island south of the outermost headland of the kingdom of Dumnonia – Cernyw. But, if she remembered correctly, there'd only been one island on the map. Was that this place, then?

Yes, indeed it was. The shepherd explained that Syllan had once been one island, but that the sea-level had risen gradually over the last few decades, making several islands out of the one. They were now standing on the main island – or the 'meen isle', as he called it.

"Wheer did you two come frum? Oover the wurter, frum the looks of you."

"That's right. Over the water. We were captured, to be sold as slaves. The storm came. The boat sank. But we managed to swim to shore."

"A miracle. Thanks be to the Lord. Glory be his name."

The shepherd made the sign of the cross, his eyes sparkling with grateful tears. Ina crossed herself too. She had to eye the girl to remind her to do the same thing. Blushing, she hesitantly copied her. She must still be in shock, thought Ina.

"I sur ships approaching, befur the sturm," added the shepherd. "It may be that theer still at anchor. Perhaps you may sail on one of them."

"Where are these ships?" asked Ina urgently.

The shepherd lifted his arm and pointed a bony hand in the direction of the breeze.

"That way! The meen purt, on the fer side of the isle."

Ina stared into the distance. If they headed for that rock that jutted out across the moorland and then carried on straight, they'd be going in the right direction. Ina gripped the girl's arm again and began to run. The girl stumbled but kept her footing, sprinting at Ina's side.

"God be with you!" the shepherd called after them.

But there was no time to return his blessing. There wasn't a moment to lose.

XX

Ina and the girl lay on their bellies and looked down over the edge of the cliff to the natural harbour beneath them. Anchored in the deep water of its bay were two big ships. One of them had a large shape on its sail. A cross? Ina narrowed her eyes to see it better. Yes, no doubt about it – a cross. Her heart leapt. Christians! So they weren't Saxon ships – or any other pagans'. But were they Britons, like them? There was only one way to find out.

Ina and the girl followed a narrow path down to the beach. On reaching it, Ina crouched behind some rocks, the girl at her side. She was very quiet now, and seemed to have gone into her shell again. It must be because she's frightened, thought Ina.

Peeking over the rocks, Ina saw two men dragging a rowing boat into the waves and realised at once what was happening. Now she had to make a decision – take a risk; or lose the opportunity. She jumped to her feet.

"Greetings!"

But the men took no notice. Either they hadn't understood or they hadn't heard her at all. Ina beckoned the girl to follow her, but she was shaking her head furiously. So Ina dragged her to her feet.

"We don't have a choice!"

Keeping a tight grip on the girl's hand, Ina ran towards the men, praying that they'd be friendly.

"Greetings!" she shouted again.

One of them turned and said something to the other. Then he turned too, watching the two girls approach. Ina slowed as she drew closer, out of breath.

"Good . . . day . . . to you. In the name of . . . God, the Almighty."

The younger man stared at her, a cheeky grin on his face.

"You came to bless us? If so, there's no need. The kindly monks of this isle have already looked after our souls." Then he saw their manacles, and his smile vanished. "We came to ask for your help," explained Ina, "and for a place on one of the ships. We're not from here. We were captured, and we have no one to defend us."

"The ships'er full," said the other man, in an accent similar to the shepherd's.

The first man turned to him. "So what if the ships are full? We can't leave them here. Look at the two of them, and have a heart – they surely wouldn't weigh much more than a sack of wheat between them."

"And how do we know theer's no sickness on them? Or, worse, plague?" asked the other, crossing himself hastily.

"Don't be stupid. The only sickness on these two is hunger."

"We'll work our passage," said Ina, hurriedly. She wasn't exactly sure what she and the girl could do to help on the ship, but it was worth a try.

"Ha! Two bitty gals like you?" exclaimed the second man, doubtfully.

"Come on," said the first, ignoring him. "Jump on board."

Ina stepped into the waves, but the other girl was standing motionless at the water's edge, looking at her feet.

"If you're coming, come at once. We can't delay further," added the sailor.

"Come on. Don't be frightened," Ina whispered gently to the girl, realising that getting impatient wasn't going to help. It worked, because the girl stepped into the waves. Then the two of them scrambled into the boat as the men pushed it out to sea before jumping swiftly into it themselves, grabbing the oars and starting to row.

"We offer you great thanks," said Ina, politely.

"That's very ladylike of you – to match your dress and that fine cloak on your arm. What's your name?" asked the man, in a friendly voice.

"Ina ferch Nudd."

"And who's she? Your handmaiden?"

"No. My friend," said Ina, surprising herself with the certainty of her answer.

"Does she have a name?"

Ina looked over at the quiet girl, who was staring at her feet once more, avoiding everyone's eyes.

"Heddus," said Ina, thinking that this would be a very good name for her, for it meant 'Peace' in Brythonic. And 'peace' always seemed to go along with 'quiet' – which she certainly was.

"Bedo ap Dyfrig, at your service. And this sullen lump is Artheg ap Cador."

Artheg tried to look annoyed, but he couldn't help a little

smile of amusement. Perhaps he wasn't as bad-tempered as he appeared. The warm relief of being rescued was beginning to seep through Ina's body. She sighed, more loudly than she'd intended.

"Don't worry. You're safe now," said Bedo.

Ina turned to the girl – or Heddus, as she must think of her from now on – and tried to give her a supportive smile. But Heddus was staring at the horizon, as if she were searching for something, just like the woman on the slave boat. Ina shivered as she remembered the ill-fated people on the boat. As the shepherd had said, it was a miracle that she and the girl had survived.

"How long will it take to reach the kingdom of Dumnonia?" asked Ina.

"A few hours," answered Bedo.

Thank goodness, thought Ina.

"But we're not sailing to Dumnonia," he went on. "Or anywhere else in the Isles of Britain. We're sailing to Britonia."

"Britonia? Where's that? Near Brittany?" Artheg laughed.

"Little Britain, you mane? We'd be theer by this avening."

"He means this evening," explained Bedo. "Forgive him – he can't help it. He's from Cernyw, poor man."

"Better Cernyw than a hool of a pleece like Caerloyw!" answered Artheg like a shot.

"Hole, Artheg. Hole of a place. Not 'hool' or 'pleece'."

This was obviously a regular subject of sport for them both. But Ina had little patience for this tomfoolery – there were much more important things on her mind.

"When do we reach this Britonia, then?" she asked.

"The day after tomorrow. Or the day after that," answered Artheg.

Three or four days on the open sea! Ina's heart – and stomach – sank to her feet.

"Where's Britonia then? Egypt?" asked Ina, worried.

"Not as far as that," said Bedo kindly, seeing her fear. "It's in Hispania."

Hispania! But that was beyond the kingdom of the Franks, even! They might as well have been sailing to Egypt after all! And to reach Hispania, they'd need to cross the treacherous Gulf of Gascony. Gwrgant had told her how dangerous this passage was. Apart from the regular, raging gales, there were sea serpents and other hideous monsters to be found, lurking beneath the water. Ina shivered in her seat. What was the point of being rescued, if they now had to endure a perilous sea-voyage to arrive at the other end of the world?

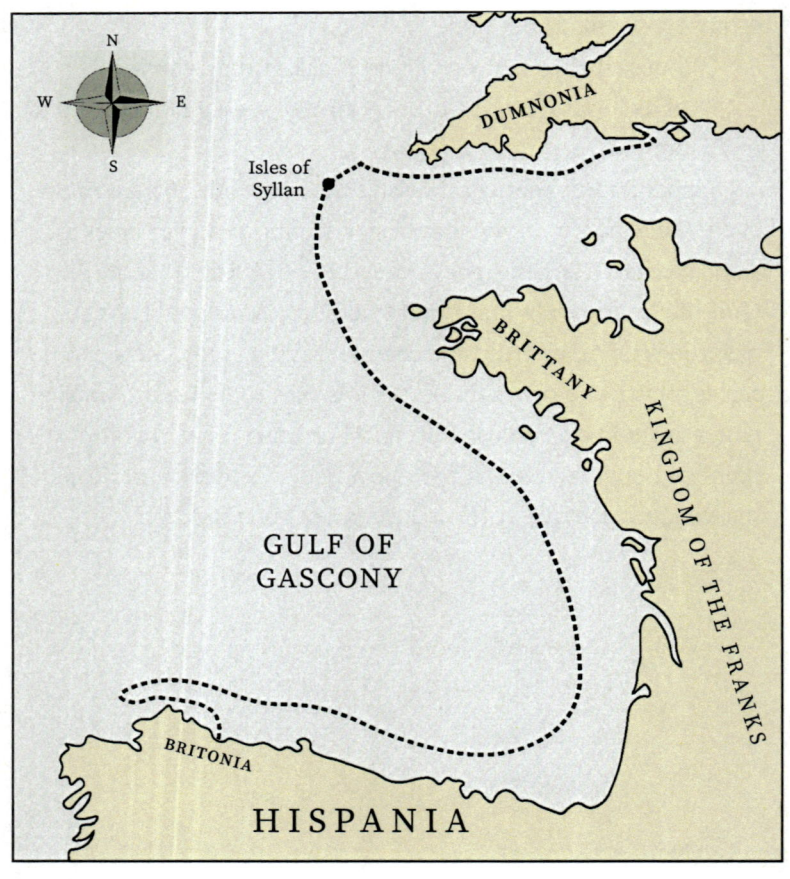

XXI

Ina stared up at the stars. She'd never seen such a multitude. The firmament above her head contained even more stars than it had that night on the veranda. That last night, before she'd left. The last time she'd seen Gwrgant. And the last time she'd ever see him again.

Were there more stars over the sea, or were they just clearer here? That was the sort of question she used to ask Gwrgant. Ina missed him terribly. But there was comfort, of a sort, in knowing that he'd be very proud of her – of how she'd escaped from the Saxons and how she'd survived the storm.

It was a pity he hadn't mentioned this place, Britonia, to her. It occurred to her that there were many things he hadn't mentioned, and that some of what he had said she now knew wasn't quite true, such as that the Saxons had slaughtered all the Britons in their path, for apparently there were Britons living free far to the east of Great Dyke, and others who had come to terms with their new Germanic rulers. She pushed the thought aside, as it seemed ungrateful. What sort of a land was Britonia? she wondered. Was it vast and powerful, like Gwynedd or Dumnonia; or small and civilised, like Gwent?

She leant back against the ship's bulwark, the hornpipe still hanging around her neck. She'd made a new vow – she wouldn't take the hornpipe off until she reached the end of the journey. She wasn't sure if it would still play after its drenching in the sea and she wasn't sure, either, when she'd lift it to her lips again, if ever. But this was the only one of Gwrgant's things she had left, and that in itself was enough of a reason to treasure it.

Heddus was sleeping beside her. She hadn't moved more than a step from her since coming on board. Soon after that, Bedo had found her a better dress and a cloak, although Ina had had to persuade her to accept them. For some reason, Heddus was reluctant to touch the clothes and, after putting them on, had plucked doubtfully at the material for ages. Poor her. Perhaps she came from a family so destitute that she'd never worn anything so fine before. Perhaps she really had been someone's handmaiden, or slave. Why not? Perhaps she'd belonged to someone on the slave-boat . . .

"Stop letting your mind wander all over the place, girl!" said Ina to herself, a little too loudly, looking about to make sure no one had heard her. She needed to be careful not to talk to herself too much, now that she was with others. The people on the ship didn't know yet that there was something strange about her – and there was no reason why they should, either.

She stared at the calm, unruffled sea and tried to quieten her thoughts. When it'd still been light, she'd watched the sky fearfully, looking for a black cloud; and the sail, to see if the wind was getting up; or the sea, to check whether the waves were beginning to swell. But her fearful lookout had been in vain. There'd been no sign of a storm, or of sea serpents.

The ship was quite a big larger than the Irishmen's boat

and seemed more solid too, for it was made of wood. But the space within it was just as limited because it was chock full of people, their belongings, and goods of all sorts – sacks of the season's first grain, bundles of leather and of wool, and bars of tin from the mines of Dumnonia.

But although the ship was full to the gunwales, everyone made a point of being friendly and everyone was full of lively stir about this journey to their new home over the sea, unlike like the captives on the Irishmen's boat. And, of course, all the people on board this ship wanted to be here, and had paid for the voyage. Some were fleeing the Saxons. Others had chosen to leave everything behind – for there were many desperately bleak places in Britain now, following the ravages of the plague. But all were full of hope at the prospect of a better life overseas, and everyone was in the same boat – not literally, of course, for there were two ships on this sea passage.

The person in charge of the voyage was one of the most prominent monks in all Britonia – a kindly man by the name of Maelog. And after introducing the girls to him, Bedo – and Artheg, fair play – had made sure they were comfortable and well provided with food and drink.

But first of all, Bedo had freed them from their manacles, with the help of Artheg, who really was as strong as the animal he'd been named for – Arth meaning 'Bear' in Brythonic. The girls' skin had scarred where the iron had cut into it, and so a sympathetic fellow-passenger rubbed ointment into their wrists to help it heal.

To begin with, Heddus had refused to eat anything – as reluctant to take food as she'd been to accept new clothes.

But after watching Ina chewing happily on a large piece of bread and a chunk of cheese, she couldn't resist any longer. She sniffed suspiciously at the cheese then took a careful nibble at the bread. And after that, there was no stopping her. There was something animal-like in the way Heddus tore into the bread with her teeth, swallowing it without chewing. Exactly as she herself had, thought Ina, when she'd ravenously attacked the rabbit's meat, and exactly like Bleiddyn. A terrible pang of *hiraeth* came over her as she remembered him. And perhaps the *hiraeth* would have got worse if Heddus hadn't suddenly doubled over, groaning in pain. She lurched to the side of the ship to be sick, Ina leaping up to support her.

That had been hours ago now. Ina stared at the strip of a girl who was still sleeping quietly by her side. Heddus. Whatever she'd been before – daughter of a poor family, handmaiden or even slave – it made no difference now. Now she was Ina's friend. Ina had said this publicly, and had given her a name.

But saying she was a friend and being a friend were two different things. Ina didn't really know how a friend was supposed to behave. She'd made a complete mess of being a young lady and she was now determined to make a better job of being a companion. Heddus seemed fond of her, which was a good start. And who cared if she couldn't speak? That'd never stopped Bleiddyn being her best friend, and they'd had such great times together . . .

"Ina, little one . . ." she sighed, just as Briallen used to. Here she was letting her thoughts gallop away with her – again!

She shook herself and lifted her eyes once more to the firmament. Briallen had told her once that the stars were angels' eyes, shining as they looked down on Earth by night. Perhaps they were all looking down at her now. Gwrgant. Her mother. Lluan. Ina felt sure her sister would be pleased she'd found a new friend, and that was a good feeling.

The stars above seemed to twinkle and shine even brighter, as she wondered once more at their multitude.

✦ ✦ ✦

The following day the sea around the ship began to surge, although the wind had not picked up. Everyone began pointing, excitedly, at something in the water. Ina peered at the waves. There, clearly visible under the surface, a terrifying shape darted rapidly through the sea at the side of the ship – almost touching it. A smooth shape, that was astonishingly long and lithe. The shape of a sea serpent.

Suddenly, steam blasted from the monster's back. Then, even worse, a powerful stream, like a huge fountain, came spurting from its head. A stream that was almost as high as the ship's mast. Everyone started to scream – everyone, but the crew. This is the end, then, thought Ina. The serpent will wreck the ship and everyone will be drowned – or eaten alive.

The screaming grew ever louder as the creature turned swiftly beneath the surface and came hurtling back towards them. Ina felt her legs sag beneath her in terror. Then she saw Heddus staring at the fast-approaching shape, captivated, in spite of her own fear. The monster erupted from the water, like a fish reeled in on a fisherman's hook, its huge, shining body glittering in the sun. It was enormous. Truly enormous. A long head on a sleek body. Grey backed and white bellied, with a mouth that was big enough to swallow a cow whole.

It spun, powerfully, in the air, and it was as if time itself stood still. The monster was looking at them all with one, huge eye. A surprisingly beautiful eye, with a thin, dark rim that went all the way up to the animal's back, like a smudge of eye makeup. Ina stared, open-mouthed, into the depths of this eye. And she saw that it was not the eye of a cold-blooded, dumb-witted monster, but that of an animal that could think and feel. Like her.

The creature dived back into the water – splash! – soaking half the people on board, and everyone shouted even louder. Amidst all the mayhem, Ina heard something she'd never heard before. The sound of Heddus, laughing.

✢ ✢ ✢

Another morning – another *fair* morning, thought Ina, stretching her arms and legs after a good night's sleep. Once again, thanks be to the Lord, the stormy weather she'd feared so much had failed to materialise. This had been her second night of sound, uninterrupted sleep. The sea air must be doing me good, she thought. And she wasn't afraid of the ocean any more – not after seeing the monster. Looking about she saw that Heddus had woken already and was at the side of the ship, staring across the sea.

Suddenly Heddus spun and ran towards her, full of

excitement, gesticulating wildly for her to get up. This was the first time Heddus had tried to say something to her – without words, of course – but as she hurried to her side Ina realised that this was another step forward, as was yesterday's laughter. Ina joined her at the gunwale and Heddus pointed eagerly towards the horizon where, in the distance, she could see the outlines of mountains. At that point, Bedo walked past them and Ina called out to him.

"Britonia?"

"Part of Hispania, yes, but not Britonia, I'm afraid. There's another day's sailing before us till we reach our destination."

A whole day? Hispania must be vast, then. Heddus was looking intensely at Ina, as if to ask whether they were sailing towards the mountains. Ina shook her head and Heddus slumped and sat down, disappointment written all over her face. Ina stared towards the mountains again before turning to Bedo once more.

"If that's not Britonia, where is it?"

"It's the land of the Basques."

Basques? Gwrgant had never mentioned them.

"The Basques are a law unto themselves – ferocious and unconquerable," explained Bedo. "Although, to be fair, they're first-rate seamen."

Seeing the fear on Ina's face, he continued, "We're too far out to sea for them to spot the ship. Don't worry, we'll keep our distance until we reach Britonia."

"Does the land of these Basques extend as far as that?"

"No . . . but the whole coast is dangerous, and the mountains behind it too. This is the most lawless stretch in all Hispania."

Ina turned back to watch as the long outline of the coast seemed to drift past the ship, trying to imagine what other kinds of savages lived there. Bedo pointed to an area further along.

"The tribe called the Cantabri live there. They aren't much better than the Basques, to tell the truth, though Latin's what most of 'em speak. Then come the Asturians. Proud people, warlike, but a little more civilised than the other lot, for all that."

"Of curs, none of them's as bad as them scoundrels frum Caerloyw," said someone behind them. It was Artheg of course, pulling Bedo's leg. Bedo laughed and Ina tried to join in, but she was too worried by what she'd just heard to do much more than smile feebly. From the sound of it, these three races weren't much better neighbours than the Saxons – and perhaps they were even worse.

She stared upwards. The sky was still blue, with not a cloud to be seen. All she could do was hope that the weather would continue to be merciful. Who knew what their fate would be, if they were forced to take shelter on this treacherous coast before reaching Britonia?

XXII

On the third day, the ship turned and sailed for land. They'd reached the coast of Britonia some time during the night but, as it was never a good idea to land in darkness, the crew had changed course and tacked gently with the wind until dawn broke. By now the sun had risen and dry land was before them. The other ship had already started out for shore and was almost completely out of sight.

Ina had never seen cliffs like these before. They were twice – no, three times – as high as the towering cliffs of the Isle of Syllan: a wall of resolute, firmly-planted hills rising in a row from the sea, their grey slopes topped bright green with vegetation. She turned to Heddus, who was also staring at them in wonder.

"Maybe giants live here!"

Ina regretted saying this at once, for she didn't want to frighten Heddus. The atmosphere on ship was strange enough already, with everyone on tenterhooks, swinging wildly from excitement to apprehension at what lay ahead.

Instead of sailing straight towards the cliffs, the ship veered to the left. As they got closer, Ina could see that parts of the cliff-tops were a carpet of gorse and heather – the yellow and the purple like a colourful crown on their summits. Just like the coast of the kingdom of Dumnonia, thought Ina, only a lot bigger.

Before very long, the giants' cliffs were behind them and the coast began to look more welcoming. They sailed past a small beach. On it, there was a large pile of stones in the shape of an egg – like a dragon's nest, thought Ina, deciding not to share this with Heddus, who was beginning to look frightened again.

"Don't worry," she said, instead. And, remembering the kindly monk who was in charge of the voyage, she added, "Maelog is sure to look after us."

She was feeling anxious too, though she wasn't about to show this to Heddus. Then, suddenly, Heddus gripped the hornpipe that hung around Ina's neck, lifting it to Ina's lips.

"Not now." Ina shook her head to make sure that Heddus understood. The last thing she wanted was to attract attention to herself – to the two of them – with everyone so agitated already. The girl pulled the strap, as if to say 'please'.

"No, Heddus!"

Heddus turned away. Ina hadn't meant to sound so sharp. She put her arm around the girl's shoulder and tried to smile at her.

"Another time, all right?"

To tell the truth, Ina wasn't sure she'd ever be able to play the instrument again, but she didn't want to disappoint her friend. The girl tried to smile back, without much success.

She was still on edge as, in truth, was Ina – the only difference being that Ina could hide it better.

The ship sailed further, and a river-mouth came into view.

This estuary looked an ideal place to land, for it formed a natural harbour. But Ina was disappointed. Although she longed for the ship to turn in, it continued on its course.

"The next harbour," said Bedo to her, as if he could read her mind. "We'll be there before long, you'll see."

Ina smiled gratefully at him before turning to Heddus and pointing towards the shore.

"Did you hear that, Heddus? We'll be there any minute now."

Heddus looked at her blankly.

"Nearly there," said Ina, louder this time.

Then Heddus smiled in relief. She'd understood the second time, obviously. But she still didn't say a word, for all that. Ina still hoped she'd start talking some time – perhaps after they arrived in Britonia and began to settle.

"I'd better help take the ship about, or Artheg will get his britches in a twist," said Bedo, hurrying to join his friend.

They sailed past white beaches. On one of them were striking, standing rocks which, to Ina's eyes, resembled the ruins of a Roman temple – like the one she'd passed as she'd fled the Saxons. It was less than a week since then, she thought, incredulously. It felt like months.

Bedo was as good as his word, because in no time another river-mouth appeared before them. This was quite a bit broader than the last, as if the river were tired out after its journey to the sea and was yawning widely.

And then – at last – the ship turned for shore.

+ + +

The beach was full of hubbub, as the other ship had recently landed too and was busy pouring all its travellers and their belongings out on to the beach. Many people had already started the second part of their journey, overland to the different settlements that were dotted across Britonia – including to the main fort, which acted as a capital for the Britons here. This was where Ina and Heddus were heading, with the second company, under the leadership of Maelog. It seemed that everyone but Ina and Heddus had family and belongings to herd together, and no one took a blind bit of notice of the two stray girls.

Not that Ina cared. She was glad for the opportunity to turn her back on all the bustle and stretch her legs to walk along the beach, with Heddus keeping tight to her heels. Just like Bleiddyn used to.

The beach made up one side of the natural harbour. Opposite, on the far side of the river-mouth, there were wooden huts and boats. Fishermen lived there, perhaps. The landscape rose steeply around the harbour like the sides of a cauldron and, in the distance, from where the river flowed, several high summits soared dizzyingly into the sky. The mainland must be very mountainous, thought Ina, as she reached the end of the beach. She stood there for a moment or two, watching the sun's reflections dance on the waves in the harbour.

Then she realised that Heddus was no longer at her side, but was crouching a little way off, using a piece of wood to carve shapes into the sand. Intrigued, Ina went to see what she was up to. But the moment Heddus noticed her approach, she scratched frantically across the shapes so they were obscured. Apart from one. This one was like a letter – the letter 'M'. Then Heddus hurriedly crossed this one out too.

"What don't you want me to see?"

Heddus stared, mutely, at her.

"M for mountain, is that what you've written? Or does your real name begin with M?"

Ina snatched the piece of wood from her, and carved another 'M' into the sand.

"That's what you wrote, wasn't it? What's your name? If you can't say it, write it!"

Then Ina pressed the wood back into Heddus's hands but, instead of writing with it, she flung it into the water.

"What's the matter with you?" asked Ina, suddenly angry. The girl turned away, walking to the water's edge. Ina stayed where she was, her mind racing. If Heddus really could write, then she couldn't be a handmaiden, or a slave. Perhaps she came from a good family after all. But if she did, why did she look so very wretched?

Ina soon regretted shouting at her. She must try to be more caring towards her –after all, they were friends now, officially. Small wonder she was a little bit odd, after all she'd been through. Perhaps Ina seemed odd to other people too.

Then, from behind her, Ina heard a voice calling.

"Greetings to you!"

It was Bedo, with Artheg at his side like some large, ungainly shadow.

"Bedo, am I odd?"

Bedo laughed.

"I don't know about 'odd'. But you are pretty . . . unusual."

Ina wasn't sure what the difference was. Perhaps this was just a more polite way of saying the same thing.

"Come on, the tuh of yuhs," said Artheg.

"The two of you," translated Bedo.

"That's what I seed," answered Artheg. "Maelog's asking after the tuh of yuhs."

"Heddus!" called Ina.

The girl didn't so much as glance back, but kept on gazing across the harbour.

"She can't hear very well," Ina explained to the others, before shouting even louder. "Heddus! We have to go now!"

At last, the girl turned and Ina beckoned frantically to her. Slowly, she began to walk towards them, then stood a little way away, keeping her distance. Then Ina realised that the two men looked a little awkward – Artheg was shuffling his feet in the sand and Bedo had an uncharacteristically serious look on his face.

"The time's come for us to say our farewells," said Bedo.

"Aren't you staying?" asked Ina, her heart falling.

"No, Ina, we're not. We sail next for the Mediterranean.

We'll be back come springtime, then we'll head home again to Britain."

"Can we come with you?" asked Ina, impetuously.

"I don't know about that . . ." said Bedo, kindly. "We might be in trouble with Maelog if you do. Anyway, who knows? Perhaps you won't want to leave by then," he went on.

At that moment, it was hard for Ina to believe this. The four of them walked forward, silently. Then Ina whispered something in Bedo's ear.

"What about Heddus? Do you think she's odd?"

"I'd say she's a tiny bit . . . unusual, too," he answered with a little grin.

Ina looked back at Heddus, who was trailing behind them. The boyish figure. The shorn head. And the eyes that darted back and forth, like a small, frightened animal. Perhaps she really is unusual, thought Ina, in the same way that she herself was unusual. Perhaps the two of them suited each other perfectly, and were lucky to be friends.

Perhaps no one else would want to be friends with them anyway.

XXIII

Only after sailing from the beach and leaving the harbour for the ria – the part of the water that was neither sea nor river – did Ina fully realise its size. The coastal inlet stretched for miles, with hills rising either side and the high mountains that Ina had glimpsed earlier looming beyond them in their full, awe-inspiring glory.

Ina and Heddus were now on another type of boat. This craft was similar to the ferry boat that plied its trade across the river Hafren – a light boat with a flat bottom, handy for sailing close to shore and up rivers. But this time Heddus made a point of keeping her distance from Ina – as much distance as was possible in a boat of this size.

They were heading for a river at the far end of the ria. Once they got there, the hope was to use the strength of the tide to pull them up it as far as possible before turning to the strength of the oarsmen, or pushing, if the water became too shallow. Apparently, when they'd travelled as far up the river as they could, Britonian settlers would be there to greet them with food, drink and pack-mules, which would help carry goods and belongings.

Maelog had explained all this to Ina and Heddus, after insisting that the two girls travel in the same boat as him. There was something about this serious, dignified man that reminded Ina of Gwrgant, though he was a lot younger. The same sincere way of speaking to her and of listening to her responses – not pretending to listen, like so many adults, but really listening.

As the boat drifted further into the ria, Ina was so lost in her thoughts and in the mountainous vista before her that she didn't notice Maelog coming to stand at her side.

"Are you afraid?"

Ina turned to face him. "A little."

"We will find you a good home. Both of you. I have someone in mind already."

"Who?"

"A lady of noble birth. I forget her name. She was on the other ship. But she, too, has suffered. Lost everything. She will be full of sympathy towards you."

"Thank you for thinking of us."

The monk smiled, staring thoughtfully before him, and Ina let out a quiet sigh of relief. She and Heddus would not be separated, then. There was no point telling her this now because she was obviously sulking. Or angry. Or sad. Who knew what she was feeling? Was being a friend always this difficult?

The boat reached the river and sailed effortlessly into the wide turning. They were now entering a broad valley, with meadows either side. Soon, this valley turned into a narrow, wooded gorge. They sailed past an old pile of fallen tree trunks, on which three children were playing. Ina called out over the water, greeting them. But the children stared sullenly at her in response. She turned to Maelog.

"I hope everyone here's not as rude as them."

"They weren't our children. They were the children of the Gallaecians."

The Gallaecians? Who on earth were they? Bedo hadn't mentioned them.

"But I thought only us Britons lived here!"

"We do. But we share the land with the native peoples. Britonia, you see, is part of Gallaecia, and that province in its turn is within the kingdom of the Suebi, who rule the whole of this part of Hispania. The Goths own the rest. The Suabians are *Ellmyn*, originally from Germania, as are the Goths. But they are Christians . . . of a sort."

Ina was horrified to hear this.

"They're *Ellmyn*? Like the Saxons?"

"Don't worry. We're on good terms with them – and with the Gallaecians, on the whole."

Ina's head swam with confusion. How could anyone who was a Briton, like her, be friendly with these Suabians, when they were *Ellmyn*? It didn't make sense! But then, there it was. Maelog said so, and he said everything was all right . . . And, somehow, Ina trusted him, though she hardly knew him.

"Do you see the mountains?" asked Maelog, pointing to the towering peaks upriver.

"Yes."

"That's Arfynydd – the land of the mountains. Your new home will be in Argoed, a land of woods, hills and pastures between these mountains and the coastal regions of Arfor, which we sailed past this morning. These are the three parts that make up Britonia."

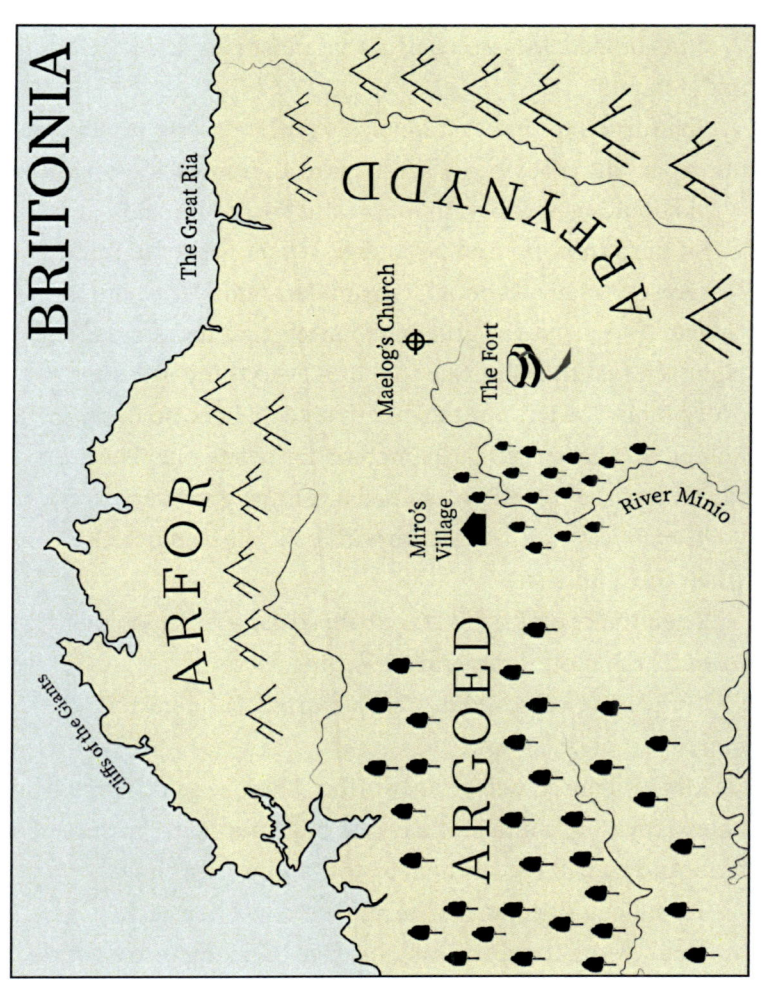

"Three is a powerful number," said Ina, repeating something she'd once heard Gwrgant say.

"It is indeed. More powerful that most people understand."

She turned to find that Maelog's probing, serious gaze was upon her. She'd obviously made quite an impression on him.

"I should like to hear more of your story," he said

So Ina's story poured out of her. It was a relief to tell this sincerest of men all about Gwrgant, her family, and life in Gwent. And about the grueling journey, that had started the night she fled the villa. She told him everything – or almost everything. She left out the fact that she'd been so nasty to Sulien, for she was still ashamed of her behaviour. The story ran and ran, and Maelog listened attentively to every word.

"*Dominus tecum* . . . God be with you," he said quietly, when she'd finished.

Then the two of them stared ahead for a time, looking towards the mountains and not saying a word.

"Why has God saved me?" Ina blurted, suddenly. "And more than once, at that?"

Maelog paused before answering. Then he said, "Only he knows that, my child. He has great plans for you, I'm sure of that. And he will reveal them to you. In his own time."

Then he nodded at the hornpipe around her neck.

"And before long," he said, his face breaking into a gentle smile, "you will be able to take up your instrument again, properly. And play it again from your heart, as you used to with your mother. Of that I am also sure."

"When?" asked Ina, earnestly.

"When the time is right. You'll know then."

Ina was a little doubtful, but she wasn't about to argue with Maelog. She'd been so absorbed in their conversation and had enjoyed Maelog's company so much, she hadn't noticed that the boat had come in to shore and was now preparing to tie up at a short wooden jetty. She felt a sudden pang of guilt for having ignored Heddus for so long, but Heddus didn't look as if she cared much – she was still staring down at the bottom of the boat as everyone about her buzzed with excitement.

After the passengers had disembarked and all the goods unloaded, Maelog went about to everyone, making sure that they had enough food and drink. As he'd promised, they'd been greeted by men – Britons – who'd brought supplies and helped the passengers load their belongings on to mules for the journey to come. Heddus sloped off to sit on her own on the river bank and Ina followed her. It was another scorching hot day but thank goodness it had started to cloud over, so the sun wasn't quite so intense.

Heddus acted as if she wasn't there, making Ina feel very awkward. Then she had an idea. Pulling the hornpipe from its strap, she raised it to her lips. Part of her still felt that she was doing something wrong, something forbidden, but remembering how much the girl had loved the lullaby she was determined to give it a go, just this once. It didn't mean she was going to take up her instrument again, properly, to use Maelog's words. But surely there was nothing wrong in playing the lullaby now and then – the song that the two of them treasured?

Ina didn't even know if the hornpipe would work again, after its dousing in seawater, but she wetted the reed and placed her fingers on the body of the pipe then, taking a deep breath, she blew. And a sound emerged, a little strident but . . . yes, it still worked! Now she began to play the lullaby. Slowly, trying to enjoy it this time. The girl was still avoiding her eyes, acting as if she wasn't listening – but she couldn't pretend for long. She turned to face Ina, humming along to the tune beneath her breath.

Then Ina stuttered to a stop. She hadn't even got as far as the chorus. She'd forgotten how much breath you needed. Her lungs were burning and her cheeks hurt, and her playing hadn't felt right, somehow – but Heddus was obviously pleased, because she wasn't frowning any more.

Ina passed a piece of bread to her. Taking it, Heddus gazed intently at her, as if she were about to say something. Ina held her breath, but not a peep came out of the girl's mouth. So Ina looked away, taking a bite of the hard crust in her own hand, and then she heard a small, hoarse voice in her ear.

"Ebba."

Ina turned to stare at Heddus.

"Did you just say something?" she asked in amazement.

"Ebba," said Heddus again, clearing her throat, as if saying the word was causing her pain. Ina was so excited she couldn't speak clearly herself.

"Ebba? I . . . I don't understand."

"I-na," said Heddus, haltingly, pointing at Ina, before turning her finger in her own direction. "Ebba."

Ina frowned. Then her face lit up.

"Eb . . . Efa! That's your name! Efa!"

Efa was a Brythonic name; Ebba wasn't – so Ina must have misheard it initially. Or the girl'd had trouble pronouncing it after being silent for so long. But she'd spoken, at last! Ina smiled to herself. If Gwrgant were here he'd insist it was all down to the hornpipe, working its mysterious magic!

The girl looked at Ina as if she wanted to correct her, before pointing at Ina again and saying "I-na," with a smile as wide as a gate.

"Efa," said Ina, pointing back at her, smiling just as stupidly.

"I-na," said Efa again, giggling.

"Efa," said Ina, joining in the laughter.

"I-na!"

"Efa!"

And here they were, telling each other their names – back and forth, time after time, getting faster and faster until they were speaking across each other, before falling on to the gravel bank of the river and laughing uncontrollably until their bellies hurt.

Ina hopped to the side of the path on one leg, before sitting and pulling out the sharp little stone that had stuck into the sole of her left foot. The other foot was sore too, after walking for hours along the narrow path through trees, climbing steeply for most of the way. She wasn't used to walking barefoot.

"Hopefully I'll have new sandals soon," she said under her breath, before noticing that Efa was at her side, staring down at her. So Ina pretended she was talking to her, rather than to herself.

"Hopefully you will too."

The girl didn't say a word, reaching out a hand and helping Ina back to her feet. It was difficult for Ina to think of her as 'Efa' and not as Heddus. But that was her name, so she'd better get used to it. And, although Ina had tried to coax a conversation out of her more than once on this long walk, Efa wouldn't say any more than her name. In fact, when Ina'd tried the last time – whilst they'd rested after an especially steep section – Efa had gone into her shell again, so Ina'd decided to give up. Efa would be sure to start talking at some point – in her own time. Until then, Ina would need to be patient – though she knew better than anyone that this wasn't one of her strengths.

At last, the steep path came to an end. Here they joined another, more level path, and then, suddenly, they were out of the woods. Before them was a wide, bare stretch of land, part of which was farmland. And right in the middle was a huge, oval hillock, lit by the sun that was by now fast setting. Ina looked closer, focusing through the sun's low rays. And she realised that it wasn't just a hillock. It was a hillfort.

Ina stood stock-still. She could almost've believed she was back in Gwent, though this hillfort was closer in terms of size to the stronghold of Caer Faddan than the hillfort near the villa. Efa was standing motionless too, as if she'd never seen such a place before.

"Here is your new home," announced Maelog before adding, with a touch of pride, "It's not as splendid as some of our biggest forts in the mother-country perhaps, but this is the main fort of the Britons of Hispania. You'll see when we go inside that it contains all the conveniences of a modern, civilised society. May you both be very happy and comfortable there."

Ina turned to Efa, glowing with excitement.

"Did you hear that?" she asked, but Efa was still staring ahead of her at the fort. Ina couldn't guess what was going through her mind. It was easier by far to see what the other new arrivals felt, for everyone had begun chattering enthusiastically, picking up their pace towards the hillfort – despite being dead tired after their long trek.

Soon, the outer dyke of the fort was within a stone's throw. At first you couldn't see the entrance – but presently it appeared, hidden in part by the clever angle of the high earth wall that was at least four or five times a man's height. Ina noticed that Efa edged even closer to her as they walked in through the high wooden gates. So Ina reached out to hold her hand and gave her a heartening little smile.

Within this outer dyke was an enclosure with cattle already penned behind its fence, safe for the night. On the other side was a large storehouse of some sort and behind that a plot for growing vegetables and an orchard. Beyond the orchard, Ina saw a row of bee hives, similar to those that Gwrgant had kept at the villa. It really was like being back in Britain.

Straight in front of them was another enormous earth dyke – covered in grass – and the path headed straight for a gap in the middle of it. This had to be the main entrance to the inner fort.

But before anyone had the chance to take a further step, a noisy, joyful crowd of people came rushing out to welcome them. It was obvious to Ina from the way they greeted them that these residents were old friends or family to many of the newcomers. There was much laughter, much embracing, and many tears of happiness, too. The rest of them – including Ina and Efa – stood awkwardly to one side, not recognising a soul.

Then Ina noticed that Maelog was talking to a woman. It was impossible to see her face because her back was to her, but there was something very familiar about her, in spite of that. And when she turned to face them, Ina gasped. Here, standing before her, was the woman who'd wanted to buy Pennata on the day that Caersallog fell, before trying to drag Ina herself off the horse!

Before she knew what was happening, Maelog and the woman began to walk towards her and Efa. Ina didn't know where to turn.

"Girls, this is Morwenna. She has, most generously, agreed to take care of you both."

Ina was too shocked to say a word. The woman smiled at her, giving a little smile to Efa too. Perhaps she doesn't remember me, thought Ina. And perhaps she isn't as bad as all that, after all. But when Maelog turned his head to wave at someone else, the smile vanished from the woman's face and she stared coldly at the two of them – with an especially icy glare for Ina.

"Yai remember you very weel, my gal, just in case yur thinking I didn't recognise you," she said, another little smile spreading across her lips – this time a very unpleasant one.

Ina's heart sank to her heels. Of all the countless people in the whole wide world, why her?

XXIV

Ina gaped at the small, round hut with the thatched roof. Could this really be their new home? It looked more like a pig sty, or a stable! To the side there was an even smaller stone building in the same style. Perhaps this was where they'd sleep. There was no proper door to the main house, just a frame made from three large slabs of stone, and Ina saw that they'd have to bend to enter through this gap. The stone walls weren't very tall, either, but at least the thatched, cone-shaped roof was high.

"Hare we are. Our hoome," said Morwenna, gesturing to them both to enter. It was impossible not to notice the bitter ring in her voice.

Ina ducked through the doorway with Efa close at her heels. It was dark inside. There were no windows. The little light there was came from the gap where the door should have been – and from a sad-looking, smoky fire, opposite the doorway. In the middle of the room was a thick, high post, which held the roof up. From this post, other, smaller beams fanned out to the wall, acting as rafters to keep the roof-straw in place. From one of them hung a chain and a large pot, above the fire. The floor was made of earth, and Ina could feel its dampness beneath her feet. Rushes were spread across it, and there was a large pile of straw between the fire and the door. Next to this was a leather travelling bag, similar to the one Gwrgant had given Ina, and a pile of clothes.

"Yai own thoose," came a sharp voice from behind them. Morwenna was pointing at her belongings – she had sneaked in behind them.

Seeing that Ina didn't understand, she said, "Theer my things. Get it?"

Ina nodded. The accent that'd sounded so charming on the shepherd from the Isle of Syllan and on Artheg the sailor was getting on her nerves already, coming from this sour woman's mouth.

"What's yur neem again? Irwen?"

"Ina . . . Ina ferch Nudd."

Morwenna turned to Efa.

"Yur neem?"

Efa stared at her, mutely.

"Are you daff?"

"Yes, she is a bit," Ina answered for her.

"Meeks no difference to me – long as she's not afreed of work. You'll need to labour too – Ina ferch Nudd. I know yur some sort of gentlewoman, from a noble line. But hare, yur nothing. Yur my property."

Ina's heart sank even further. It was obvious that this woman was going to make her pay dearly for challenging her that day. She, Ina, would not be much more than a maid to her. Nor would Efa.

Thank goodness, a knock on the door broke across this dismal thought. Ina recognised the bald head straight away: Elfryn ap Berddig. She'd met him earlier, with Maelog. At that

point, Ina had taken it for granted that Maelog was the head of the hillfort. It had been a shock to realise that Maelog didn't even live here permanently – his home was a few miles away, next to the Britons' most important church.
Apparently, this man, Elfryn, was in charge; he was the fort's keeper and part of his job was to make sure that newcomers were settling in all right.

"Hail, cherished pilgrims!" said the bald man in a cheery tone, stepping inside with a large bundle of fur-skins and a full sack.

"Behold," he went on, "fur-skins, to keep you warm at night. And, behold! Food and drink for your supper."

He put the sack and the bundle on the floor, before turning to Morwenna.

"Allow me to explain once more, my most respected lady, that this accommodation is but a temporary arrangement; for you have, most generously, agreed to take care of these two, dear girls."

So that was why Morwenna had been willing to take them in, then – so she could get somewhere better to live! Ina had already suspected that she hadn't done it for their good. Meanwhile, Elfryn's formal, flowery language flowed on.

"It is, indeed, a most lamentable fact that we have been unusually busy this summer, due to the unfortunate events in our mother-country. But, my lady, I dare to be confident that there will yet be a dwelling place worthy of your esteemed self, renovated and ready, within the year."

"Within the *yare*?" thundered Morwenna. "Yur telling me we have to stay in this hool for a whole yare?"

"Greetings to you, fair lady!" was Elfryn's only response, and he stepped back, bowing deeply. He was surely glad to be leaving. More than anything in the world, Ina wished she could leave too. But she had nowhere else to go.

✦ ✦ ✦

Ina awoke to the sound of snoring from the other side of the room. It was Morwenna. She hadn't stopped all night, after drinking the whole flask of wine that had come with the supper of bread and cheese. She'd grown ever angrier and more self-pitying the more she'd drunk – jabbering on about how she'd lost everything and how great her life had been before she'd had to flee from the Saxons. Then she'd ordered the girls to prepare a straw bed for her and had collapsed on to it in an unhappy heap. At least Ina and Efa had had a little time to themselves before going to sleep. Not that they'd stayed awake for very long either – for they too were completely exhausted.

During the night Efa had tossed and turned in her sleep, whimpering like a small animal. Ina had whispered in her ear that everything was all right, that she was safe now. But Efa was in such deep sleep that she was impossible to reach. Sinister sounds came from her, as if she were reliving some dreadful experience – alien sounds, harsh, like the voices of the Saxons. Ina held her tightly, wrapping a fur-skin coverlet about her. In the end she'd quietened and Ina had managed to catch a snatch of sleep herself, despite Morwenna's loud snoring.

She was still at it now, like a sow with a head-cold. There was no end to it!

"Are you awake?" Ina whispered to Efa, who lay on her side beneath the fur-skin on the pile of straw. Efa turned to face her.

"Ina," she whispered back.

"Let's get up and leave the sow to snore in her sty," suggested Ina, getting to her feet as quietly as she could. Efa followed her example and the two of them tiptoed towards the makeshift door – a frame of woven branches, leaning against the stones that formed the doorway. As Ina carefully shifted the frame so she could squeeze herself through the gap, a hoarse, angry voice screeched from the other pile of straw.

"Ina ferch Nudd! Get back hare, now!"

And that was the end of that. The girls were made to collect together all the straw and put it in a tidy pile out of the way, while Morwenna helped herself to breakfast. By the time she'd eaten her fill, just two small pieces of hard crust were left for them.

Next, Ina was expected to dress Morwenna's hair, while Efa shook the fur-skins outside, folded them tidily and put them away. Luckily for Ina, Briallen had taught her how to dress hair, though she'd never expected Ina to do her own. That had been Briallen, the maidservant's, job.

Ina began to braid Morwenna's hair as best she could. It wasn't easy, because the older woman tut-tutted continually and made a point of squirming dramatically every time Ina grasped her hair even a tiny bit hard.

"Watch it!" shouted Morwenna, as Ina worked a plait a little more tightly than the rest. Then her hand flew out, like a claw, seizing a chunk of Ina's hair and pulling it, hard, until Ina was whickering in pain. Staring on in horror, Efa dropped the fur-skin she'd been folding to the ground.

"See, you idiot? It hurts, doesn't it."

Then the woman turned to Efa.

"Teek up that fur-skin at once. If you had any heer left on yur baldy head I'd be pulling it too!"

Efa hurriedly bent to pick up the fur-skin, her hands shaking. Ina was motionless with shock, her eyes watering in pain and her whole head burning.

"Compliments of the morning to my dear young ladies!" came a familiar voice from outside. "Are you all decent?"

"One moment!" called Morwenna in an over-friendly voice, hurriedly primping her hair whilst hissing at Ina in a voice that wasn't friendly at all, "You – on yur best behaviour, ur else. Open that dur."

After a moment's puzzlement, Ina realised that Morwenna meant door, so she stepped across to move the woven frame aside. A round face appeared, smiling kindly at her. It was Elfryn, with more things for them. He strode inside, a spring in his step. Ina longed to tell him what had just happened, but what if he didn't think Morwenna had done anything wrong? She had every right to discipline them, worse luck.

"And was Somnus kind to you last night?" asked Elfryn.

Ina was surprised to hear him refer to one of the Roman gods, him being a Christian. Somnus was the god of sleep.

"Yes – thanks to Bacchus," answered Morwenna, giggling

coquettishly. Elfryn laughed politely too. Bacchus was the god of wine.

"And what has Hercules in store for us today?" asked Morwenna in a little girl's voice. Hercules was the god of strength. Ina realised that she was flirting with Elfryn. How embarrassing was that?

"I don't know about Hercules, but I do bring you lunch," he said, handing a sack full of vegetables to Morwenna. "And I would like, if I may, to most sincerely extend the warmest invitation to tonight's feast in the great hall, where we hope to welcome you and all others recently arrived at the fort," he added.

"Yur too kind," simpered Morwenna. She'd obviously decided that charming Elfryn would be a better ploy than complaining.

"And so, farewell!" said Elfryn heartily, raising his hand to wave goodbye as he stepped out of the hut.

The smile on Morwenna's face lasted until Elfryn was out of sight, and not a moment longer. She thrust the sack of vegetables at Ina.

"Meek the fire, and cuck some fud."

Then Morwenna turned her back on the girls, wrapping herself in one of the fur-skins and sitting down. Ina could make a fire easily enough but, apart from roasting rabbits and the like over a camp fire, she had no idea how to cook. However, Efa grabbed the sack without a word and, taking up a knife from beside the fireplace, began skilfully peeling and dicing vegetables. Obviously *she* could. Thank goodness for that, thought Ina, coaxing the sparks into flames then collecting water from the water butt outside the door. Before long the pot was boiling and the tasty smell of soup filled the room.

Morwenna took more than her share, though she complained throughout that the soup was like pigswill. And after eating her fill, she ordered the girls to be silent while she rested. When Ina plucked up courage to ask if they could go out and explore, she received a bark of "No!" in response, and so Ina and Efa had to sit there, doing nothing and saying nothing, all afternoon. At least they had tonight's feast to look forward to, thought Ina. It would be a chance to see Maelog and explain to him that Morwenna wasn't at all suitable as a guardian. It'd also be an opportunity to meet other children. After all, no one knew who she was here. No one knew that she'd survived the plague; that she was 'different'.

But as evening time approached it became clear that Morwenna didn't want them coming with her to the feast, even though the three of them had been invited. As she stepped towards the door, she turned to Ina.

"Yai've bane thinking . . . I'd rather wear yur cloak. Yai sharl borrow it from you – and the brooch. Give them me."

Ina felt breathless with shock, hating this idea, hating the thought of Morwenna even touching the cloak that had been Gwrgant's gift, the brooch that had been her mother's. But at the same time she realised it would be better not to refuse, in case Morwenna lost her temper again and hurt the two of them.

"You will be careful, won't you? It's my mother's brooch."

"How appropriate. It sharl suit me perfectly then, sharn't it."

A crooked smile spread across her face. Reluctantly, Ina handed her the cloak and the brooch.

"Meek shur that everything's cleaned and tidy by the time I'm back. And don't you deer go out – don't you deer meek so much as a peep of sound. Especially with that shoddy old instrument theer," said Morwenna, pointing at the hornpipe.

With that, Morwenna pinned Ina's cloak across her shoulders and stepped out of the hut.

Ina was glad to see the back of her. Because, for the life of her, she didn't know how she was going to bear one more day in the company of Morwenna, never mind a whole year.

XXV

Ina woke to the harsh, repetitive sound of snoring. Again. Opening her eyes, she stared over at Morwenna, who was lying, fully dressed, on the pile of straw opposite her. She hadn't even bothered to take off her cloak – or rather, Ina's cloak – and her hair, that had looked so elegant last night, fell in dishevelled locks across her face. Her mouth was open wide, as if she were expecting someone to feed her. The most hideous snorting sound was coming from it – much worse than the previous morning.

Morwenna had returned very late last night, waking them up to brag in a slurred voice about how much everyone had admired her and had wanted to get to know her, before collapsing on to her straw bed, still rattling on about this and that. Ina hadn't understood much – whether this was because of Morwenna's strong accent or all the wine she'd knocked back, she couldn't say. Probably a combination of the two.

Turning away from her, Ina moved closer to Efa. "Are you awake?" she whispered.

Efa didn't answer. So Ina gave her a little shake. Still no answer. Then, at last, Efa turned to face her. Her cheeks were wet and her eyes full of tears.

"Efa, dear . . . It's no wonder you're sad, is it? Come here. We're going to put a stop to all this, right now."

Once Maelog learned of how badly Morwenna was treating them he'd be sure to put them under the protection of someone more suitable. It was clear by now that Morwenna wasn't fit to look after chickens, never mind children.

Cautiously, Ina got to her feet, making as little sound as possible. So did Efa. Then the two of them tiptoed to the door. Ina gripped the wicker frame that leant against it, shifting it a little to the side. But this time, Morwenna didn't wake. She was sleeping as soundly as a hog. Or, rather, a sow.

Ina stepped outside the hut and Efa came after her, both of them blinking in the early sunlight. This was the first time they'd been out on their own since arriving. They saw at once that their house was on the outskirts of the inner fort, standing back to back with the inner defensive dyke. In the morning sunshine they could see, through the gaps between houses, that a strong wall of stones reinforced the earth of this dyke. At the front of their house was a path, which wound in a circular direction around the edge of the inner fort. Ina beckoned to Efa to follow her, then began to walk purposefully along the path in the direction of the main entrance.

They passed buildings of all shapes and sizes, Efa sticking close by her side. Some buildings were round, like their hut. Some were oval-shaped, and some were square. Most of them formed connected groups of two or three or four, and obviously served different purposes – as people's homes, storehouses, workshops and places to keep chickens and pigs.

Though it was early, there were a few people out and

about already, and many were already at their work. They came to a junction where one path led off from the circular path, and Ina realised that it led towards the centre of the fort. So they followed it, walking past grander buildings now, buildings with red-tiled roofs, very like those on the villa that had once been Ina's home.

"Good morning," said someone from inside one of the buildings. It was a man, about forty years old. A hammer was in his hand, and a large moustache above his lips. Sulien and his blackberry-juice moustache came flashing into Ina's mind and she cringed inwardly at the memory, wondering if she'd ever stop feeling embarrassed about it.

"I haven't seen you two before. Did you come on the last boat?"

"Yes, we did. Do you know where Maelog is, please?" asked Ina. "We need to speak to him."

"Maelog? He left with the dawn."

Ina's heart sank.

"Then, have you seen Elfryn yet this morning?"

"I'd say he'll still be snoring abed, after last night's feast," answered the man, giving them a wink. Elfryn's not the only one, thought Ina.

"Thank you. God be with you," she said politely, trying her best not to show the crushing disappointment she felt.

"God be with you, also," he answered, treating them to a warm smile that made his moustache dance.

They'd need to have a word with Elfryn as soon as they could, then. But for now, they'd better get back before Morwenna woke. Hurrying forwards to a wider path, Ina saw that this was the main thoroughfare, going all the way from the main entrance through the centre of the fort to the back entrance. Straight in front of them was a grand building – the grandest they'd seen yet. This had to be the fort's great hall. They might have seen inside it, had they been at last night's feast. Ina seethed to think how unfair it was that Morwenna had stopped them from coming. How unfair everything was.

A gang of children was approaching down the path, joking about, noisily. All the shouting and laughing stopped as they set eyes on Ina and Efa, and they stared suspiciously at them.

"Hello," said Ina, trying to sound friendly.

The gang walked past them without saying a word. Just like the children of the hillfort back in Gwent, thought Ina, with an inward sigh.

"Come on," she said to Efa, trying to hide her disappointment and hurrying back to the little round house.

On arrival, Ina pushed herself through the narrow gap in the doorway. To her surprise there was no sign of Morwenna, only an empty straw bed. Then, suddenly, a hand whipped out, grabbing her hair and dragging her into the room. Morwenna had been lurking just inside the door, waiting for them. Ina writhed in pain and fell to her knees as Morwenna yanked her hair yet harder, twisting it mercilessly.

"Who geev you permission to go out?"

"No one," gasped Ina, her voice shaking – with anger more than pain.

The next moment, Morwenna was staggering backwards, stunned, as Efa flew from the doorway, flinging herself against her and shoving wildly at her. Letting go her grip on

Ina and screaming in outrage, Morwenna grabbed the slighter girl then gave her such a slap that Efa staggered too, falling to the floor. Morwenna's black-rimmed eyes were blazing. She towered threateningly over Efa, pulling her leg back to deliver a vicious kick. Then came a voice from outside the door.

"Greetings, on this beautiful day!"

It wasn't Elfryn's voice this time. Hastily smoothing back her hair, Morwenna pushed the wicker frame aside. There stood a thin man, with two fat pigs.

"Sadwrn ap Tangwyn. At your service. My lady, I should like to provide you and your household with sustenance. Pray you, allow me to offer these two pigs."

Morwenna smiled a fake smile at him, making his face light up. It was obvious from the goggle-eyed way he was looking at her that he found Morwenna very attractive, despite the fact that she'd just woken up and looked pretty dishevelled after last night's excesses.

"Respected gentleman, greet are my thanks. Pree you, give me a moment to compose myself."

Morwenna turned to Ina and gesticulated furiously at her to do her hair, at once. Although her own head was still burning from Morwenna's brutal treatment, Ina did her best, for Efa's sake. At all costs, she had to avoid giving Morwenna another reason to strike her friend.

"That'll do," said Morwenna abruptly a short while later, staring at herself in the mirror. After dabbing more makeup on her face, Morwenna invited the man into the hut. He'd been standing outside patiently the whole time, without a word.

"It's an honour and a pleasure to cross your threshold," said Sadwrn, before ducking to step inside. He held a large wooden staff in his hand.

"This will be handy for keeping the pigs in order," he said, passing the long piece of wood to Morwenna.

"And fur keeping these two in order," she answered playfully, pointing the staff at the girls. Then she brushed her hand lightly across Ina's hair, as if they were the best of friends. But Ina knew the truth of her words and her actions. She was giving the two of them a subtle warning.

Then Morwenna and Sadwrn talked for ages and ages, while the girls had to sit, fidgeting with boredom and unease, listening to their nonsense. Morwenna was putting on her most velvety voice to create an alluring, ladylike impression – and as for Sadwrn, Ina didn't like him at all. Not just because he was staring at Morwenna like a bong-eyed mooncalf, but because his eyes kept flitting towards her, Ina, all sly and shifty. She noticed that he took no notice of Efa, who was crouching beside her and staring at the floor.

At last the man left, but not before promising to call again. Once he'd gone, Morwenna turned to them.

"Yai hope you've learned yur lesson. Teek the pigs into the wood so they can find fud. And when you return, come straight back to the house. Don't go bothering anyone else."

Then Morwenna gripped the heavy staff and thrusted it, menacingly, at Ina.

"Yai don't have to tell you what'll happen if you don't do as I see, do I?"

Ina looked at her then shook her head. This wasn't an

empty threat, like dear Briallen's endless warnings. Ina knew full well that Morwenna would beat them without a moment's hesitation with this staff, given half a chance. But before leaving, Ina had to say something. She cleared her throat.

"May I have my cloak back, if you please?"

"You mee not. Ya i'm caping it. And the brooch. You don't deserve them."

Ina knew there was no point arguing. The horrible truth was now out in the open. She wasn't a servant to Morwenna – she was a slave. Not officially, perhaps, but as good as. And so was Efa.

Without another word, Ina put the hornpipe around her neck, nodded to Efa to follow her and walked out of the hut, grasping the staff tightly in her hand.

Swinging the staff, Ina beat the air black and blue as she walked through the wood, going through all Gwrgant's fighting moves until her arms ached and sweat poured down her face. In her imagination, her opponent was Morwenna – and she was giving her a real thrashing. She was completely out of breath by now and had run out of moves, but she felt much better for it.

Ina had made a promise to herself. A promise that Morwenna wouldn't get the better of her and Efa. She wasn't sure yet how they'd stop her, but she knew that she'd have to be very careful from now on and do nothing rash. The two of them were very vulnerable – they owned nothing in the world and there was no one here to protect them. So they needed to be very patient, and very cautious.

Efa had been walking behind her with the pigs, a safe distance from the staff's blows. Now she stopped, letting the animals rummage for food on the woodland floor.

"Thanks for trying to defend me earlier, but don't do it again. I don't want her hurting you," said Ina.

Efa looked at her, wordlessly. She'd gone into her shell again after Morwenna's blow. One of the pigs sauntered over and rubbed its snout against Efa's leg – just like Bleiddyn used to, thought Ina. There was something quite sweet about the pigs. One had a black ear that flopped over her snout and the other had a crossed eye, so she looked as if everything was a big surprise to her. It wasn't their fault that they'd belonged to that creepy man, Sadwrn.

The girls had had no trouble finding the wood, which was visible from the back of the fort. They'd simply followed the path leading from the fort's back entrance and here they were, right in the middle of its sheltering trees. Efa had stared down at the ground the whole way. Before she'd started on her fighting manoeuvres, Ina had done her best to coax a smile from her. But even her bright idea of naming the pigs 'Mora' and 'Wenna' hadn't worked.

Now Ina drove the pigs yet further into the wood, using the staff to gently direct them, so they were surrounded by thick, tall trees in all directions. Efa walked behind her, treading so quietly that Ina had to make sure from time to time that her friend was still with her.

Then Ina heard a rustling in the undergrowth behind them, twigs snapping underfoot, as if someone was following them through the trees. She stopped, stock-still, gripping the staff tightly. Perhaps it was Sadwrn himself, come to interfere. A creeping feeling of unease filled her and she almost called out for Bleiddyn, before remembering that he now lay, lifeless, on a faraway beach. Ina strode forward, her heart beating fast, motioning to Efa to keep up with her.

And after a bit, the trees opened out and the sound of running water filled the space. They'd reached a river. On its bank there stood a tall, old tree – a silver birch. A small, stony beach lay beneath the tree and rushes grew thickly at the river's edge. Ina stared in astonishment. It was just like her favourite place in all the world, near to her home in Gwent! Without a moment's hesitation, she ran to enter the shade of the silver birch's canopy and sit down beneath it.

Shortly, Efa came and sat down next to her. Then she gestured at the hornpipe around Ina's neck. Ina shook her head.

"I'm not in the mood to play it today."

The disappointment was obvious on the girl's face, but Ina wasn't about to change her mind.

Then, suddenly, came a musical call, echoing through the trees. The sound of another hornpipe! The notes were penetrating but their tone was warm, less strident than Ina's. Ina and Efa turned to each other, their eyes wide in astonishment. And the tune continued – a beautiful melody; the piper so talented that Ina could almost see the notes as they wove through each other in the air about them.

The song drew to a close and Ina held her breath. Silence. Efa's eyes were like saucers and her pale cheeks were for once flushed pink. She clapped her hands in joy.

"Mora," said Efa suddenly, pointing at one of the pigs, before pointing at the other. "Wenna." And she started to laugh.

Here was Efa, saying two new words! Perhaps this other, mysterious hornpipe was magic too.

"Good day!" called Ina, loudly, to the unseen piper – not sure where exactly to direct her voice.

But not a peep came back and, although the two of them searched painstakingly, there was no sign of the mysterious hornpipe player. It was as if the wood had swallowed them alive.

XXVI

It was difficult to know who was snoring loudest – the two pigs in the little sty at the side of the house, or Morwenna. At least if Morwenna's snoring she can't tell us off, thought Ina, who had just woken up. Efa was awake too, pressing her hands against her ears.

Morwenna had been in a better mood when they'd arrived back from the wood yesterday. Elfryn, the keeper of the fort, had arrived at their door, bringing supper for them again – plus a pitcher of milk for breakfast. He was a kind man and he knew that, as recent arrivals, they wouldn't yet be able to sustain themselves. However, there'd been no chance for Ina to pull him aside and have a quiet word with him about Morwenna.

Now she found herself unable to lie quietly in bed, and not just because Morwenna was snoring like a hibernating bear. Hearing the hornpipe yesterday had awoken her in a way that she couldn't properly describe. And, very suddenly, a desperate need came over her to see her sister Lluan's face again. And just as suddenly, she had an idea how.

She got up and crept on tiptoe to the edge of Morwenna's bed, picking up the small mirror before returning, just as quietly, to her own pile of straw. Perhaps if she were to look into the glass she'd see Lluan again, as she had when she'd worn her emerald dress for the very first time. And this time, she wouldn't look away.

"One, two, three . . ." whispered Ina, before lifting the mirror. But although she looked at it from every direction, there was no sign of Lluan's beautiful face. The only face she could see was that of a scrawny twelve-year-old, with eyes that were too far apart and a neck that was too long. Ina dropped the mirror in disappointment, dismayed with herself for having such a stupid idea.

Efa had been watching the whole time. Now she too lifted the mirror and stared, hesitantly, into it. She held her breath, open-mouthed, as if she didn't recognise herself at all. Then she put her hand to her shorn head and stroked it. Tears began to roll down her cheeks. This made Ina feel even worse. She reached out and took the mirror from her swiftly, without saying a word.

Then she crossed the damp earth floor and put the mirror in its original place. Staring down at Morwenna she had to admit that, even in her sleep with her hair all over the place and her mouth wide open, she was beautiful. How could someone so lovely to look at behave in such an ugly way?

✦ ✦ ✦

Breakfast was yesterday's bread soaked in a large dish of milk. Ina had to eat hers standing up, hurriedly, piece by piece, because Morwenna wanted her hair done as soon as possible in case the pig-man, Sadwrn ap Tangwyn, called by. (Or Snorty ap Hog-face, to give him the name Ina had recently coined for him.)

"Greetings! On this lovely morning!" called a shrill voice from outside. Speak of the devil. Morwenna primped her hair and opened the door. Sadwrn stood there, dressed in his finest clothes – which were a little too big, him being as thin as a rake. He tried to smile, wrinkling his nose like a nervous hare.

"I wonder if I may have the pleasure of escorting you around the fort, my gracious lady?"

Morwenna extended her hand towards him.

"You mee."

As Sadwrn took it, he threw a crooked little smile in Ina's direction, which Ina did her very best to ignore.

Morwenna turned to the girls, barking, "Teek the pigs to the wud. You nade not return till supper."

Then she pulled one of her fake, girlish smiles at Sadwrn, whose own smug face said he'd won the most valuable prize in all Hispania.

✢ ✢ ✢

Ina and Efa had been sitting under the silver birch on the bank of the river for ages, hoping to hear the magical music again. But not a sound came from the wood. Nothing but the enthusiastic grunting of the two hogs – Mora and Wenna.

Ina looked up at the sky. It had been cloudy all day. And it was at least some relief to Ina that summers here seemed no better than back in Britain. With a bit of luck, Morwenna's mood would've improved too. It was obvious that Sadwrn wanted her as his wife and just as obvious – to Ina, at least – that Morwenna wasn't that keen on him. Probably, she thought she could do better. However, Ina was sure that Morwenna would have no scruples about using him to improve her life. What if she went so far as to actually marry him? Ina shivered at the idea of having to share a house with such a loathsome man and his roving eyes . . .

She stood up, turning to watch Efa, who was playing with pebbles at the water's edge. Ina saw that she'd placed the stones in a particular order – just as she had with the shapes she'd carved into the sand that time – but Ina couldn't see any pattern that made sense. Perhaps Efa was just creating pretty shapes.

"Come on, we'd better get back."

Efa kicked the piles of stones, scattering them, before climbing up the river bank.

Then, a note came echoing through the trees. One, single note, floating out into the woodland air between the river and the leaves. A second note arrived to follow it, and this one too was long and playful. The mystery piper was here, invisible amongst the trees on the opposite bank.

Efa grabbed hold of the hornpipe and pushed it into Ina's hands. Ina hesitated, just for a moment, then she lifted the instrument to her lips and piped exactly the same note in response. There came another note, and again Ina answered. And again. And again. The piper was skillfully leading Ina along a song-path. And whilst she didn't recognise the tune, she knew the song from the atmosphere it created, from the feel of it. It could so easily have been one that her mother had played with her. And so, she felt, the piper had to be a Briton. Just like her.

She felt the notes diffuse within her, becoming part of her. How thrilling it was! She'd felt nothing like this since she'd accompanied her mother, all those years ago. But when she remembered her mother – pictured her, playing the hornpipe – her throat went dry and she had to pull the instrument from her lips, her heart beating hard.

The song came to an end. Efa seemed unaware of the commotion in Ina's chest. Her eyes were closed and she was smiling gently, completely lost in the song, although its closing notes had already sounded.

"Good day!" called Ina, across the river. The response was the first note of the song again. Ina longed to join in a second time, but she was afraid to. Afraid of the thrill. Afraid of remembering her mother. So the piper played unaccompanied, and the notes formed by their dexterous fingers danced across the water's surface towards the girls.

Suddenly Efa gave a little scream and hid behind Ina. There, between the trees across the river, was a figure, watching them.

A closer look revealed a boy about the same age as Ina. A hornpipe was in his hands. Not exactly the same kind of hornpipe as Ina's, but similar. The biggest difference, from what Ina could see, was that the pipe was stuck into some sort of bag.

"Good day!" called Ina again, surprised that such an accomplished piper was so young.

"*Salve!*" answered the boy.

Ina was even more astonished to hear him answer in Latin. He most likely wasn't a Briton, after all. Was he one of the Gallaecians, then?

Before she dared to answer, the boy turned his head, like a deer picking up the wind-borne scent of hunters, and disappeared from view.

Fear crept along Ina's spine. What had made the boy flee?

One thing was for sure – she didn't want to hang about to find out.

✦ ✦ ✦

Ina and Efa had just driven Mora and Wenna in through the gate of the fort's outer wall, when the pigs suddenly froze and began to squeal, loudly. Had they injured themselves, somehow? Ina crouched to check them over, running her hands down their legs.

Then "Ina!" Efa screamed in warning, from behind her.

She turned to see a young horse galloping wildly towards her. So that was why the pigs had set up the alarm. They couldn't see very well but they could smell danger – literally.

Every sinew in Ina's body wanted to run away, but she knew from experience – from learning to handle Pennata – that you had to hold your ground. And that's what she did, though it was far from easy. The horse slowed, but his eyes bulged, wide open, wild, and he beat the ground with his front hooves, squealing furiously.

Then, to Ina's horror, Efa stepped forward, placing herself between Ina and the horse. The horse began to pound the ground even harder, shaking his mane and sidestepping wildly, bunching the muscles in his hind legs, threatening to rear up and bring his front hooves down, hard – on to Efa.

But calmly, slowly, Efa was walking towards the horse. Placing her hand gently on his muzzle, she stood on tiptoe to whisper something into his ear. In an instant, the stallion calmed, shaking his head and neighing, as if in recognition of a friend. And then he stood, motionless, allowing Efa to stroke his long neck before she leant against him and rested her forehead against his nose, murmuring quietly to him the whole time.

Ina stared at her, open-mouthed. "How in the world did you manage that?"

But Efa didn't answer. Either she hadn't heard, too absorbed in the horse, or she was ignoring her. Ina was so taken by how Efa had subdued the horse that she didn't notice the man running towards them.

"Valens has never let anyone near him, never mind stroke him," he panted, out of breath and as full of wonder as Ina.

Valens was the name of this powerful stallion, then. A Latin name, which meant 'strong and healthy'. Efa took no notice of the man. She was in another world, a world where nothing existed but her and the horse. Perhaps she can't hear after all, thought Ina. She turned to see that it was the man with the moustache who'd spoken.

"Maelog was absolutely right. You two girls are very special."

The man smiled kindly at Ina before watching Efa with the horse, his gaze full of admiration. Ina felt a tiny pang of jealousy, though she knew she shouldn't. Then the man approached the horse, which at once began to squeal in protest and throw his head. The man laughed, making his moustache dance once more.

"I do declare he doesn't want to leave you," the man said to Efa, before turning to the horse and speaking in a consoling voice, "Come, Valens. You'll see your new friend again."

As the man led the horse away, Ina went over to Efa, who was waving farewell to the animal.

"Why can't someone like him come to court Morwenna, instead of that stupid Snorty ap Hogface?"

Efa didn't respond, just stared longingly after the horse. The fact that Efa so often ignored her was beginning to get on Ina's nerves.

"If you can speak to a horse you can speak to me, can't you?"

Efa stared downwards, as she did in every difficult situation.

"Fine. Don't speak to me then." And Ina turned tail and walked away, completely losing patience. She didn't bother to see whether Efa was following her. She was sure to be, like a shadow. She might as well be her shadow. Here she was, with a friend – at last – but one who refused to talk to her, though she was happy enough to talk to animals! What a friend!

Then Ina turned her thoughts to the man with the moustache. If he was as kind as he seemed, he'd be a much better husband to Morwenna than Sadwrn the creepy milksop, and definitely a better guardian to the two of them . . .

An idea came to her. But first, there were two things to sort out. One, she had to find out whether the man with the moustache was already married, and two, if he wasn't, she had to make sure that he and Morwenna met as soon as possible.

XVII

Ina had not the slightest desire to be anywhere near the house when Sadwrn next called. So she made sure to dress Morwenna's hair very early the following morning, giving her and Efa time to leave before he came over. When Morwenna had mentioned the night before that he'd be dropping by, Ina had almost referred to him as Snorty but, thank goodness, she corrected herself in time.

Instead of driving the pigs straight towards the gate at the back of the fort, Ina headed towards the house where the man with the moustache lived, hoping she'd be able to discover more about him. She knew full well she wasn't supposed to do this, and there'd be a high price to pay if Morwenna came to learn of it, but this was important.

From her confused appearance, it was obvious that Efa didn't understand what was going on when Ina veered off the main path through the fort.

"You only have to ask, you know."

For a moment, Efa opened her mouth as if she was going to say something. Then she closed it again. Something was stopping her, something that seemed beyond her control.

If Ina'd been in a better mood, she would've felt sorry for Efa. But a fairly good night's sleep hadn't made Ina feel any less irritable as she strode impatiently in front of her. As ever,

Efa followed her, as silent as a shadow.

They reached the house, but there was no sign of the man so Ina decided to hang about for a bit. Then someone come out of the front door. Not the man, but two children – a boy and a girl. Ina sighed in disappointment. He was married, then. What a shame. No, more than a shame. A tragedy. The children stared at them inquisitively.

"Was it you who tamed the horse?" one of them asked Ina.

"No. It was her," she answered, pointing at Efa.

Efa smiled shyly at the children. Everyone stood, saying nothing, for a second or two. It was obvious that they all wanted to say something but no one was very sure what.

Then came the noisy crowd of children – the same gang they'd encountered before – heading down the path in their direction. As soon as they noticed Ina and Efa, they sneered and began to grunt loudly like pigs – "Oink! Oink! Oink!" – waving their arms in the air as if they were herding Ina, Efa, Mora and Wenna down the road before them.

Ina grabbed Efa's arm and pulled her quickly away, driving the pigs towards the back gate as the shouting children mocked them from afar.

"Oink! Oink! Oink!"

✦ ✦ ✦

Smack! Crack! Smack! Mercilessly, Ina pounded the tree with her staff until the bark began to split. She roared with each blow, her voice thundering through the wood. Whack! Crack! Whack! She struck at the trunk again and again and again.

Struck it until her body shook with fatigue. With one last shout, Ina aimed a savage blow, smashing one of its branches to splinters. Then she dropped the staff and rubbed her sore hands. They were red – as red as her face, which was dripping with sweat.

Getting her breath back, Ina walked down to the river to wash. The water was beautifully cold. She gulped down a mouthful or two as she splashed her face, noticing how very quiet the wood was. Perhaps she'd frightened the birds. And then she realised that she hadn't heard the familiar snorts and snuffles of the pigs for some time. Putting the hornpipe back around her neck, she grabbed the staff and walked quickly to the spot where she'd left Efa to watch over them.

But the pigs weren't there. Neither was Efa. They must have wandered off, and Efa must have gone with them. They wouldn't have gone far. Then Ina heard a splash, from the direction of the broad old silver birch. There was Efa, skimming stones across the water, looking longingly at the other side of the river. She's hoping to see the mystery piper again, thought Ina. In her rage and frustration, she'd forgotten all about him – just as Efa had evidently forgotten all about the pigs.

"Where are Mora and Wenna?"

Efa turned to look at her, and her eyes grew suddenly fearful. Ina raised her voice.

"The pigs! Where are they?"

Paling, Efa climbed the river bank and hurried past Ina without daring to look at her.

"Mora! Wenna! Mora!" called Efa, her voice shaking.

"Wenna! Mora! Wenna!" shouted Ina in panic, running to and fro amongst the trees. After searching fruitlessly and shouting until they were hoarse, Efa approached Ina, worry etched all over her face.

"You were supposed to be keeping an eye on them!"

Her eyes fell to the ground and she stood there, mutely.

"This is all your fault, you hear?!"

Ina turned on her heel and walked away and, although she continued to look everywhere, there was still no sign of the pigs – not a trotter, not an oink. Perhaps whatever had frightened the young piper yesterday had frightened them away too . . . perhaps it had even killed them and torn them to pieces.

✦ ✦ ✦

"The pigs! Lost?" spat Morwenna, her eyes flaming. Ina had expected her to go mad and so she'd steeled herself against the harsh words, but she could see that Efa was trembling in fear.

"Yai expect you were too busy playing that stupid old instrument. Or did dumbo here fall aslape?" hissed Morwenna, pointing at Efa.

"Efa wasn't asleep."

Morwenna rushed at Ina, spitting into her face.

"Yur to blame, then?"

This time, Ina stared back at her. This time, she wasn't going to give in and, for sure, she wasn't going to blame Efa, even though they'd fallen out.

Then, without warning, Morwenna grabbed the hornpipe, breaking the leather strap that held it around Ina's neck.

"Don't you dare!" shouted Ina instinctively. Then she regretted her words, immediately.

"*Don't you deer?*" repeated Morwenna, incredulous. "Did you just say 'Don't you deer' – to me?"

"I meant, please don't . . ." said Ina, quickly corrected herself. "If you please . . . do not take it from me. The hornpipe was Gwrgant's. It's the only thing I've got left of him."

"Yai've heard about enough about yur stupid family. Yai'm yur family now!"

"Say what you like – you'll never be a mother to me!" Ina yelled back, unable to control herself.

An overwhelming silence descended. Ina couldn't believe she'd just shouted at Morwenna. Neither could Morwenna, from the look on her face. Nor could Efa, who was standing stock-still, holding her breath. It was as if time itself had stalled, just as it had when the sea monster had risen from the sea on the journey over to Britonia. The three of them stared, wordlessly, at each other.

And then Morwenna turned on her heel and smashed the hornpipe against the iron cooking pot with all her strength. The hornpipe split into fragments, and so did a part of Ina.

"No . . .!" she screamed.

Efa began to sob, uncontrollably, hunching over and hiding her face in her hands.

"You got what you dayserved," said Morwenna, icily, before turning to Efa. "And you – stop that wretched whining, at once!"

Then Morwenna grabbed the staff and raised it swiftly, about to smash it down on to Efa's back. At that moment Ina snapped, hurling herself at Morwenna. She was too light to knock her over, but she knew from Gwrgant's training how to fight a heavier opponent. Using her height and the element of surprise to snatch the staff, she spun Morwenna, who was still grasping the other end of it, like a top before throwing her off with all her strength. Morwenna lost her grip on the staff, and fell backwards, hitting the back of her head so hard against the cooking pot that it came free from its chain and crashed to the ground. Now Morwenna was lying on the floor, moaning in agony. Ina turned to Efa.

"Out of here!"

Ina rushed for the door, but someone was standing in her way. Sadwrn ap Tangwyn. Fearlessly, Ina stepped towards him, threatening him with the raised staff and feeling sure, in that moment, that she could deal with a milksop like him. Sadwrn stepped back and Ina threw herself at him, but Sadwrn surprised her by deftly grabbing the staff and tearing it from her hands. For someone so thin, the man was surprisingly strong. Before she had the chance to retreat, Sadwrn had whipped the staff across her legs, tripping her up and decking her. Then he raised the staff high above his head, ready to bring it down upon her. Hard.

"No! Don't!" called Morwenna, trying to stand.

Sadwrn stared down at Ina, before letting the staff fall to the ground.

"You're a very, very lucky girl," he said, before rushing to Morwenna and helping her to her feet.

Ina had no idea why Morwenna had stopped him, but she was very glad for it. She knew that Sadwrn would've beaten her mercilessly.

Holding tightly to Sadwrn, Morwenna staggered unsteadily out of the house, without looking in Ina's direction. Was she afraid of her? A thrill went through Ina at the thought. It was a very sweet possibility.

Getting shakily to her feet, Ina cursed herself for ignoring, yet again, one of Gwrgant's golden rules – never lose your temper in battle. Would she never learn? Efa was staring at her in a mixture of fear and admiration.

Then came a sound from outside the house. A familiar, snorting sound. Efa rushed out, only to return almost straight away.

"Mora! Wenna!" she said excitedly, before disappearing through the door again to shoo the pigs into their sty for the night.

So the pigs had returned by themselves. If only they'd arrived ten minutes earlier . . . But Ina knew better than anyone that no one could turn back time. She crouched down to collect the shattered pieces of the hornpipe together. It would be impossible to fix it. She sank to the ground, turning her face to the cold, stone wall of the hut. Shut her eyes. She felt empty – completely empty.

Then Ina heard a voice, humming a lullaby – her lullaby – quietly, so quietly – as if from far, far away. Soon the voice began to sing the words – words that Ina hadn't heard for many, long years.

> "Heavy with acorns from the glade,
> His nose as dirty as a spade,
> The fat young pig comes from the grove
> And seeks the straw of its sleeping cove,
> Good night, Ina,
> Good night . . ."

The voice was lovely. As if from another world. And the familiar words wrapped themselves about her, making her feel all warm and snug.

> "A river bank, a fishing boat,
> And all the dreams around them float;
> A shadow comes from the prowling night
> With tales to tell by the fire light,
> Good night, Ina,
> Good night . . ."

"Lluan . . ." whispered Ina, turning over and opening her eyes, but it was Efa who stood before her, Efa who was singing. Her blue-green eyes were sparkling and her face shone as brightly as her voice.

"Don't stop . . ." whispered Ina.

Efa paused. Then, with a shy little smile, she sang the last verse.

> "The great white rock is mountain dark,
> The young green leaves embrace the bark,
> And only the mist, without a sound,

> Through trees and meadows whirls around,
> Good night, Ina,
> Good night . . ."

The song ended. Efa cleared her throat. "Ina. Not. Sad," she said, stumblingly.

Efa had astonished Ina with the lullaby. Now she astonished her even more. She'd just spoken more than one word. Three words, all together, at the same time. At last!

"Ina not sad," said Efa again, adding, "Efa here."

"Yes, you're here. Thank goodness for you. My friend," answered Ina, their quarrel long forgotten.

"Efa not friend," insisted Efa. "Sister."

With this, Efa embraced her. And although she was squeezing Ina tightly, her touch was as light as a feather. Perhaps she's an angel, thought Ina. A star, who has fallen to Earth.

XXVIII

It had rained during the night, making the path through the wood muddier than usual. Ina knew this because she'd woken several times to the pitter-patter of raindrops on the thatched roof of the hut. She'd slept badly, and not just because of the rain. Morwenna hadn't returned, but Ina had been too afraid to sleep heavily in case she came back to take her revenge. As soon as the sun had risen, Ina had decided that the best thing to do was to take the pigs to the woods early to avoid Morwenna for as long as possible.

By now, she regretted losing her temper. She'd have to live with the results, whatever they may be. Part of her was still furious with Morwenna for trying to hurt Efa and for breaking the hornpipe, and the other part was full of happy excitement, in spite of the situation, because Efa had at last begun to speak in sentences – of a sort.

Sister. That's what she'd said. Ina's sister. She spun the word about in her head. Sister. Did she have a right to think about this girl – this girl who, in truth, Ina knew almost nothing about, as something more than a friend – as a sister? Lluan wouldn't mind, Ina was sure of that, but was this still a step too far . . .?

"Wenna! No!" called Efa, interrupting Ina's thoughts as the pig with the crossed eye began to roll in the mud.

Efa prodded the pig gently with a stick. "Time to get up!"

But Wenna was enjoying herself too much to obey. Efa poked her harder.

"Naughty girl! Time to get up!"

At last, the hog stopped rolling and got to its trotters.

"Good girl," said Efa, smiling.

She speaks to the pig exactly as you'd speak to a little child, thought Ina.

But all Wenna did was join Mora, who was also rolling contentedly in another mud bath a few paces away. Seeing this, Ina laughed loudly and Efa joined in.

"Silly piggies!" she giggled.

Efa hadn't stopped talking since they'd arrived in the wood, but it was impossible to ignore the fact that she couldn't string more than a few words together, and not always in the right order. The individual words sounded odd too, as if they'd rusted within her. Ina decided not to say anything, in case she went into her shell again. She didn't ask Efa about her own story either, or about her family. Whatever had happened to Efa must've shaken her so badly that the words weren't flowing easily, yet. Ina had to be patient with her.

"Lazy girl! Time to get up!" said Efa, trying to sound as strict as possible – which wasn't strict at all – and waving the stick. Then the two pigs stood up together, suddenly, and ran as fast as their short legs would allow in the direction of the river.

"Piggies listen Efa." Efa grinned proudly, then set off after them.

"No wonder. I'd be frightened of you too," called Ina playfully, tight on her heels. But if Efa understood the joke, she gave no sign of it.

Ina didn't know that pigs could run so fast. By the time they'd reached the river she and Efa were panting so hard they could scarcely breathe, but Mora and Wenna did no more than snuffle about happily beneath the trees.

While the girls had recovered their breath, a single note from the mysterious hornpipe sounded from across the river. What with all the trouble with Morwenna, Ina had completely forgotten about the young piper. Here he was again – and her own hornpipe in pieces . . . Last night, hearing Efa singing the lullaby, something had awoken deep inside her, making her long to play along with the boy today. But it was too late for that.

Ina and Efa hurried to the riverside. There, opposite, was the boy, playing the same melody he'd played the last time, on his strange-looking pipe. At Ina's side, Efa began to hum the song in accompaniment, her voice as clear and bright as the sunshine that dazzled their eyes as they peered across the water. And the piper's notes were just as nimble and fleeting as the sunlight's reflections, dancing on the river. Ina wondered once more at the boy's talent, knowing from experience how difficult it was to create such a full, rich sound.

The tune came to an end and Ina saw the skilful musician dissolve before her eyes as an ordinary boy appeared in his place. In the same way it was hard to believe that Efa owned such a magical singing voice, it was hard to believe that this ordinary-looking youth could play the hornpipe in such a heavenly way.

"Salve!" called the boy, greeting them in Latin and raising his hand.

"Ave! . . . Greetings!" answered Ina. *"Quis est tuum nomen?"* What is your name?

"You can speak Latin!" said the boy in surprise, in Latin – forgetting to tell them his name.

"Yes, I can. I am not a barbarian."

"That's for sure. You speak our tongue like a real lady! Who's the girl beside you, with the beautiful voice? Your sister?"

Ina paused before answering.

"Yes. My sister, Efa."

Here she was saying it out loud, and it felt completely natural. Efa pulled at her sleeve.

"What Ina say?"

"So you don't speak Latin?" Ina asked her.

Efa shook her head.

"I told him . . . that you're my sister," explained Ina. It felt more of a thing, somehow, to say it in her own tongue. Efa smiled so hard Ina was afraid her cheeks would split.

"Salve!" the boy called to Efa.

"Sal . . . be!" answered Efa, trying to get her mouth round the word, without much success.

"She does not speak Latin," explained Ina.

"Why not?"

"Long story."

"I'd like to hear it some time."

"Tomorrow? Same time?"

"*Same time tomorrow,*" confirmed the boy, turning to leave and lifting his hand to wave farewell.

"*You have not told us your name yet!*" shouted Ina after him.

"*Rodomiro. You?*"

"*Meum nomen Ina est.*" Ina is my name.

"*Ina,*" Rodomiro repeated, smiling. Then, "*Vale, Ina and Efa!*" he called, saying goodbye properly this time and raising a hand in farewell.

"*Vale!* . . . *Farewell, Rodomiro!*" answered Ina.

The boy melted into the trees. Ina turned to see that Efa's large, blue-green eyes were even wider than usual. Ina wasn't sure if this was from hearing so much Latin or from seeing the boy again, but she had a pretty good idea that Efa wouldn't tell her the reason – even if she asked.

✝ ✝ ✝

Morwenna wasn't there when Ina and Efa reached the house. Looking around the dark, damp hovel of a place, Ina couldn't think of it as her home. If it'd been hard to do so earlier, it was impossible after last night. From the looks of it, Morwenna hadn't come back at all. The cooking pot was still on its side on the floor and the hearth was cold.

Ina began making the fire, while Efa prepared the sad-looking vegetables that were left in the sack. So Ina was crouching at the hearth when Morwenna strode into the house, followed swiftly by Sadwrn. Instinctively, she jumped to her feet.

"Calm down, girl. There's no call to get upset," said

Sadwrn, holding up his hands, but keeping his distance.

"I'm not upset," answered Ina, though her heart was beating hard.

"That's good. Because nobody wants a repeat of what happened yesterday."

Alarmed, Ina saw from the corner of her eye that Efa had also stood up and was holding the sharp knife she used for peeling vegetables tightly by the handle, pointing it at the intruders. She gestured swiftly at her to drop it and Efa opened her hand, the knife falling to the floor.

"Yai thought theer was oonly one poisonous snake around hare – turns out theer's two," said Morwenna.

"Beloved . . ." said Sadwrn, trying to sound calming, "what's the point of stirring the waters? Remember – our purpose here is a joyful one."

He smiled expectantly at Morwenna and received a smug little smirk in return.

"God's grace fur reminding me, my swateheart. Yes, I have glad tidings of greet joy. Ware to be married," she announced, staring icily at the girls.

Ina's heart sank to her heels. So Morwenna had managed to hook her claws into Sadwrn. And she and Efa would be forced to live under the same roof as this creepy sneak, Sadwrn – also known as Snorty. Not just creepy, but violent, too. But before anyone could say another word, someone else came to the door.

"Good greetings!" called a hearty voice.

Morwenna turned, frowning.

"Is this the home of Ina and Efa?" continued the voice.

"Fur now, yes," answered Morwenna. "What have they done this time?"

"They've done no wrong. Quite the opposite. My debt to them is great. I didn't have the chance to thank them properly the other day."

"Then you'd better come in."

Morwenna stepped aside and a tall, upright man ducked through the doorway. The man with the moustache.

"Caradog ap Meurig, at your service."

"Morwenna ferch Peder," she simpered, offering her hand so he could kiss it.

"We are to be married," announced Sadwrn possessively, swiftly putting his arm around her and sticking out his bony chest.

"Congratulations," said the man, smiling. "If I'd've known I'd have brought a present for you too."

Then he passed a leather bag to Ina, as she was the nearest to him. "This is for you both," he said. "For stopping Valens escaping and bringing him back to me, meek as a lamb."

Astonished, Ina opened the bag and glanced inside to see a slate and two sets of small, smooth stones – some white and some black. *Ludus latrunculorum!* The game she'd played so often with Gwrgant! Her favourite game ever.

"Are you familiar with latrones?" asked Caradog.

"I am," said Ina, smiling from ear to ear. "Thank you."

"Thank my children," replied Caradog. "They insisted that I give you two a present. And quite rightly. You both deserve a reward."

"Thank you," said Efa too, shyly. At the sound of her voice,

Morwenna and Sadwrn gaped at her in surprise. Caradog was none the wiser of course, unaware that Efa hadn't spoken properly until yesterday.

"So, farewell!" he called, ducking out of the hut.

Ina was half expecting Morwenna to take the leather bag from her, now that the man had left, but she didn't. Instead, she turned to Ina and pointed at Efa.

"How long's shay bane talking?"

"Ask her yourself," answered Ina shortly, unable to help answering back.

"Maybe that cuff I geev her did some gud, then. Maybe I shouldn't have stopped Sadwrn giving you a bating yesdee either."

"Stopped him giving me a beating yesterday, you mean?" asked Ina, impudently.

"That's what I seed."

"My beloved, you haven't shared *all* our joyous news with the girls," said Sadwrn hurriedly, keen – for obvious reasons – that things didn't deteriorate again.

"That is true, my own treesure," replied Morwenna in a sugary voice, before turning to Ina and Efa. "You won't be coming to live with us after our wedding. It wouldn't be a gud idea – fur anyone. Yai'll be spaking to Elfryn in the next few dees, and he can organise another, better hoome fur you."

For once, Ina didn't know what to say.

"Yai sharl be having supper with my intended tonight," she went on, flashing a self-satisfied smile at Sadwrn. "Yai believe we sharl be dining on venison. Enjoy yur vegables."

Then she cackled with laughter, took Sadwrn's arm and

disappeared with him through the door.

"Did you hear that, Efa? We don't have to live with Morwenna and Snorty!"

It wasn't clear from her confused face whether Efa understood or not.

"Efa! This is great news! No more Morwenna! No more Snorty!"

Efa's eyes lit up. At last she seemed to have got the message.

"Efa do vegables," she said, smiling.

"Please do. As long as you say 'vegetables' from now on," joked Ina. Efa gave an uncertain little smile as if she hadn't understood the joke, and went on with preparing supper.

Ina couldn't believe it. No more Morwenna, once she was married! She could stand her until then. Better not say anything about her to Elfryn now, until everything had been organised and the two of them were safely somewhere else, just in case.

The possibilities began to crowd into her mind. Perhaps it wasn't a coincidence that the man with the moustache's name was Caradog. Caradog had been the name of the king of Caersallog. He was supposed to've been her guardian – and he would've been, if only the Saxons hadn't come and ruined everything. Those barbarians were to blame for all the bad things that had befallen her ever since. I wonder if this Caradog will adopt us? she thought, unable to stop herself hoping.

Perhaps, at last, her luck was beginning to turn . . .

✦ ✦ ✦

Ina awoke suddenly in the pitch black of night, realising at once that something was wrong. She lay still, listening carefully, but she couldn't hear a thing. Not even Efa's breathing at her side.

"Efa?"

She reached for her in the darkness, but the bed was empty.

"Efa?"

No answer this time, either. She wasn't there.

Ina began to worry. Efa had seemed fine as they went to bed and had even said 'sleep well' to Ina. But now she had some memory of waking earlier and hearing Efa tossing and turning. Perhaps she hadn't been able to sleep.

Rubbing her face hurriedly with her hands, Ina forced her tired body up from the straw bed. She went to the door and realised at once that the wicker frame had been moved. Stepping out of the house she saw that the night was clear and cloudless and the stars were shining brightly, in all their glory.

Then she saw Efa, standing stock-still and staring up at the sky. Carefully, so as not to shock her, Ina approached. Her friend was completely lost in the firmament, her face gleaming in the light of the moon, a shadow of a smile on her lips. Her eyes, deep green again by night, shimmered. Ina saw that there were tears on her cheeks.

"Thinking of home?" asked Ina, softly.

Efa nodded her head, without taking her eyes from the

stars. Ina stared upwards too. Suddenly, she wanted to find the North Star. Yes – there was the crown-shaped cluster of Caer Arianrhod. Ruling a line with her finger, she came to the milky strip of Caer Gwydion and, within it, the constellation of Llys Dôn – Dôn's Court . . .

But she didn't get any further. Seeing this M-shaped cluster of stars, she remembered the 'M' that Efa had carved on the beach and a shiver went through her. Perhaps she really is an angel, she thought. An angel that Lluan has sent down to me.

Tearing her gaze from the stars, Ina looked at Efa from the corner of her eye. Efa took no notice of her. She was far, far away.

XXIX

Rodomiro was as good as his word. The following day he was there by the riverside. What's more, he'd crossed the water to their bank and was waiting for them under the great silver birch.

"*Salve!*"

"*Ave! Quo modo venisti huc?*" asked Ina, amazed. Greetings! How did you get here?

"*Volavi,*" he answered, with a straight face. I flew.

Ina laughed. Efa pulled at her sleeve.

"Why Ina laughing?"

Ina translated it for her, and Efa laughed too.

"*Where's your hornpipe?*" the boy asked Ina as she sat down at his side, with Efa next to her.

"*As we are all sitting comfortably now, I will tell you, Rodomiro.*"

"*Everyone calls me Miro. You can too.*"

"*Great – Miro, then. I warn you, it is a long story. But it will explain why Efa cannot speak Latin too, and lots of other things besides.*"

Efa looked at her as if to ask why she'd said her name. Ina explained to her that she was going to tell their story to Rodomiro, or Miro, as they should call him from now on. And then Ina began at the beginning: her last night at the villa, how she'd been supposed to join the court of Caradog as a fosterling and about everything that had happened since then.

+ + +

Miro listened attentively and Efa did too, though she didn't understand anything except her name and the names of the other people she knew. As the story came to a close, Ina found Miro looking from one to the other of them, wide-eyed.

"So you're not real sisters? You and Efa?"

Efa pulled at Ina's sleeve again and Ina translated his question. Efa frowned.

"Efa sister Ina."

"Yes, you are," said Ina, comfortingly, before turning to Miro and adding in Latin, *"Sisters by choice. Not by blood, but sisters just the same . . . And what about you? What is your story?"*

Miro laughed.

"My story won't take long – it's very small fry in comparison to yours. But before I tell it, how about something to eat? I'm starving after hearing such an epic saga."

Miro grinned as he pulled bread, cheese and fruit from a large leather bag and placed them on a nearby rock. At the sight of this feast, Ina's mouth began to water, and so did Efa's. Ina realised that they were desperately hungry – neither of them had eaten much more than boiled vegetables for days.

"Food!" exclaimed Efa happily.

Miro smiled at her, then turned to Ina for a translation. So she explained to him what 'food' meant.

"Foo-ud," said Miro, smiling again at the unfamiliar sound of the word. Efa clapped her hands and laughed happily, her blue-green eyes sparkling at him. Then Miro asked if the girls had any food to share and Ina had to explain that their leather bag contained not food, but a board game. Latrones. As she pulled out the slate and the pieces, Miro's eyes lit up in recognition. But he was confused as to how Ina could play this game, until she reminded him that Britain, too, had been part of the Roman Empire, and that the Roman traditions still lived on in many aspects of their lives – apart, of course, from those parts that were now in the hands of the Saxons. Ina hissed the name, with all its repellent s's – Saxons! – and she noticed that Efa cowered, her eyes growing wide and fearful, at the word.

"Don't worry. They can't get you here," she said to her, comfortingly.

But Efa had obviously been shaken. Please don't go into your shell again! thought Ina, regretting her mention of the enemy.

"Do you know how to make fire?" Miro asked Ina, suddenly.

"Of course."

Miro gave her a piece of flint and a knife, before walking towards the river.

"What Miro do?" asked Efa.

"We'll surely find out soon enough," said Ina, setting about to collect dry leaves and sticks, arranging them on the riverbank's pebbles then coaxing the sparks into a small fire.

After a bit Miro came back into view, carrying a large, fat fish.

"Fysc!" shouted Efa, clapping her hands again, before

paling, as if she'd said something wrong, and staring down with fearful eyes.

"That's right. *Fish*," confirmed Ina, without making a show of correcting Efa and embarrassing her. Ina turned to the boy.

"How did you catch the fish?"

"With these," he answered, waving his hands and accidentally letting go of it. The fish wriggled to the ground and Miro had to crouch quickly to grab it before it jumped back into the river. Ina laughed, glancing over at Efa and expecting her to join in. But, to her dismay, Efa's face was pale and she was trembling slightly.

"Efa? What's the matter?"

Efa shook her head frantically, as if to say 'nothing', but Ina didn't believe her. Something was wrong. Something big. And Efa didn't say another word after that. All they got was a half-smile when the fish was ready to eat, after roasting to perfection over the fire and giving off the most mouth-watering smells.

And how delicious it was! Ina had eaten nothing like it since the farewell feast at the villa. She felt a pang of *hiraeth*, although she'd felt nothing when telling her story to Miro earlier. Then, it'd been as if she'd been talking about someone else. But now, as the tender flesh of this fresh, bountiful fish melted in her mouth, it hit her how much she still missed her home – though, of course, it was now in Brochfael's hands. How much she still missed Gwrgant and Briallen, Bleiddyn, her mother, and Lluan. Everyone she'd ever lost. But she had Efa, thank goodness. And remembering this, the hunger overcame the *hiraeth* and she began to tuck in again, eagerly.

There was friend material in Miro too, if the boy really was as kind and agreeable as he seemed. Who knew, though. Perhaps once she'd got to know him better Ina would find him an annoying big-head, like Sulien – although, perhaps, Sulien hadn't been as bad as all that, really. Sometimes, she feared she'd simply misjudged him, but perhaps this was just her conscience, pricking her ... But here she was, as ever, letting her thoughts wander away! She made a promise to herself. She was going to give this boy more of a chance ...

"No need to ask whether you enjoyed it," said Miro, interrupting Ina's thoughts.

"The fish was fantastic," answered Ina, choosing not to mention her *hiraeth*, nor the fact that she'd decided he was a nice person, for a boy.

"And everything else, obviously," said Miro, grinning.

Ina realised, to her horror, that she and Efa had also scoffed the bread, the cheese and the fruit, leaving almost nothing for Miro.

"I am so sorry. We did not realise!"

"No worries. I'll have plenty to eat tonight."

"Unlike us," said Ina, without thinking.

At that, the boy passed the last piece of bread to her, telling her to share it with Efa. Perhaps he's even kinder than he seems, thought Ina. And as the two of them chewed slowly, savouring the fresh, wholesome bread, Miro began to tell them something of his own story.

XXX

On the far side of the main river there was a network of smaller rivers and many large pools of still water. Miro lived in a small village on the banks of one of these pools and, because of this, he was a skilled boatman – and a good fisherman too, as he'd just proved. Everyone else in the village had at least one brother or sister, but Miro was an only child. His mother, Marina, had been very ill after she'd given birth to him – she'd almost died during the labour – and so she didn't dare to have any more children. His father, Felix, was a carpenter.

No one in his family had played an instrument, but a renowned piper by the name of Magnus the Blacksmith lived locally and, when he'd come to play at a special occasion, all the village children had taken a turn to play the pipe. To everyone's astonishment, Miro had been the only one to create a true, pure note straight away, on his very first attempt. The village children – including Miro – used to make simple instruments from gourds or rushes, but none of them had ever been able to play an adult instrument like this before. Of course, he'd had to practise hard at his craft but, by now, people were saying that he was as good – if not better – than the old master, Magnus the Blacksmith himself.

Though Miro had been happy to talk about his family and

his village, he was less eager to boast of his musical talent and Ina had had to coax the story out of him bit by bit, for she was afire with curiosity to learn how he achieved the magic of his playing. Miro was just as curious about her: he wanted to know how she and her mother used to play together and why she'd sworn an oath to give the instrument up – until the voyage in the slave-boat.

Through all of this, Ina was very aware that Efa couldn't follow the conversation and so she'd tried to make her part of it all by translating as much as she could. However, as she'd feared earlier, Efa had retreated once more into her shell. For the life of her, Ina couldn't understand why. But whatever she did to try and make Efa smile, nothing worked – so in the end she gave up translating too.

"It is such a shame I do not have a hornpipe any more," said Ina in Latin, sighing more loudly than she'd intended.

"I could make you one," offered Miro.

"Are you serious?"

"Many cattle will go to slaughter in the killing season before winter, and there'll be plenty of choice of a suitable horn then. It won't be exactly the same as your old one, of course. But it should be close enough."

"Thank you, Miro. That would be so great!"

Ina could hardly believe it. She turned excitedly to Efa.

"Miro's going to make me new hornpipe!"

Efa managed a smile, but it was a pretty feeble one. Ina turned back to Miro.

"She is not herself today. She goes through phases like this."

She felt awkward talking about Efa in a tongue she didn't

understand, but at the same time it was important that Miro understood, in case he thought Efa was like this all the time.

"*What about a game of latrones?*" *he suggested.* "*Perhaps that will cheer her up.*"

"*Good idea. She does not know the rules – but if I play with you I can teach her as I go.*"

After explaining the plan to Efa, Ina placed the slate board on the large stone. It was impossible to say whether she was happy about it or not. Perhaps she couldn't be enthusiastic about anything today.

Ina poured the pieces – the smooth, small stones – on to the slate.

"*What colour?*" she asked Miro.

"*Black.*"

Ina gathered the white pieces and put them in two rows on the squares that'd been carved into the board. Miro did the same thing with the black pieces.

"*Ready?*" asked Miro.

"*Ready.*"

Ina moved one of her pieces. Miro pondered for a moment, studying the board, then moved one of his. Ina shifted her next piece without hesitating.

"*You've played this game a lot, I see,*" said Miro.

"*Yes, I have – in the past. But not for ages.*"

"*You could've fooled me. I'd better concentrate.*"

"*Yes, you had better,*" said Ina, smiling.

Latrones was one of those games that seemed easy because it was so simple. But there was a world of difference between a simple game and an easy game. The aim was to take the other player's pieces, by moving one piece at a time in a straight line over as many squares as was necessary – up, down or across – until there was no other piece in the way. To take a piece, you had to move your pieces until two of them lay either side of one of your opponent's, like a sandwich. Then that piece was taken off the board. The game ended when one player's last piece was surrounded and couldn't move. So, the trick wasn't in learning the rules – you could do that in two minutes – but in playing expertly.

No one could beat Ina – no one but Gwrgant, and even he only succeeded sometimes. Gwrgant had been convinced that latrones helped people think strategically and that – according to Gwrgant – was as powerful a weapon as a good sword.

"I didn't realise that one was in danger!" exclaimed Miro, as Ina took yet another of his pieces.

Ina grinned at him. *"You had better concentrate even harder, then."*

She was pleased to see that Efa was beginning to take an interest as, bit by bit, Ina interpreted Miro's pattern of playing and won even more pieces.

Suddenly, a stone landed to the left of Ina, missing her by an inch. Then another, landing behind her. Looking up from the board she saw a row of unfamiliar, unfriendly-looking children on the other side of the river.

Snatching up one of the stones, she leapt to her feet and hurled it back over the river at them. Miro had jumped to his feet too.

"Stop it, you idiots!"

The children dropped the pebbles in their hands and gaped over the water in surprise.

"*Miro! It's you! What you doing on the other side of the river?*" called one of them.

His face darkened with a frown, Miro opened his mouth to respond, but his words were drowned out instantly by a terrifying cry that came from the woods, as if someone – or something – was skewering the pigs alive. Then Mora and Wenna burst into view, running hell for leather on their short legs and squealing for all they were worth. Behind them came a huge goat, leaping as fast and as far as possible but lagging behind the pigs because it was lame. It was the biggest goat Ina had ever seen – at least twice the size of the goats they'd had at home, with huge, powerful horns on its head, sticking straight up above its ears before curling back across its nape. The goat stared about ferociously and its alarming, slitted eyes lighted on the three of them before it hurtled past.

"*Cabralos!*" shouted the children on the other side of the river in terror, scrambling away despite the wide water that separated them and the creature.

"*Cabralos? Is that its name?*" Ina whispered to Miro, but Miro did not reply. His face had turned completely pale, as had Efa's, who was taking shelter behind him.

"*Look,*" hissed Miro.

Ina turned. Chasing the goat was a creature similar to a wild cat. Once again, Ina had never seen such a huge animal and, not for the first time, she was sorry that Bleiddyn wasn't here to defend her. The wild cat was just as big as the goat – though not so heavy – and it had long legs, dark spots all over its grey-yellow body and a short tail with a black streak along it. Its head was extraordinary – a wide, striking face with piercing yellow eyes, long, pointed ears and some sort of beard under its chin.

In a blink, Ina realised that the expression in the goat's eyes hadn't been fury, but terror. It was still limping away, then it fell, scrambled to its hooves and leapt once more as the big cat pounced, narrowly missing. Then it disappeared into the trees with the cat bounding after it.

The pigs were still squealing fit to wake the dead. Efa went over to comfort them, bending to whisper something in a voice too low for Ina to hear, and they began to quieten. Perhaps Efa really could communicate with animals, thought Ina. She wouldn't've been surprised. Who knew what went on in that head, under the short, ragged hair?

Then came the sound of agonised bleating from amongst the trees. Efa clasped her hands to her ears and turned instinctively to Miro, who put his arm protectively around her. After an especially heart-breaking scream, everything went quiet. The cat must have killed the goat.

And that's when Ina had the idea. Grabbing Miro's sharp knife, she began to run towards the trees.

"Be careful! Wait!" yelled Miro, reaching out to grab her arm, but missing.

"Ina!" shouted Efa fearfully.

"Don't worry! I've got a plan!" shouted Ina, not even bothering to look back.

And into the woods she disappeared.

XXXI

Ina gulped down the last mouthful of goat's-meat soup and sighed contentedly. She was so full she was afraid she'd burst. She and Efa had been feasting on goat's meat for days. Days during which they'd seen neither hide nor hair of Morwenna. Sadwrn's welcome had obviously been too warm to refuse – plus she was probably making grand preparations for the wedding, thought Ina. She didn't give a fig that Morwenna wasn't there. In fact, she didn't give a fig whether she saw that peevish face ever again.

Ina looked over at Efa. She could've sworn she'd grown a centimetre or two over the past few days, thanks to all this nourishing food. Her fair hair was definitely longer and looked more like real hair – instead of like a field of straw scythed too close by some careless serf – and her face was a tiny bit rounder. Ina wondered at the colour of her hair. She'd never seen a more golden hue.

At that moment Efa glanced up, noticed her attention and said, shyly, "Efa little yellow-feathered chick." She really did say some odd things sometimes.

There'd been two reasons for Ina's plan that day by the river. First of all, to have goat's meat to eat and secondly, to take its magnificent horns. Surely they'd be able to make a hornpipe from one of them – a real treasure of a hornpipe, at that. That way, she wouldn't have to wait till autumn for Miro's village to slaughter their cattle – Miro would be able to make one for her right now.

Using tracking skills learned from Gwrgant, Ina had had no trouble following the trail of the goat. When she'd burst on to the scene from between the trees, the great cat had turned, snarling ferociously to defend its conquest, but Ina's instinct was true. She knew that the predator would slink away if she made herself as big as possible, waving the knife and making plenty of noise. But whatever'd happened, Ina was so starving – especially after tasting the fish – that, even without the knife in her hand, she'd have fought the wild cat tooth and nail, tearing the goat from its jaws, if needs be.

Afterwards, as she walked back to the river, Efa had been pacing up and down, chanting something to herself as if she were trying to ward off evil spirits, her crystal voice now brittle and breathy, her face pale.

But as soon as Efa saw Ina, the colour flowed back into her cheeks and she ran to her, throwing her arms about her and hugging her tightly.

"Hey . . . I'm fine," said Ina, trying to sound comforting and making a point of smiling.

"Efa worried . . ."

"See? There was no need. Come on, you two. I've got a surprise," Ina added, dragging Efa and Miro into the trees.

As he helped Ina cut the goat into pieces after they'd hung its body from a branch, Miro explained that the children had run away because they'd mistaken the goat for one of the old gods of that area, Cabralos – the holy mountain goat. This goat had been an ordinary mountain goat, though it had been unusually big. The only reason the big cat – or 'mountain cat', as Miro called it – had dared attack the goat was because it was lame. And Ina had been right to assume that it would run away on seeing her – though they looked fearsome, mountain cats were afraid of people. Ina translated all this to Efa because by now she'd come right out of her shell and insisted on understanding everything Miro said.

Whilst she'd been gone, Miro had suggested that he and Efa play latrones, to take her mind off her worries for Ina. Indeed, it had worked for while, until Efa's distress got the better of her and she'd started that strange singing. In the time it took for Ina to track the goat, chase the big cat away and leave a trail on her way back, apparently Efa had beaten Miro at the game. Ina assumed that Miro had let her win, but Miro insisted he hadn't.

In the days that followed, when Ina and Efa weren't filling their bellies every mealtime, they were playing latrones non-stop in the wood, making sure this time not to let the pigs roam too far. However, after their close encounter with the giant mountain goat and cat, the pigs had been keeping close by anyway. The girls played at night too, in the little round hut by the light of rush candles. And it soon became obvious that Miro had been telling the truth about Efa beating him because Ina was beginning to marvel at how good she'd become, in so short a time. When they'd played just now before eating, it'd been touch and go for Ina. She'd almost lost.

Ina sighed again. She'd stuffed her belly so full it felt like lead.

"Oof. I can hardly move . . ."

"Latrones?" asked Efa, hopefully.

"Again? I'm too full – really."

But she soon gave in when she saw the disappointment on Efa's face. Efa eagerly set the pieces in their places. And, after only five minutes of play, Ina felt the tide turning on her. This time Efa was always two or three turns ahead of her, able to predict by now what Ina would do. In an attempt to trip her up, Ina suggested a bit of Latin practice as they played. Efa wanted to surprise Miro tomorrow by speaking a few words to him. *Salve!* And the new hornpipe would be ready! Ina could hardly contain her excitement about this and she could see that Efa was, in her quiet way, just as thrilled at the thought of seeing Miro again too. *Meum nomen Efa est. Vale!*

After ten minutes, the game was over.

"Efa win!"

Efa laughed and clapped her hands, as she did every time she felt happy. Which wasn't often, especially in recent days – despite the fact they now had enough food. Ina realised that whatever was worrying Efa – whatever it was that had happened to her – still lurked, threateningly, just beneath the surface. Sometimes, it was as if something was tearing at her from the inside, as if she were struggling against its terrible claws.

But, for now, Efa's smile lit up the little round house as brightly as the rush candles, and so Ina didn't care about losing. In fact, quite the opposite. She was very proud of Efa, her sister of choice.

And so, impulsively, Ina lifted one of the goat's bones – that had dried to a bleached white and was shaped like a half-circle

– and held it ceremonially in both hands. Imitating Elfryn, the keeper of the fort, she offered the bone to Efa as a crown.

"Most honoured lady! Great was your feat. May the bards sing praise to your conquest throughout Britonia – nay – throughout all the lands of the Britons!"

Efa was by now giggling uncontrollably.

"Ina – enough! Belly Efa hurting!"

But Ina wasn't giving up as easily as that. She lifted the bone yet higher.

"With this bone, I crown you . . . Latrones Champion of all Britonia!"

Still cracking up with laughter, Efa obediently bowed her head and Ina placed the bone on to it.

"Hear you, o hear you! I announce to all present that the name of the prize-winning conqueror is – Efa ferch - daughter of . . ."

Ina paused, realising that she didn't know Efa's full name.

"Efa daughter of . . ." she said again, so that Efa could finish the sentence.

"Nudd," said Efa, after a long pause.

"Nudd is my father's name, isn't it?" said Ina kindly. "You need to say *your* full name."

Efa stared at her wordlessly and Ina saw the shine fading from her eyes, the smile disappearing.

"Efa daughter of . . ." said Ina again, though she knew by now, deep in her heart, that asking again wasn't a good idea.

"Nobody," said Efa quietly, taking the bone from her head and giving it back to Ina, avoiding her eyes.

The fun had faded and a heavy dullness had fallen in its

place. Ina could almost see Efa wilting before her and she bitterly regretted putting pressure on her to say her name. It had only been a bit of fun, something to celebrate the fact that Efa had beaten her at latrones for the very first time.

"Whatever, well done you for winning," said Ina in her normal voice, not knowing what else to say.

Efa tried to respond, but although her lips were smiling her eyes looked strained and grim.

"Shall we go out?" Ina offered, jumping towards the door. Perhaps leaving the house might help pull Efa's thoughts from whatever it was that tortured her.

Efa shook her head.

"Come on! We could call on Caradog's children, to see whether they want to play latrones. We can show them how good you are."

But Efa shook her head again. Perhaps she wanted – needed? – to be alone. And although she didn't like to leave her like this, Ina thought it might be better to give her a bit of space and leave her in peace for a while.

"I'll go out for a walk, anyway. I won't be long."

Efa said nothing, just nodded her head. Ina wasn't sure if she'd even heard.

As she stepped outside the house she had to shade her eyes from the low light of the sun, which was busy sinking towards the horizon. Those clouds left in the sky had started to blush pink in preparation for sunset. Ina walked down the path between the houses, noticing how the last rays of the sun lit up the red tiles on the roofs, revealing every crack and defect. Poor Efa, thought Ina. She's broken too. Hopefully they'd find a way to put her together again.

XXXII

To stretch her legs and give Efa the chance to come back to herself, Ina decided to walk around the fort's outer defensive dyke. To the west was the great wood which embraced the fort in a wide half-circle. In the middle of the wood was the river and, beyond that, Miro's village. Although she couldn't see the village from here, Ina tried to imagine it. But she didn't know enough about the place to form a proper picture in her mind. Perhaps, someday, Miro would invite her and Efa to his home by the pool.

Ina strode onwards. To the north and east the summits and crests of mountainous Arfynydd were outlined sharply on the horizon. To the south, Ina knew (thanks to Miro) that the river, though invisible from here, meandered over a hundred and fifty miles to the western coast of Hispania and into the sea. The Minio, that's what Miro and his people called the river. It was sure to be longer than the Wysg. Was it even longer than the Gwy? Or yet the Hafren? Ina felt another pang of *hiraeth* as the oh-so-familiar names of these rivers surfaced in her memory. Would she ever see the banks of the Hafren again?

The sun was sinking fast now and there was a strange, unsettling feeling in the air. Ina strode towards the fort's wide gate, just because she could, now. It felt good to be able to come and go as she liked, without having to worry about being punished by Morwenna. Turning back, she headed for Caradog's house. There, playing outside, were his two children.

"Thanks for the latrones game," said Ina. "I'm sorry. We should have thanked you earlier."

"That's all right," said the boy, looking embarrassed.

"What are you playing?" tried Ina, though she too felt a little awkward by now.

"We've got to go in now. Mam's calling us."

And then the two of them disappeared inside the house. Ina hadn't heard anyone call. Perhaps they're shy, she thought. She decided to visit Elfryn, to find out whether he'd decided who their new guardians would be. After asking a passerby – a woman who answered her abruptly then went swiftly on her way – she learned that Elfryn was busy in the great hall.

On the way there, her heart sank as she saw the gang of children who'd mocked her and Efa. As they stopped and stared at her, Ina held up her head and stood her ground. She was ready for them this time. But to her surprise they all changed tack, heading back the way they'd come. One of them – a girl with hair almost as unruly as Ina's – was staring at her over her shoulder. Ina had seen that sort of look before. Back in Gwent. On the faces of the children of the hillfort.

By now, an inescapable sense of something being wrong, very wrong, was skewering Ina's bones. She hurried to the great hall and her heart sank yet further as she registered the pained expression on Elfryn's face, who was outside the hall, watching her approach.

"Good day to you, Elfryn, in the name of God Almighty."

"Good day, Ina," he answered, shortly.

"Has Morwenna spoken to you yet?"

"Yes, she certainly has. I am sorry that she had to, but she had no choice, under the circumstances."

"About getting married?" tried Ina, not really understanding what Elfryn was talking about.

"Ina. I have seen the bruises, and I have heard everything from her."

Bruises? Morwenna must have gone to him after Ina had pushed her against the cooking pot!

"I can explain . . ." said Ina, but Elfryn cut across her.

"I have heard more than enough already. There is no justification in the world for turning against someone who is simply doing their best for you both. For swearing, threatening and striking that person. I am desperately disappointed in you, Ina. In the two of you. We are all – the good people of this whole fort – deeply saddened."

"But . . .!"

Elfryn lifted his hand to silence her.

"We have decided, after some discussion, that the best thing would be to separate you both and send you from here to other settlements. You will be sent to one of the communities in Arfynydd, and Efa to another in Arfor."

At this, Ina shook in the same way she had when she'd heard that Gwrgant had been killed. Her legs seemed to stagger, dizzily, beneath her.

"Everything has been organised," Elfryn continued. "You will leave tomorrow."

"Tomorrow?!"

"There's no sense in delaying. Autumn will be upon us soon enough."

"But it was Morwenna who abused us!"

Elfryn shook his head, sadly.

"My child, can you deny that you struck Morwenna?"

"No. But . . ."

"God be with you, Ina. And with poor Efa too."

Ina's head was spinning. There must be something she could do. Then came a tiny flicker of hope.

"Does Maelog know?" she asked.

"Brother Maelog does not usually involve himself in the day-to-day running of the fort. This is a matter for us." He sighed. "All this protestation is to no avail, Ina. You must now accept your fate."

And with that, Elfryn turned his back on her and walked away. This was more of a blow than any beating. If Ina had been able to cry, she would've done, without a doubt.

She looked up at the sky. By now, the clouds were soaked in red and orange and the sky was indigo. The sun was so low that you could stare right into its face. Ina frowned at it. The sun had no right to be so beautiful this evening. Nor the sky.

Accept her fate. That's what Elfryn had said. But could it be possible that God had saved her – and Efa – for this? To punish her, after all the two of them had had to suffer already?

She began to walk, faster and faster, until she was running for her life towards the small, round house on the edge of the fort. By the time she arrived, her legs were trembling and her lungs were burning.

"Efa!" she shouted as she scrambled into the hut. "We have to leave! Now!"

Instead of asking why, Efa turned her back on her, as if she were trying to hide something.

"Efa! Did you hear me? They're going to separate us! And send us away – tomorrow!"

But still Efa wouldn't face her. What was wrong with her?

Ina seized her by the shoulders and spun her about. And that's when she saw the knife in her hand. And the marks on her arms. Bloody patterns, carved into her flesh with the blade of the knife – the same patterns she'd seen her making on the beach and by the river and, yes, there was that 'M' again, outlined in red against her pale skin.

Ina held her breath in fear, and Efa stared at the floor. Her eyes were red from crying.

"Efa, dearest!"

Ina tried to put her arm around her, but Efa pulled back, exactly as she'd done that first time, on the slave-boat. Then Ina reached out her hand.

"The knife," she said firmly, though she was still shaking with shock. Efa handed the knife to her, avoiding her eyes.

"Why in the world would you do such a thing to yourself?" asked Ina, sorrowfully.

Efa looked away.

"What do these patterns mean? Are they letters?"

"Saxon," said Efa at last, so quietly that Ina could hardly hear the word.

"The Saxons did this to you? Before? They cut you, did they? Is that what you're trying to say?"

"Saxon . . ." said Efa, louder this time, the tears pooling in her eyes. "Saxon words."

"Efa, my darling – I don't understand . . ."

Efa took a deep breath.

"Ebba daughter of Ealdwulf," she said, sitting up straight.

"What? Who?"

"Ebba's name . . . Ebba ferch Ealdwulf."

"Efa, I'm sorry, I don't . . ."

Efa cut across her, fiercely.

"Not 'Efa'. Ebba! Me Ebba."

"Your name's Ebba? Not Efa?" asked Ina in surprise.

"Ina says Efa, but me Ebba! Ebba! Ebba!" shouted the girl, the tears by now flowing down her cheeks. "Ebba ferch Ealdwulf."

Ealdwulf? What sort of a name was that?

"Ealdwulf father Ebba. Hilde mother Ebba. Ebba . . . Saxon."

"Don't talk nonsense. Of course you're not a Saxon," said Ina, angrily.

"Ebba Saxon," repeated the girl, insistently.

"But . . . that's impossible! For one thing – you know the words of the lullaby!"

"Branwen teach Ebba."

Branwen? Thank goodness for that. Ebba definitely wasn't a Saxon, then. Because Branwen was a Brythonic name.

"Who's Branwen? Your sister?" asked Ina.

"Branwen not sister. Branwen . . . *wâle*."

"What?" asked Ina, trying to understand. "What's that?"

"*Wále* . . . catched. Like Ina and Ebba on boat."

"A slave-girl?" asked Ina, horrified.

"Branwen slave-girl Ebba."

"You had a slave, and she was a Briton?!"

"Branwen like mother Ebba. Love Branwen," said the young Saxon girl, and the tears rolled once more, uncontrollably this time.

But Ina didn't hear her. She felt sick to the stomach. So Gwrgant had been right to hate the Saxons all along, if they kept her people as slaves.

"But . . . Ebba sister Ina. Yes?"

Efa reached out her hand to Ina, but Ina struck it away in fury.

"You . . . you deceived me! I thought I'd found a friend. At last. More than that – a new sister. But the whole time, you were using me . . ."

"No! Ina sister Ebba now!"

Ina gripped the girl's shoulders and shook her.

"We're not sisters any more. You hear? And we never will be!" spat Ina, shoving her away.

"What's all this racket?" asked a voice at the door. Then Morwenna appeared, staring at the two of them in astonishment.

"She's a Saxon!" cried Ina, wildly.

"What?" exclaimed Morwenna.

"That's why she couldn't talk to start with. Because she couldn't speak our language properly!"

"The lying little . . ."

"Get her out of my sight! Now!" shouted Ina, her eyes flaming.

"With pleasure!"

Morwenna stepped towards the cowering girl then dragged her by what little hair she had towards the door.

"You sharl pay dearly fur what yur people did to Caersallog. What they did to me."

"Ina! . . . Ina! . . . Ina!" begged the girl.

Ina turned her back on her. She stood, motionless, as the sound of the girl's wretched howling retreated into the evening, a sound as heart-breaking as the bleating of the goat when the cat sank its sharp teeth deep into its neck, choking it. Ina clapped her hands to her ears to try to stop them, but the desperate cries continued. Then everything went quiet.

XXXIII

Ina opened her eyes to the song of a blackbird. Other birds would soon come to join the early-morning choir. But for now the only voice was this songbird's magical chatter. When the weather turned and autumn arrived, the blackbird would quieten again, until the spring. Where would Ina be by then? And where would Efa?

Ina squirmed wretchedly at the thought of her. She could not think of the girl as 'Ebba' – her real name – any more than she could get used to the fact that she was a Saxon. She could still hear her cries, echoing through her head. Begging her. Ina tried desperately to convince herself that she shouldn't care about her any longer, shouldn't be bothered, because she was a lying, savage pagan. Yes, that's what she was. A treacherous, barbarian foreigner. And yet . . .

She dragged herself from the straw bed. Her body hurt all over, from barely sleeping. Every time she'd managed to drop off, she'd woken at once in a dripping sweat. She knew she'd had more than one nightmare, but she couldn't remember them – only the feeling of horror that still flowed through her body and a bad taste in her mouth, like poison.

Her thoughts were completely scattered. The only thing she knew for sure was that she couldn't stay in this desolate hut for one more second. She stumbled to the door and crept out on to the street. The fort was deathly silent. The sun hadn't risen yet, so the heavy gates across both entrances to the stronghold would still be locked. But there was enough of a gap between the back of the house and the inner wall for a thin person, like her, to climb up it, then drop down, unseen, on the other side. Luckily the pigs hadn't woken yet and sounded the alarm, and neither had any of the fort's dogs.

She walked quickly to the next outer dyke. This one was harder to climb and Ina scraped her knee, painfully, in the process. But something deep within her was driving her on, would have driven her over a dyke twice this size if it'd been in her way.

In no time she was in the wood. She realised with a pang that this was the first time she'd ever been here by herself, without Efa. It felt strange without her, in spite of everything. Perhaps this was the last time she'd be here at all, if what Elfryn had said was true. If being sent into exile to Arfynydd really was her fate, perhaps she'd never again return to the wood, or the fort, or Miro . . .

Then Ina froze in place as a loud noise drowned the twitter of the birds in the trees. An angry, impatient roar. There it was again. It was the bellow of a stag. At once, Ina remembered the first time she'd hunted deer with Gwrgant – she'd been a little girl then and had been frightened by the harsh, strident sound. Thanks to Gwrgant, she'd learned enough about woodcraft to survive in the wild for weeks, if not months. Perhaps she should escape and dwell like a hermit in the forest, with only God's creatures for company . . .

Ina walked on and joined the path that twisted through

the trees towards the river and the great silver birch. The sun was dappling the river by now, and small flies were swarming lazily above it in the sleepy warmth of the dawn. Ina sat beneath the shelter of the tree and leaned back against its sturdy trunk. She closed her eyes and heard the splash of fish, surfacing now and then to catch unwary insects.

She stayed like this, quietly, for ages. She didn't have the energy to do anything else. She felt as dry and desolate as an egg sucked empty, nothing but a shell. And then, little by little, familiar snatches of familiar songs lifted from somewhere deep inside and began to fill the empty space within her. It was as if all the songs she'd kept under lock and key since Lluan and her mother had died were now bursting out and insisting on being heard in her head – all at the same time. The melodies surged without stopping, spilling forth in a cascade of countless, jarring notes.

She pressed her hands tightly to her ears to try to dampen the sound. But the muddled music was part of her and it wasn't possible to get rid of it. Suddenly, across all this noise came a voice. A pure voice, clear as crystal. An otherworldly voice, entreating her:

"Ina . . . Ina . . ."

Ina was afraid to open her eyes. Perhaps it was Efa's spirit calling her – perhaps she was dead; perhaps Morwenna had killed her during the night. Or perhaps it was an angel, with shining wings and a long sword, come to drive her from this life and lead her to the next world, to take her place in the firmament amongst the stars. Ina had been told that there was a reward for everyone in heaven, and that all her family were waiting for her there. Perhaps the time had really come.

Taking a deep breath, she opened her eyes. The angel was trying to say something, but the music in her head was so loud by now that she couldn't hear it. She struck her head back against the tree trunk to try to get rid of the sound, and the pain. She felt hands gripping her to stop her doing it again. Suddenly, the music quietened as abruptly as it'd begun, and Ina realised that the person looking at her was Miro.

"Ina! What in the world is the matter?"

"Efa . . ." said Ina, unable to say more.

"What about her? What's happened?"

Before she could answer, two familiar pigs came out of the trees. Mora and Wenna. They hurried towards her, snorting and shaking their short tails, before nudging her playfully with their snouts. Ina flung her arms around their broad backs – she'd never been so pleased to see them in her life.

"Ina, answer me," persisted Miro.

Ina gave the pigs another hug before turning to Miro.

"They want to send me far away. Efa too."

"Why?" asked Miro, incredulously.

"Morwenna. She told lies about us."

"I-na . . . I-na!" called a voice from within the wood.

"I-na . . . I-na!" called another voice.

"She is here!" cried Ina, full of panic. *"And Sadwrn! They must have let the pigs out to find me!"*

"Quickly! To the boat!" said Miro at once.

The two of them rushed to the river's edge, where Miro's round, skin boat was tied up. Ina curled up on its base, making herself as small as possible, and Miro flung a sack over her then pushed the boat into the current, crouching beside her and holding the little craft still with his oar. The next moment, Morwenna and Sadwrn came into view.

"Boy!" shouted Morwenna. "You sane a gal hare in the wuds?"

"*Salve!*" Miro called back, trying to hide the agitation in his voice. "*I'm sorry, I don't understand you.*"

"*You girl see?*" asked Sadwrn, in broken Latin.

"*Girl? No. I haven't seen anybody.*"

Under the sack, Ina's heart beat like a drum. She prayed they wouldn't demand to search the boat.

"*If you girl see, you come to hillfort, tell me. You . . .*" Sadwrn stopped mid-sentence and turned to Morwenna. "What's 'reward' in Latin?"

"No idea," she answered brusquely. Then Sadwrn remembered.

"*You . . . reward have.*" Before adding, dishonestly, "*Girl maybe lost. We worry.*"

"*Fine. If I see her, I'll let you know,*" answered Miro.

"*Vale!*" called Sadwrn, before turning to Morwenna. "With luck, the boy'll lead us to Ina. In the meantime, we need to get rid of the Saxon. I'll send her to my cousin in Arfor – he can sell her as a slave. I've no doubt he'll give us a nice little commission to help pay for our wedding, my precious."

Under the sack, Ina heard every word. Their plan filled her with disgust. Perhaps it was true that Efa deserved to be punished, but being kept as a slave for the rest of her life was another matter.

"Sadwrn, my treeshur, yur even craftier than may."

"Thank you, my own treasure. From your sweet mouth, that's high praise indeed."

From the sound of it, they were moving away now. Ina took a cautious peep out from under the sack and almost cried out in shock. There was a huge bruise on Morwenna's face. She must have hit herself to create it, or asked Sadwrn to. No wonder Elfryn had been so ready to believe her!

Miro waited until Morwenna and Sadwrn had disappeared into the trees, herding the pigs before them. Then he steered the boat back to the shore.

"You can come out now," Miro said. *"They've gone."*

Ina sat up, and he helped her out of the boat.

"You're as pale as a ghost. There's no need to worry – they didn't suspect a thing."

"You do not understand . . ."

Miro looked expectantly at her and, drawing in a deep breath, Ina told him everything.

Now it was Miro's turn to turn pale. He stood there motionlessly, staring down and saying nothing. Exactly like Efa did. But there was a chill to his silence. Ina could sense him distancing himself from her.

"Miro . . .?" she tried.

"How could you?" asked Miro, finally.

"How could I what?" asked Ina, surprised.

"Behave in such a way!"

"Me? You mean Morwenna! I did nothing wrong!"

"You betrayed Efa. That's what you did."

"She betrayed me. Pretending she was one of us. She is a

Saxon – do you know what that means?"

"I'm a Gallaecian. Not a Briton. I'm not one of your people either."

"But you are a Christian. Like me."

"I never said I was a Christian."

"But . . . I thought you Gallaecians were Christians!"

"Not all of us."

"If you are not a Christian, why did you not say?"

"Why should I?"

"Because . . ."

Ina couldn't finish the sentence. Her thoughts had all scattered and she couldn't gather them together again.

"You are not the same thing as a Saxon, anyway," she protested. "It is not your people who are destroying our towns and taking our land."

"True. It's your people who're stealing our land."

Ina stared at him, stunned.

"Why do you think the children of my village threw stones at you over the river? Because your people landed here and behave as if they own everything!"

"But that is different!"

"Why? Because you're Britons?" countered Miro, furiously.

Ina had no answer to this. Miro had muddled her completely by now.

"And to think I spent days making this for you," said the boy, pulling something from the boat. A brand-new hornpipe, splendid, its horn and mouthpiece crafted from mountain-goat horn; its body of applewood. Ina had forgotten all about it. Miro handed the instrument to her.

"*It is beautiful . . .*" said Ina quietly, in wonder.

"*I was looking forward to playing a duet with you,*" he said, just as quietly, "*but you'll have to play it on your own now. Goodbye, Ina.*"

With that, he turned his back on her, exactly as Elfryn, the keeper of the fort, had the day before. But the disappointment Ina felt now was a hundred times worse. Miro jumped into the boat and began to row across the river.

She'd betrayed Efa, that's what Miro had said. But Efa wasn't Efa – she was Ebba. And again, before that, Heddus. So who was she really? And what exactly was she to Ina?

Ina sank to her knees. She'd never felt so lonely or so lost. If Lluan were here, she would've known what to do. Then Ina caught her own reflection in the river's water. She looked away, her heart beating fast.

"Uinseann, my friend – if you can hear me, ask God if I may see my sister . . ." she pleaded, under her breath.

She was afraid to turn and face the river. Afraid that Uinseann hadn't heard her. And even more afraid that God had chosen to ignore her.

"One, two, three . . ." she whispered, before turning to stare into the water. She held her breath. It wasn't her reflection that was staring back at her! But nor was it Lluan's.

It was Ebba's.

Ina jumped to her feet, shouting across the river.

"*Miro! Wait! . . . I need your help!*"

XXXIV

A hunting horn sounded and, from her hiding place near the fort's outer dyke, Ina heard a commotion from within the walls. Her plan must've worked, then. And yes, shortly afterwards, Ina saw figures hurrying through the back gate: Miro – then Morwenna and Sadwrn, swiftly followed by a large group of men, all of them heading towards the wood. Miro had pretended to call for the reward after all, promising to show them where the wicked girl was hiding. And this, in turn, gave Ina the chance to rescue Efa . . .

Once they were completely out of sight, Ina climbed over the inner dyke, dropping down the other side behind the little round house – exactly where she'd escaped earlier this morning. She crept past the back of the houses in the direction of Sadwrn's house, reaching it before anyone had spotted her.

Although she'd never been there before, she knew exactly where it was and what it looked like because Morwenna had bragged so much about it. Yes, it had a roof of red tiles. Yes, it was much larger than the little round house – for three buildings had been joined together to form Sadwrn's 'palace' – as Morwenna insisted on calling it – and a smaller, barn-like extension had been built on to the side for animals. Ina couldn't help a little delight in the fact that the 'palace' wasn't any bigger or more luxurious than Caradog's house, although the dream of being adopted by him had long since died.

Looking about to check she was still alone, Ina hurried to the door and tried to push it open. It didn't budge. Then, with a sinking heart, she saw the little hole in its wood and realised it had been locked. She bent down to look through the keyhole and saw nothing but darkness. Then she went to the door of the barn, which was held shut by a beam. Carefully she pulled the beam along and squeezed herself through the crack in the door into a dark cowshed. A high-pitched squeaking assailed her immediately and before she had the chance to close the door properly she'd been surrounded by a litter of piglets, all clamouring for attention. Spotting a bucket hanging on the wall, brimming with food slops, she poured its contents on to the ground and their squealing quietened immediately as they crowded round to gobble it up.

There were no other animals apart from a calf in a stall at the other end. Beyond the stall was a door. This had to lead into the house. Ina hurried towards it, praying that it wasn't locked. As she passed the stall, the calf lowed, plaintively. Ina took in its wretched appearance and instinctively tried to stroke it but the animal jerked back its head in fear. Ina could only imagine how badly Sadwrn had treated it for it to react in this way.

Then Ina saw another creature lying in the straw at the feet of the calf. She was horrified to see that it had been tied up with thick rope. She was even more horrified to see that it wasn't an animal, but a girl, her clothes torn to rags. She couldn't see her face but Ina knew exactly who it was.

She fell to her knees and reached out to her. The heap on the floor jerked away from her as much as the rope allowed, exactly as the calf had, a moment ago.

"It's me . . . Ina . . ."

The heap moved again. Two thin arms came into view, one of them covered in bloody marks that had started to dry. And then a face. Even in the wan light of the cowshed, Ina could see the huge bruises that were beginning to swell over her left eye, and the chunks of short, golden hair that were soaked in blood.

"Ina . . ." said the girl, beginning to shake.

"Shh . . . You mustn't be afraid any more . . . I've come to rescue you," answered Ina, doing her best to smile. "I'm going to get water and clothes for you to change into," she added, before hurrying to the door. It didn't have a lock, thank goodness, and in no time Ina had collected what she needed from the house.

Hurrying back to the cowshed she set about cleaning the girl's wounds. It must have hurt, but she didn't make a sound.

"Ina . . . came back . . ." said Ebba, as if she could hardly believe it. "Morwenna say Ina go."

"I couldn't leave you, Ebba daughter of Ealdwulf . . ."

"Ina say name Ebba." And Ebba smiled, despite the pain.

"You're Ebba to me from now on."

Ina helped her from her rags and into the clean clothes she'd just taken from Morwenna's clothes chest. Then she gave her a piece of bread.

"Eat it slowly. I've got more, but better you don't eat too much at once."

Ebba stuffed the bread into her mouth, chewing it ravenously while Ina pinned on the cloak that Morwenna had stolen from her. She fingered the fine weave of the woollen cloth and stroked the brooch that had been crafted so skilfully. She would never let anyone take it from her again. Ever. Nor would she let anyone hurt Ebba again. Never, ever again.

Ebba began to choke.

"Go easy, Ebba, or the food will turn your stomach."

But Ebba was too hungry to listen, and Ina was just glad she hadn't given her a bigger piece.

"Come on. We don't have much time."

Ina looked at Efa, and almost smiled. If there'd been some way to cover her wounds, she'd have looked like a young princess in Morwenna's grand clothes. Then she put her arm around her friend and led her to the door, carefully pulling it open a crack. The last thing they needed was the piglets – who'd almost finished off the food scraps – escaping and causing a commotion.

"I'll go first," said Ina, pushing herself through the crack in the door. But as soon as she let go of Ebba she collapsed in a heap on the ground. She wasn't even strong enough to walk out of the cowshed, never mind escape from the fort.

So Ina squeezed back in and slammed the door shut. She needed to rethink her plan, and that quickly.

"Do you think you're strong enough to ride Valens, Caradog's horse?"

Ebba nodded her head.

"Ebba strong. And Valens like Ebba."

Ina smiled. However frail she may look, there was something very steely about Ebba.

Then Ina opened the door and herded the piglets out. The little animals burst free in one squealing crew and, sure enough, the girls soon heard the sounds of shouting and swearing from every direction as they created havoc in the street outside.

"On to my back! Now!" said Ina, urgently.

Ebba managed to do so and the two of them crept out of the cowshed – as fast as Ina could manage with a girl on her back – and down the narrow path back to the little round house. Thank goodness she doesn't weigh much, thought Ina. And thank goodness for the rampaging piglets. Anyone they passed outside the houses was too busy trying to catch them to notice the two fugitives.

Soon they'd reached the place behind the hut and, with some effort, Ina managed to pull Ebba up the wall of the inner dyke and support her down the other side. Sticking close to the dyke, Ina carried Ebba in a half circle around it, until they reached the fields on the other side of the fort that were sandwiched between the inner and outer dykes. Here there were vegetable gardens, orchards and several livestock enclosures – and in one of these paddocks a lordly, magnificent stallion stood on his own. Valens.

As Ina crept towards the paddock with Ebba on her back, Valens turned his head to watch their approach. Then he spotted Ebba, and he began to pace up and down in excitement, blowing and shaking his head. Tumbling from Ina's back, Ebba managed to walk unsteadily towards the fence.

"*Gōdne morgen, hors!*" greeted Ebba tenderly, wishing the stallion a good morning in her own tongue. There was no need for her to whisper her Saxon words any more. What's more, they didn't sound half as frightful or threatening coming from her, thought Ina. The horse lowered his head so that Ebba could stroke him. Then she put her nose against his, speaking to him all the while in a low voice, until he quietened down completely, standing obediently still. Ebba turned to Ina.

"Ebba horse at home," she said, her eyes beginning to sparkle with tears. "Like Valens. Strong horse. People fear horse. But horse love Ebba."

"The slave-girl . . . Branwen. Was she really like a mother to you?"

Ebba nodded, and more tears sprung to her eyes.

"Mother Ebba die. Branwen kind, like Ina. Branwen beautiful, like Ina."

Then Ebba brushed the tears from her eyes and, with Ina's help, she climbed over the fence and into the paddock. Clinging to his neck for support, she whispered into Valens's ear and he went down at once on to his knees. Efa pulled herself on to his back and beckoned to Ina – who was watching in amazement – to follow her.

She leapt over the fence – a little too quickly, because Valens squealed in fear – and mounted the horse behind Ebba, keeping a tight grip on her waist while Ebba took hold of the horse's mane.

"*Ga! Scynde!*" commanded Ebba – Go! Hurry! – and Valens hastened to his feet, rocking the girls on his back. Then he strode to the far end of the enclosure before turning and cantering towards the fence, jumping it with no trouble at all. Although Ina was used to riding Pennata, she found this stallion's speed and power frightening, but Ebba was in her element, controlling him easily and naturally.

Crouching low on his back, Ebba drove Valens at the great gate of the outer dyke. Men were working in the fields by the gate and, seeing them, they began to shout, dropping their tools and running to stop the horse escaping. But Valens flew through them at full pelt, scattering them before him like sparrows.

And then they were out of the fort, free and safe.

For now.

XXV

The sun was scorching. Today of all days. It was at its highest by the time they reached the main church of Britonia, and by now Ebba could hardly stay on Valens's back, never mind control him. It was as if the stallion realised that Ebba was suffering, because he'd slowed to a careful, even walk.

"Better wait a minute," said Ina to the slumped girl in front of her.

"*Stoppa*," whispered Ebba into the horse's ear, and Valens obeyed at once.

Although autumn was just around the corner, the sun still beat down ferociously, and today had been especially hot. After their long journey from the fort to Maelog's church, Ina felt light-headed too, and her stomach was churning strangely.

Shading her eyes to look across the landscape before her, she saw the *llan* – the wooden church set in the centre of a level, oval piece of ground on top of a hillock, surrounded by an earthen wall like a miniature hillfort. To its left, just below the hillock, there was a collection of round stone huts and other buildings. Ina prayed that Maelog was there, for this godly man was now their only hope.

"Onwards," said Ina.

And the horse strode ahead. He must have understood my command, thought Ina, for Ebba was by now too exhausted to speak. As they approached the path up to the church, a monk came out of one of the buildings, stopping as he saw them.

"Good day, in the name of God the Highest," called Ina.

"Good day, in the name of the Almighty," answered the monk, hurrying towards them. From the look of him, he was only about eighteen years old. He had to be a novice. His eyes widened with alarm as he approached and took in Ebba's terrible condition.

"Your friend . . . Is she injured?"

"Yes. Someone attacked her. That's why we're here. To tell Maelog what happened."

"Maelog? I doubt that he . . ." began the youth, but Ina interrupted him.

"You've got to listen to me. Maelog knows us."

The novice gaped at her in surprise.

"And you'd better help her, now – instead of standing there like a mooncalf."

"Of course. Forgive me," said the young monk, awkwardly helping Ebba off the horse. As soon as her feet touched the ground, she fainted. Somehow, the novice managed to catch her before she hit the ground. Meanwhile, Ina slid from Valens's back to kneel beside her.

"Ebba! . . . Ebba! . . ."

But Ebba was unconscious, her face deathly white. The youth had paled too. He obviously had no idea what to do. Ina lifted her head to see that another monk was hurrying towards them. Thank goodness – he wasn't a fledgling like this one, but a capable-looking, middle-aged man.

"Bring her into the shade," said the monk authoritatively, brushing the novice aside and lifting Ebba into his arms. The young monk had frozen in place.

"Fetch water," ordered the older monk. "And reviving herbs from the garden. At once!"

The novice sprang into action, running back to the buildings while the older monk hastened after him with Ebba hanging limply in his arms. Ina followed, gripping the horse's mane.

"Will she be all right?" asked Ina, fearfully.

"After some rest, yes, she will. We will apply ointment to ease her bruises, and give her medicines to strengthen her."

Ina closed her eyes and breathed a silent prayer of thanks. Aloud, she said, "Thank you for taking care of her."

"You did the right thing by coming here. What is your name, child?"

"Ina . . . Ina ferch Nudd."

"I am Pedrog. Where have you come from?"

"From the main fort."

"But you were not born there."

"No, I wasn't. I was born in Gwent."

"I thought I recognised your accent. I myself come from the lands of Caerfaddon, on the other side of the Hafren. Tell me, what is the name of this girl?"

Ina paused before answering.

"Efa."

She didn't have to explain everything to the monk. At this moment, it was easier by far just to give her Brythonic name.

"Is she related to you?" asked Pedrog.

"Yes. She's my sister," said Ina, regretting that she hadn't corrected the young monk earlier, when he'd assumed that Ebba was just her friend. She comforted herself with the thought that, at this moment, Ebba could no longer hear her words.

Another monk appeared from somewhere, carrying gardening tools.

"Iestyn!" called Pedrog. "Come and take care of this horse."

The monk dropped the tools and hurried towards them.

Pedrog saw the concern on Ina's face and hastened to reassure her.

"Brother Iestyn is an old hand, don't worry. No one in all Britonia is as good with horses."

No one but Ebba, thought Ina. But this wasn't the time or place to argue the toss. Iestyn slowed as he approached Valens, walking calmly towards him. Completely ignoring Ina, he began talking to the horse in a calm, gentle voice, like Ebba had done. To Ina's astonishment, the stallion listened to him, obediently following the man to the monks' stables.

"You'd better come with me too," said Pedrog to Ina. "Your eyes have a drowsy look. I'm afraid that you have sunstroke."

In truth, Ina had a splitting headache by now – but there was no time to rest. They were outside one of the buildings by now and though the cool shade within looked desperately inviting, Ina didn't go any further. "I have to see Maelog. At once," she told the monk.

Then she began to walk away.

"But you can't! He's extremely busy," called Pedrog after her.

"Not too busy to see me – I'm sure of that!" Ina called back, starting on the path to the *llan*.

By the time she'd reached the hillock, the pain in her head was even worse and her stomach felt terrible – as if there were a stone inside it, growing bigger and heavier with every moment. Around the top of the *llan*'s earthen wall there was a wooden picket fence with a gate in it. Ina opened the gate and walked through. The flashing reflections of the sun against the church's little glass windows pierced the back of her eyes like spears, though she tried her best to shade them with her hands. She was shaking all through. She could hardly see the two monks who were striding towards her. But she heard their voices.

"You have no right to be here!" barked one of them.

"I'm here to see Maelog," said Ina, the sound of her own voice making her head throb even more painfully.

"Out of the question," said the other man. "Our respected brother is holding a conference with the representatives of all the churches of Britonia."

"When will the conference end?"

"When God decides," said the first monk, piously.

"If you come back at night-fall, I'm sure we'll have finished by then – or nearly finished, perhaps," added the other, a little more kindly.

"But I can't wait! I have to see him now!"

"You have to wait – and not here. Outside the fence with you," said the first monk, taking Ina's arm, pulling her unceremoniously back to the gate and pushing her out. Then he turned his back on her and walked away. The other man hesitated for a moment then came over to offer Ina a drink from his goat-skin flask.

"Drink this water. You need it."

Ina took the flask and swallowed a long draught from it. She had been so very thirsty, without realising it.

When she'd finished, the monk said, "Come back in a few hours. Until then, go and rest – out of the sun."

"That will be too late . . ."

The monk shrugged apologetically before turning and walking back to the church. Ina knew that what she'd just said was true. She knew, deep in her bones, that the men working at the fort's gate had told the others at once, and some would surely have followed them. If they'd guessed that she and Ebba had gone to Maelog, they'd be here before long.

This was it, then. This was the end. All that effort, hers and Ebba's, in vain. They'd be dragged back to the hillfort and punished. Perhaps Ina would also be sold as a slave-girl, for daring to help Ebba. For sure, there would be no more hope of them staying together. Even if their fate was to be being sent away to remote settlements in Britonia – to Arfor and Arfynydd – they'd be separated, come what come may.

Then she heard a dreaded sound. The bleak, cruel blast of a hunting horn, calling in the near distance. So, the men of the fort had hunted them down, then. And, from the sound of it, they'd be here within minutes. Ina felt the will flowing from her body. She was so very, unfathomably, tired. So tired that she swayed on her feet. Battling to stay conscious, Ina summoned her strength. This wasn't the time to lose hope! There must be some way to get Maelog's attention . . .

Then, through the haze in her mind, through the relentless pounding in her head, Ina remembered her new hornpipe, the one that Miro had made for her. She pulled the instrument from the leather bag over her shoulders and lifted it to her lips.

She blew. The hornpipe grumbled, letting out a harsh blare, and Ina pulled it from her mouth. Then she tried again. Perhaps the reed was dry. She wetted her lips and blew a second time, and a clear note sounded, powerful, echoing all across the *llan*. Ina trembled all through. Was it her that had just created such a glorious sound? Yes, it was. Her and this marvellous hornpipe. Miro was as good a craftsman as he was a player.

She lifted the hornpipe to her mouth for a third time and this time she began to play. From the heart. She felt the music flowing effortlessly, without thought, from her memory to her fingers, just as it had when she'd played with her mother, years ago. Of course, her cheeks hurt and of course, her lungs ached. But, despite that, she played the lullaby right up to its chorus and then she continued, playing on until she reached the end of the entire song for the very first time since she was a little girl.

Then Ina took a deep breath and lifted the hornpipe to her lips once more. Another melody flowed from her. A few hours ago, all these tunes had been a horrible hotchpotch in her head. Now they poured from her in a stream of spellbinding notes.

She played, and played, and played. Played until her cheeks were bursting, her lips were bone-dry and her fingers had knotted stiff. She played to honour all the people who meant so much to her. For Briallen. For Gwrgant. For Bleiddyn. For her mother. And for Lluan.

But first and foremost, she played for Ebba. The foreigner with the blue-green eyes. The pagan with the heavenly voice. Ebba, her sister. Her heart filled with light. And the hold she'd kept, like a steel grip, on her grief loosened – the grief that she'd buried so deeply within herself. Ina closed her eyes, playing the hornpipe and swaying from side to side as if in a trance. In her mind, she saw her mother. And Lluan. They were smiling at her. Ina knew they had come to say farewell. She felt the music embracing them. It was embracing her, too. The feeling was good – so indescribably good. The two of them waved to her, disappearing, but the notes were still there, wrapped warmly about her.

Then came the awareness of shouting and the sound of people approaching. And the awareness also of how very tired she was – she was all fought out, dripping with sweat from her efforts. Ina put the hornpipe down and closed her eyes. She could hear the flap of footsteps running towards her. Opening her eyes, through the haze in her vision she recognised Maelog at the head of the approaching crowd.

"My dearest child!" he called, his voice sore troubled as he gripped her shoulders. "You are shaking from your crown to your heels! . . . Whatever has befallen you, I assure you, everything will be fine now. All will be well . . ."

Ina nodded her head. She had no strength left to speak. With her palms, she wiped the sweat from her face and rubbed at her eyes. They were all wet. That was when she realised that it wasn't sweat running down her cheeks after all, but tears.

XXVI

The autumn came, the winter came, the spring came – and then summer came again. Through it all the leaves on the great silver birch by the river turned golden, then withered and fell. The naked branches froze and shivered in the teeth of the wind before putting out buds and covering the whole tree in its mantle of green once more, as happened every year without fail.

On this, the longest day of summer, the sun was dancing on the surface of the river. For once, there wasn't a cloud in the sky. Under the shade of the great silver birch, Ina stepped through the rushes by the water – carefully, so as not to dirty her new sandals. She was searching for the perfect stem. Not too thick, and not too thin.

From the corner of her eye, she caught a flash of colour and turned to see a kingfisher dart across the river, shimmering in the sun before disappearing from view.

"Did you see that bird?" she called to the golden-haired girl who was sitting under the tree, leaning back against its sturdy trunk.

"I did! So pretty!" answered Ebba, smiling.

Ina turned her attention back to the long, pointed rushes that surrounded her. Making up her mind, she chose two stems and cut them with her small, sharp knife then walked towards the tree. There, Ebba was deftly folding and weaving her own stems.

"You've nearly finished them already," said Ina, proud of her.

"I had one good teacher," answered Ebba.

Her Brythonic was much more fluent by now, although she still made one or two mistakes. But Ina had no wish to spoil the afternoon by correcting her.

She sat down at her side and took up one of her stems. As she worked at it, she caught a glimpse of herself in the river: a tall girl in a smart woollen dress, her dark, curly hair falling across her shoulders. Her neck wasn't especially long, and her eyes weren't especially far apart. She knew that some people thought she was beautiful – especially her adoptive mother, Eleri – Caradog's wife. But, in Ina's opinion, beauty was everywhere to be seen, if you were only ready to look for it. More than this, true beauty was something that you lived, that you created, that you shared with others – rather than admiring it from afar.

Ina took up the stem again, weaving quickly, not allowing her thoughts to wander. There was something lovely about this sort of concentration, about losing yourself so completely in the moment. Especially when it was shared with a favourite companion, a soul-mate. Ebba was weaving away too, just as fast, although she had to hold the stem up sometimes because she couldn't see very well through her left eye. Morwenna's blows had left their mark on her for ever.

But, thank the Lord, the scars that Ebba had carved on to

her own arms had faded over time. And Ina understood, now, what they'd meant. Ebba, desperate and afraid, had been trying to express herself, to say who she was, in her own language. The patterns had been Saxon letters, and what had looked to Ina like an 'M' had been an 'E' – E for Ebba . . .

Ina shook her head to clear her thoughts and put a kink in the mast of the rush boat in her hands.

"Ready, sister?"

"Ready, *sweostor*," answered Ebba.

Officially, the two of them weren't sisters yet. In order to be adopted legally by Caradog and become a full member of his family and the community, Ebba had to go through a sort of trial period and be baptised – for she was a foreigner, and a non-Christian. But Ina didn't give a fig about the law. Ebba was her sister. Her sister of choice. And, in any case, something thicker than blood connected them.

The two of them stepped to the shore. Ebba bent and reached for something under the water.

"Look. A piece of the sun."

She turned a shining, golden pebble in her hand, before putting it aside. Ina laughed. Ebba still did strange things sometimes.

"What funny?" asked Ebba, innocently.

"Nothing. Come on."

Ina placed her rush boat on the surface of the water. Ebba did the same.

"One . . . two . . . three!"

Ina let her boat go, and so did Ebba. The girls raced towards the large grey stone that stood in the turn of the river, as fast as their new sandals would allow. The two boats had nearly reached the turn already. Which one would win the race? The one without the kink in the mast sailed triumphantly past the turn, the other trailing in its wake. Ebba laughed and clapped her hands.

"I have win today!"

"Damn. I must've taught you too well," said Ina, pretending to be annoyed.

Then she heard the approach of easy laughter and saw a gang of children on the other side of the river. She and Ebba had played with them many times, but there wouldn't be time for that this afternoon.

"*Salve!*" called the children.

"*Salve!*" called back Ina and Ebba.

One of the children pushed a boat into the water and rowed effortlessly across the river. Miro landed the boat on their shore, smiling from ear to ear.

"*Ready?*" he asked in Latin.

"*Ready,*" answered Ebba, before Ina had the chance. Ina shook her head in surprise. Since when had Ebba known this Latin word? Every day, she surprised her more and more.

"Miro one good teacher," said Ebba, with a cheeky little smile, noticing Ina's reaction. Yes, he must be, thought Ina. Ebba sounded just like one of the Gallaecians – unlike her who, according to Miro, still sounded like some high-brow lady. On hearing his name, Miro grinned comically.

"*Are you talking about me again?*"

"*Do not flatter yourself. You are not that interesting,*" answered Ina, pulling his leg.

"*Incipiamus?*" asked Ebba. Shall we start?

Ina and Miro set about stretching and flexing their lips and fingers, while Ebba warmed up her voice with a set of sweet-sounding scales. They were rehearsing each of their songs, one by one, for the last time before the big performance. Because this evening, on the shortest night of the year, the people of the hillfort and of Miro's village would be meeting properly for the first time, to celebrate together in the clearing further up the river, near the old Roman bridge. It was to be a long night of feasting, singing and dancing. And to crown the occasion a special concert was planned, featuring two hornpipes and a voice. The three of them, as one. Ina smiled. Three was indeed a powerful number.

Everyone would be there, including Maelog. Everyone, that is, but Morwenna and Sadwrn – for they had been banished from Britonia for two years. In addition, they'd been ordered to give the two pigs, Wenna and Mora, to Ebba, to make up for the wrong they'd done her. Ina had received a cow, which was worth much more. If Ebba hadn't been a foreigner, she would've had a cow too. Some said that Morwenna and Sadwrn were in Asturias. Others claimed they'd travelled down the Minio river to the town called Portus Cale. The only thing everyone knew for sure was that no one missed them.

The celebration had been Ina's idea. And, although some had been unsure to begin with, the plan had grown quickly, thanks mostly to the efforts of Caradog and of Elfryn, the keeper of the fort. Miro's parents, Felix and Maria, had been just as enthusiastic. And with a little persuasion from the renowned piper himself, Magnus the Blacksmith, all the citizens of the Gallaecian village had come round to the idea too. Indeed, Magnus had offered to join the three young musicians by playing an encore with them at the end of the celebration, as a special surprise.

Ina stared up into the brilliant, blue sky. There was still not a cloud to be seen. It would be a spectacular night, in every sense – she was sure of it. And, somehow, Ina also knew that when darkness finally fell this evening the stars would shine especially bright.

Acknowledgements

It takes a village, or a hill fort, to raise a book. My heartfelt thanks therefore to the following: Iwan Rees, David Callander, Sara Elin Roberts, Marged Haycock, John Rea, Patrick Rimes, Simon Young, Pablo Carpintero, Xosé Antonio López, Manuel Gago and José Sanchez Pardo. They are all experts in their field – historians, archaeologists, musicians, linguists and more – who were extremely generous with their time and whose advice was invaluable. It goes without saying that any mistakes are mine.

My sincere thanks also to Anne for the cover, to Greg for the maps, to Eleri for the design, to Anwen for her meticulous work once again, to Myrddin for his unfailing support (and for Ina's lullaby!), and to my editor, Llio, for the fun and fruitful collaboration.

Lastly, a special thanks to Jane for making the story sing in Ebba's tongue, and the immensely enjoyable Zoom sessions discussing the book.

About the Author

Gareth Evans comes from Penparcau, Aberystwyth, but has lived in Cardiff for very many years after a decade in Spain and Germany. He worked first in radio, with BBC Radio Cymru, before becoming a scriptwriter for television, mostly for the long-running Welsh-language BBC series, *Pobol y Cwm*. This novel is his second. His first, *Gethin Nyth Brân*, was shortlisted for the Tir na n-Og prize 2018.

Novels steeped in history

Exciting and subtle stories based on key historical events

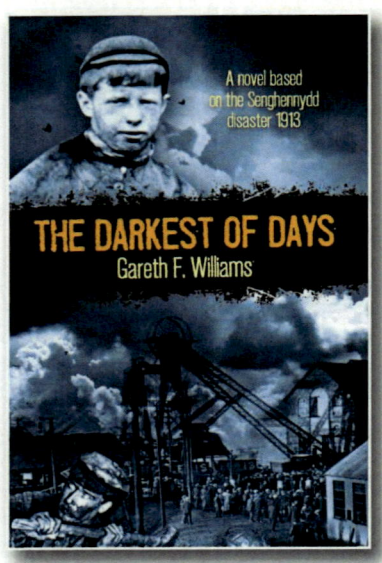

Winner of the 2014 Tir na-nOg award in the original Welsh

THE DARKEST OF DAYS
Gareth F. Williams

A novel based on the Senghennydd disaster 1913

£5.99

Shortly before 8.30 on the morning of 14 October 1913, 439 men and boys perished in a horrific explosion at Senghennydd coal mine.

John Williams was only eight years old when he and his family came from one of the slate mining villages of the north to live in Senghennydd, in the South Wales valleys. He looked forward to his thirteenth birthday, when he too would commence work in the coal mine. But he was unaware of the black cloud that was heading towards Senghennydd ...

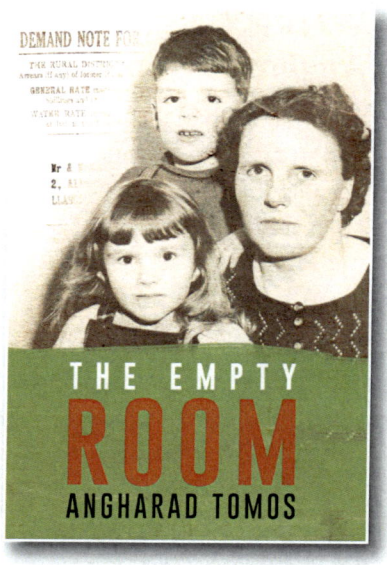

THE EMPTY ROOM
Angharad Tomos

The true story of one Welsh family's sacrifices in their fight for equaliy during the 1950s.

£5.99

Shortlisted for the 2015 Tir na-nOg award in the original Welsh

PAINT!
Angharad Tomos

Why are they painting roadsigns in Wales? Why are they painting the town?

It's the summer of 1969, and a turbulent time in the history of Wales.

£8.50

Shortlisted for the 2016 Tir na-nOg award in the original Welsh

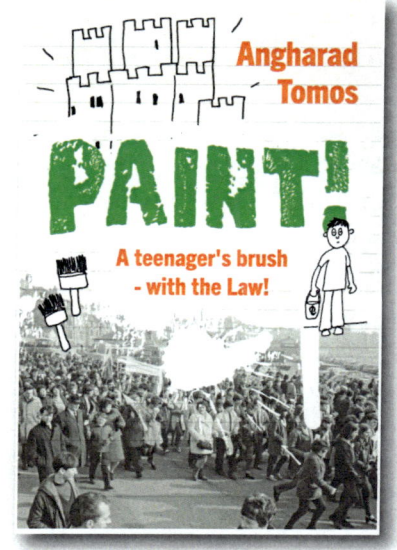

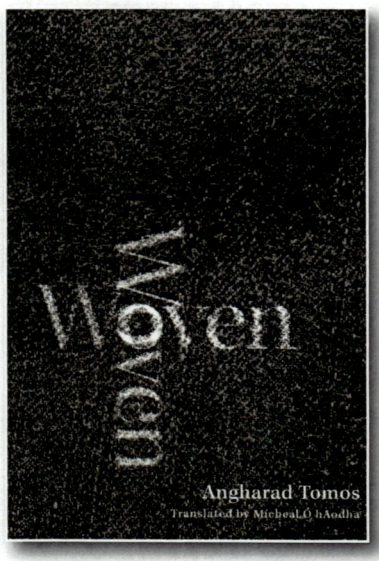

WOVEN
Angharad Tomos

A shocking story of a slave girl in the West Indies and a servant maid in Wales, and the terrible suffering of both characters.

A historical novel that faces facts and greed and violence ...

£8.50

Shortlisted for the 2021 Tir na-nOg award and Book of the Year in the original Welsh

---

THE IRON DAM
Myrddin ap Dafydd

A novel full of excitement and bravery about ordinary people battling to save their valley from being flooded.

£5.99

Shortlisted for the 2017 Tir na-nOg award in the original Welsh

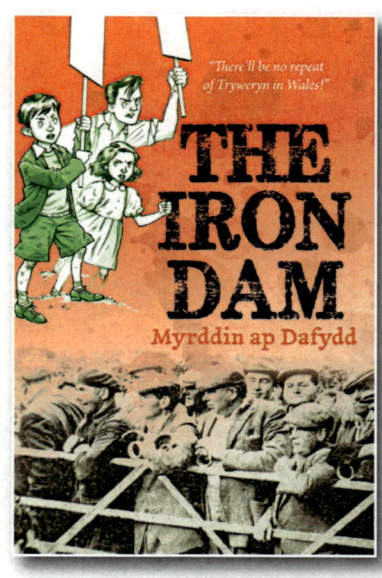

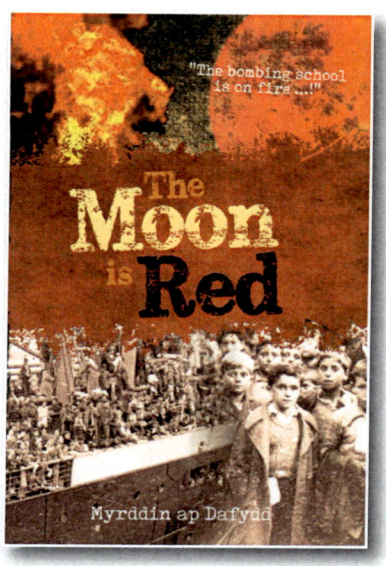

THE MOON IS RED
Myrddin ap Dafydd

A fire at an RAF bombing school in Llŷn in 1936 and bombs raining down on the city of Gernika in the Basque Country during the Spanish Civil War – here's the story of one family at the centre of both events.

£6.99

Winner of the 2018 Tir na-nOg award in the original Welsh

UNDER THE WELSH NOT
Myrddin ap Dafydd

"you'll get a beating for speaking Welsh ..."

Bob starts at Ysgol y Llan at the end of the summer, but he's worried. He doesn't have a word of English. The 'Welsh Not' punishment for speaking Welsh is still used at that school.

£7.50

THE CROWN IN THE QUARRY
Myrddin ap Dafydd

The world's largest diamond … in Blaenau Ffestiniog

The story of evacuees and moving London's treasures to the safety of the quarries during the Second World War.

£7

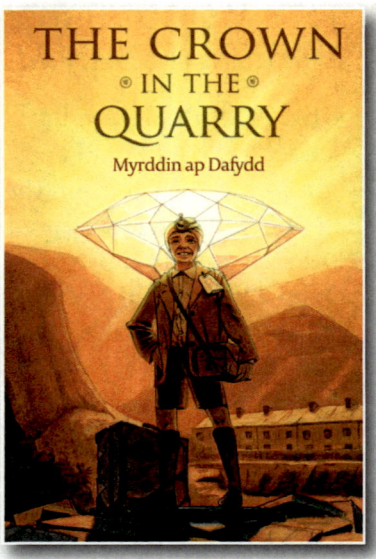

THE BLACK PIT OF TONYPANDY
Myrddin ap Dafydd

It is 1910, a turbulent time of disputes, strikes and riots in Cwm Rhondda, when the miners are fighting for fair wages and better working conditions.

People from different backgrounds are thrown together, resulting in friendships and conflict …

£7.99

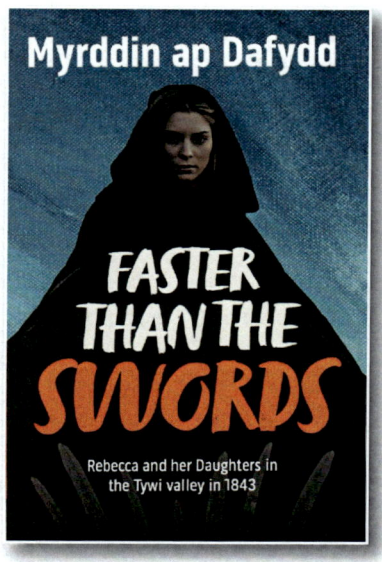

FASTER THAN THE SWORDS
Myrddin ap Dafydd

It's Summer 1843 – the time of the Rebecca Riots. The teenage twins of Tafarn y Wawr in Llangadog find themselves caught up in the struggle and they need to learn from the gypsy Mari Lee how to run faster than the swords ...

£8.50

BLACK RIVER
Louise Walsh

(*suitable for Young Adults*)

Harry Roberts is a Cardiff journalist haunted by his failure to cover the Aberfan disaster.

Black River is a powerful piece of investigative drama that draws on the feelings of a wounded nation to show the good and bad aspects of journalists, politicians and villagers alike.

£7.50

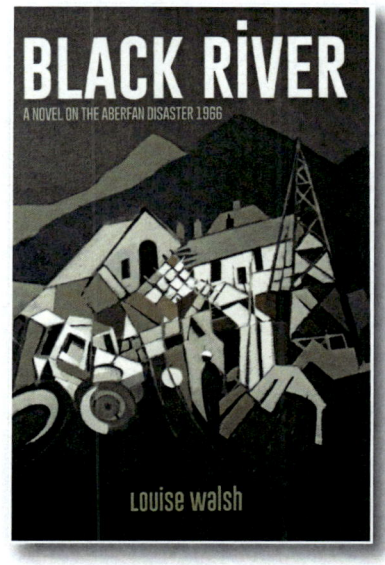

WESTERN WILDFIRE
Ifor Wyn Williams

Gruffudd ap Cynan, the fighting flame against the Normans

The story of Gruffudd ap Cynan's fight to regain his kingdom in Gwynedd.

£7.95

THE MAGIC HORNPIPE
Gareth Evans

A gripping story set in Britain, 552 AD, following 12-year-old Ina's perilous journey escaping from her enemies. Her only company is Bleiddyn, her wolfdog, and in her bag, the magic hornpipe.

£8.50